MINE TO HAVE

Harlow

I promised him I would be there for the best day of his life.
Not thinking I wouldn't be the one standing next to him.
But here I was attending the love of my life's wedding day.

I smiled when I saw him and pushed back the tears that
wanted to come out.

This was his day and I was going to fulfill my promise.

Travis

It was supposed to be the best day of my life. But the
second I got up, things started to fall apart.

Caterer cancelled.

Flowers were from a funeral.

My bride-to-be just had an allergic reaction leaving by
ambulance.

Oh, and my ex-girlfriend just walked in the church.

They say you have to see the signs when they are right in
front of you.

Maybe she was just mine to have.

BOOKS BY NATASHA MADISON

Southern Wedding Series
Mine To Kiss
Mine To Have
Mine To Cherish
Mine to Love

The Only One Series
Only One Kiss
Only One Chance
Only One Night
Only One Touch
Only One Regret
Only One Mistake
Only One Love
Only One Forever

Southern Series
Southern Chance
Southern Comfort
Southern Storm
Southern Sunrise
Southern Heart
Southern Heat
Southern Secrets
Southern Sunshine

This Is
This is Crazy
This Is Wild
This Is Love
This Is Forever

Hollywood Royalty
Hollywood Playboy
Hollywood Princess
Hollywood Prince

Something So Series
Something Series
Something So Right
Something So Perfect
Something So Irresistible
Something So Unscripted
Something So BOX SET

Tempt Series
Tempt The Boss
Tempt The Playboy
Tempt The Ex
Tempt The Hookup
Heaven & Hell Series
Hell And Back
Pieces Of Heaven

Love Series
Perfect Love Story
Unexpected Love Story
Broken Love Story

Faux Pas
Mixed Up Love
Until Brandon

mine to HAVE

Southern Wedding Series

NATASHA MADISON

One

Harlow

"This is it," I announce, looking out the window and pointing at what is my new apartment. The butterflies in my stomach are starting already, and I can't help but smile.

"It's so pretty," my mother says from the front seat, and it just makes me beam. "You did good, Harlow." She looks over the passenger seat and smiles at me. Her eyes start to fill with tears. "I can't believe you are leaving us again."

"Darlin'," my father says softly. I roll my eyes as my mother looks at him; he leans over and kisses her lips, and I shake my head. My parents' love affair was what you see in movies and read about in love stories. It got annoying when I was growing up, but now that I'm older,

I know I want a man who will love me like that. "It's a couple of months, and she'll be back for Thanksgiving."

"Maybe," I mumble under my breath, getting the stink eye from my father and a glare from my mother. Laughing, I open the door and step out of the car, the heat from the sun hitting me right away.

I put my hand over my eyes and look up at the red and white building. The minute I saw the online ad, I knew this would be amazing. I hear my parents behind me and turn to see my father taking out my three pieces of luggage from the trunk. "I'm going to go ahead and meet the girls before you guys come up and scare them off." I turn to walk up the concrete stairs, stopping at the red front door.

A little sitting area is on each side of the door under the covered porch, so you can sit out here and either work or just relax. I push open the door, my stomach fluttering as I see the picture in my head come to life. Just inside, two white doors with the number one and two are located on each side. Walking up the staircase in the middle of the room, I head to the second floor and see the same doors with the numbers three and four.

Another reason I chose this apartment is that there are only four units in the whole place. I hold up my hand to knock, and I see it's shaking with nerves. I laugh at myself right before I knock. "Coming." I hear from the other side of the door as I shake out my hand, the thumping of my heart making my stomach feel like it's on a roller coaster.

The door opens, and the girl who stands there smiles

at me big. Her blonde hair is piled on top of her head, and she wears short white overalls with a peach T-shirt. "Harlow," she says, and her blue eyes light up. "Rachel." She points at herself, and then I step forward, and we go in for a hug. The two of us have been chatting over text for the past two months, preparing for me to come down. "It's so good to finally meet you," she says, letting me go and taking a step back into the apartment. "Welcome home." She opens her arms wide.

I can't even contain my excitement as I walk in. "It's perfect," I say, looking around and seeing that the living room is attached to the kitchen. It's smaller than it looked in the pictures, but that's okay. The only thing I was really set on was having my own bedroom and bathroom. The rest wasn't important to me.

"The movers just left," she says. "They just put everything in there." She stops talking when we hear footsteps coming from the hallway and look over to see my parents walking in.

"These are my parents," I state, and I wait for it.

"Is that...?" she asks, and I glance over at her as she looks at me and then back at my mother.

"That's my mom, Olivia," I confirm, and she just smiles in shock. My mother was a big-time model before she even met my dad. My mother looks around the apartment, and I can already tell that she is planning to decorate it. She turns and looks back at Rachel, smiling at her. "And that's my dad, Casey." I point at my father, who just nods to her, and he does his own sweep of the apartment. "This is Rachel."

"Hi," she says, waving her hand awkwardly. "Nice to meet you guys. Let me show you your room." She turns and walks down the long white hallway. "Every room is the same size." She opens the first door we come to, and I see my stuff there filling up the room. "And of course your bathroom is in the corner."

"Oh my," my mother says. "We have our work cut out for us."

"Oh, no," I say, shaking my head. "This is where you guys look at me and say we love you and call us if you need anything."

"What?" my mother asks, shocked, making Rachel roll her lips to stop from laughing. "But…"

"Darlin'," my father announces. "Time to say goodbye." He looks at me, and I smile.

"It's just like camp," I say, walking to her and putting my hands on her shoulders. My mother is about five feet eleven, and we are almost the same height. I look exactly like her, just with green eyes instead of blue eyes and my hair is just a touch darker.

"It's just so many boxes," she says as she furiously blinks away tears. "Cowboy, who is going to put up her bed?"

"She's got this," my father declares. "And if she needs any help, she can call us, and we can come back."

"Okay, fine," my mother huffs. "But I insist that we take you and your roommates out to dinner tonight before our flight tomorrow."

"Deal," a different voice says, and I look over to see another girl walking in. Her black hair is in a high ponytail, and her eyes are covered with white sunglasses. She smiles, moving the glasses on top of her head to show us her brown eyes. "We can totally do dinner." She is dressed in jean shorts and a tank top with Birkenstocks on her feet. "I'm Lydia." She smiles at me and then at my parents, and I look behind her and see one more girl walk in carrying bags.

"We got booze," she states, happily holding up the white bags in her hands as if she just won a prize. When her eyes find my parents, her big smile vanishes, and her eyes go wide as she tries to backpedal. "Oh, I don't mean *booze* booze. It's code word for..." she stutters, looking at Lydia.

"It's code word for creamer for coffee." Lydia turns around, clapping her hands together. "That's Victoria." She points at Victoria, who shrugs and walks to the kitchen.

"I like them," my mother says. "You girls are going to get along just fine." She walks to them. "If you guys want, you should ask Harlow about her grandfather's sweet tea."

"No," I reply, shaking my head. "My last roommate was out for two days after drinking that." I smile at the girls. "No offense but..."

"Challenge accepted," Lydia says, winking at me. "Also, what time is dinner?"

"Oh, we should check out that new Mexican restaurant," Victoria says. "They have the two-for-one special."

"Sounds amazing," my mother agrees, and she looks

over at my dad, trying to drag out her time with me. My father reluctantly grabs her hand and tells me to text him the address, and they'll meet us there.

"Sorry about that," I say nervously as I pick up a box of stuff. "They can be all in your business, but they..."

"Oh, please," Lydia says, coming into my room. "My parents camped out in the car the first night I got here."

"My father slept in the hallway," Victoria adds. "On a chair. He looked like a bouncer in a club."

"My parents set up a neighborhood watch," Rachel chimes in, and my eyes widen. "And then bought a house around the corner." She puts up her hand. "I win." We all laugh as the girls help me set up my bed.

After I put the sheets and comforter on it, I start putting my clothes away. Luckily for me, my mother is a professional packer, so each box just needs to be put away. "So are you dating anyone?" Victoria asks when she sits in the middle of the floor and starts to unpack the lighting box. She takes out the string of lights I brought from home to hang around my bed.

"No." I shake my head. "I'm too busy to date," I admit.

"What about you guys?" I ask the room, and everyone is single.

"I feel good about this year," Lydia says, looking at us. "Really good."

"Same," we all agree, even though I'm still nervous and just a touch shy.

When dinner comes around, I'm shocked by how in sync we all are. We laugh at the same jokes, and they all get along with my parents. It takes Victoria a while before she looks over at my dad and says that he looks familiar. I groan out loud, making everyone laugh. "He's on the cover of *Forbes*. Can we move on?" He shakes his head, grabbing his beer and taking a pull.

"Shit, if I knew you guys were *rich* rich, I would have suggested the better restaurant," Rachel says, winking at me and making me laugh.

"We are not *rich* rich," I say, looking over at my father. "He's *rich* rich." I point at him. "Yet he still wears Levi's and does his own cattle work."

"That's why we are *rich* rich," he jokes with us.

When it's time to say goodbye, my mother hugs me just a touch longer than normal.

"You'll call me," she says, not even trying to hide her tears this time. "At least once a week." She holds my face in her hands. "Or whenever you feel like it."

"She's good," my father assures her. "She can take care of herself." He winks at me and kisses my forehead.

"Bye, girls." He holds up his hand, and they stand with me as I watch my parents drive away. I secretly wipe away the one tear that escapes my eye and then turn to look at the girls.

"Okay, what kind of creamer did you buy for coffee?" I ask them, knowing I need a shot to relax.

"Stuff for margaritas." Lydia laughs, and I just nod.

"Okay, time to introduce you guys to some sweet tea," I say, and they all clap their hands. When we get back into the apartment, I walk to my bedroom and take out the secret bottle my grandfather gave me. My heart pings a little when I think of my time making this batch with him.

"Here we go," Victoria says, grabbing the shot glasses.

I pour four shots and look at them. "Only one, then I'll make something else." They all look at me. "I tend the family bar," I tell them, and they all smile. "To a great year," I toast, holding my glass up.

They all swallow down the shot, then look at me. "That was smooth," Lydia says, trying not to breathe. "Burns, but it's sweet at the same time."

"I like it," Rachel confirms, bringing her glass to her mouth and making sure nothing is left in it. "Can we have one more?"

"Fine, but two is tops." The second shot goes down smoother. "Okay, I'm off to shower," I say, grabbing the bottle. "My first class is at eight," I announce, and they all groan. "Night."

"Damn, she was smart enough to take the bottle," Rachel says, laughing. "She definitely is the smartest."

I can't help but laugh at her as I hide the bottle away where they will never find it, behind the books on my shelf.

When the alarm goes off the following morning, I groan as I get out of bed, seeing that it's just after seven.

When I scheduled this veterinary anatomy class at eight o'clock, I thought it would be fine, but I was wrong. Grabbing my white yoga pants, I struggle to get them on. A morning person, I am not. I grab the first shirt I see and slide it on over my sports bra. The light pink crop top fits loosely, and when I walk out to make my coffee in my to-go cup, I groan at how bright it is. "We really need curtains," I say with one eye closed as I walk back to my bedroom. I tie my hair on top of my head in a ponytail after I brush my teeth. "It's too early for anyone to look good," I confide to my reflection in the mirror. After grabbing my bag, I walk out of the apartment while everyone else sleeps.

The walk to campus takes me no more than ten minutes, and I really wish I remembered to bring my earbuds so I could listen to music instead of the sound of traffic from nearby. It would definitely help me calm down about the first class. The nerves are hitting me like I ran into a brick wall. *"It's going to be fine,"* I think out loud as I look down for a split second. Walking up the steps, I reach out for the door when my hand falls on someone else's. "Oh my gosh, I'm so sorry," I say, looking up, and it's almost as if time stands still, or at least it feels that way to me. "I wasn't watching where I was going," I admit, gazing into the nicest eyes I've ever seen. His green eyes are bright on top and golden yellow on the bottom.

"Sorry, my fault," he says. His voice comes out deep, and his black hair looks like he was just running his hands through it. "Go ahead." He motions with his hand for me to walk ahead of him.

I smile at him, taking a step into the entryway. "I guess chivalry isn't dead after all," I say over my shoulder, and the smirk that fills his face makes the nerves in my stomach just multiply.

Two

Travis

$\mathcal{I}$ watch the girl in front of me take two steps into the building as she looks over her shoulder, and all I can do is smirk at her and then shake my head. *It's too early in the morning for her to be flirting*, I think to myself. But the second she smiles at me, my feet stop moving, and everything in me holds still. There are no words for how gorgeous she is, and even if I did come up with the words, nothing would do it justice.

I wait for her to take a couple more steps before I start walking. She must be new here. She has to be because I would never have forgotten seeing her, let alone meeting her. I fix the strap of my bag over my shoulder, my tongue itching to ask her what her name is. My head screams at me to just ask her. What's the worst that can happen? My eyes are on her ass as she walks in front of me, and there is nothing that isn't perfect on her.

I turn right at the hall, and I'm shocked when I see her hand opening the door to the class.

She stops in front of me, and it's a good thing I'm paying attention. "Are you following me?"

I'm shocked she is in my class, and then I'm stunned she is blocking the doorway, and I can't even form words to answer her question. "Um," I stutter, my tongue so dry in my mouth. "No," I finally say, and I can see the twinkle in her eyes as she laughs. "You're trouble." That just makes her laugh more, and even her fucking laughter is perfect.

"You have no idea." She winks at me and walks into the class, and I follow her.

Five rows of seats face the whiteboard in front of the class. "Excuse me," a guy says, walking past me. I have no idea why, but I move just a touch faster than he does. I watch her take a seat in the third row and the fourth seat in. She places her travel cup in the middle of the desk.

I walk behind her and sit down in the second seat. She puts her bag on the floor, takes out her laptop, and opens it. She turns toward me and catches me watching her. "That's not creepy at all." She laughs, and it's as if all the words have been taken out of me. I remember nothing at all, and if I wasn't mortified, I would actually laugh. "So, Romeo," she says as people start coming into the class. Everyone is pretty much dragging their feet. "Do we have a name?"

"My name?" I ask, pointing at myself.

"Well, considering you followed me all morning long," she teases, and I laugh, and I can feel the little nerves leaving me.

"It's not even eight in the morning." I look at my watch. "So all morning long is a stretch." She turns in her seat to look at me. "More along the lines of at least five minutes," I say, finally able to find words. "I'm Travis." I lean over the desk and hold out my hand.

She slips her hand in mine and smiles. "Nice to meet you, Travis." The smile fills her face again.

"Do you have a name?" I ask when she lets go of my hand, and I turn, putting my arm over the back of the seat between us.

"I do," she says, her voice soft. "It's Harlow." She smiles and takes a sip of her coffee. I'm about to ask her if she is new here when the door to the room slams shut, and we both look forward as the professor starts the class.

I turn my head to the front, grabbing my own laptop and opening it to take notes. During the whole class, I'm half focused, and she catches me every time I look over at her and gives me a soft smile, making my palms all fucking sweaty. When the class ends, I put my laptop away and get up, trying to make it seem like I'm not waiting for her, but in reality, I'm trying to get the courage to ask her to go for coffee.

Walking as slow as a turtle, I look over and see that she's on her phone typing something. I'm about to go to her when my phone buzzes in my pocket. Taking it out, I see it's my mother. I think about sending it to voice mail, but looking back down at the phone, I press the green button as I walk out of the class. "Hello," I greet, putting it to my ear.

"Well, at least I have one child who answers my call." My mother's voice comes out dramatically, and I have to laugh. Ever since she lost my dad six months ago, she's been on a never-ending level of needy. But then, when you try to do something for her, she gets angry and says she is independent. Giving a whole new meaning to damned if you do, damned if you don't.

"Good morning, Mom." I look back at the door and then proceed to walk ever so slowly out of the building, hoping I can catch her again. "What happened?"

"You know me, Travis," she starts. "I'm not one to complain." I can't help but laugh.

"Yes, Mom, you are the last one to complain." I stop and sit on a bench under one of the trees. Putting my bag beside me, I look over at the front door and watch as people come in and out. "I can't remember the last time you complained about anything. I mean, there was that issue last week when you were complaining that no one invited you out anymore."

"I was not complaining. I was merely pointing out the fact that no one has time to have lunch with me anymore," she huffs. "Anyway, your sisters are not talking to me."

"Oh, here we go," I mumble, watching Harlow walk out of the building with her bag slung over her shoulder. She looks left and right before walking down the steps and heading in the opposite direction of me. "Which sister is it?" I have three sisters. Shelby is the eldest, older than me by ten months. Twelve months after me is Clarabella and then fourteen months after her is the baby of the family, Presley.

"It's all three of them!" she shouts. "They are ganging up on me. All I want is what is best for them and their business." Two years ago, my sisters started a wedding planning business called Happily Ever After. I didn't know how big that industry was. Not that I ever gave it a second thought, but the three of them have worked it up from a small family business and are getting ready to buy a colonial house for office space with an adjoining barn to fix up and use as a venue. From the pictures they showed me and the work they plan to put into it, it will be beautiful. "They know they can ask me for anything, and instead of asking me to give them money," she says, "they decided to apply for a loan." She shrieks, her voice going even louder, "A loan. I have this big-ass house." She mentions the house passed down from my great-grandfather to my grandfather and then to my father. "And the three of them not once think to come to me."

"Okay, well, maybe they just want to do this on their own." I try to play devil's advocate. "Or they are going to use you as a backup plan."

"What?" Her voice goes softer.

"Well, they are trying to see if they can do it by themselves, and then after, if they can't, they know they have you to back them up," I explain, grabbing my bag and getting up from the bench. I look over to where Harlow was walking, but she's gone.

"Why didn't they just say that? Why are they so

secretive?"

"They get that from Dad," I say, chuckling. "I have to get to my next class."

"Call me later," she says. "Love you."

"Love you, too," I reply softly and hang up with her.

Taking my phone out, I pull up the group text I have with my sisters.

Me: Would you guys please talk to Mom? She said no one is talking to her.

Clarabella: ARE YOU KIDDING ME?

She uses all caps, so I know she's pissed. Actually, all caps means she's beyond pissed.

Shelby: She went to the bank and told them to cancel our loan application.

I want to say I'm shocked, but then, I'm surprised I didn't see this coming.

Presley: CANCELED, which means we have no money, which means we have no money.

Shelby: Oh, we have money, according to Mom. We just need to ask her. Who does that?

Me: Have you guys not met Mom? She needs to feel wanted and needed.

Clarabella: Then you should call her more and ask her to come and stay with you. I'm sure your roommates would love home-cooked meals and your mother waiting by the window for you to come home.

I laugh and shake my head. They would love the meals, and it would end there.

Me: I guess I have to come home this weekend, then, and make sure everyone plays nice.

Shelby: Kiss ass.

Presley: Mamma's boy.

Clarabella: Fuck you.

Me: Is that any way to talk to your big brother?

I laugh, knowing that if I was in front of her, she would flip me off.

Clarabella: Bye.

I receive a notification.

Clarabella has left the conversation.

Shelby: Now you've woken the beast.

Presley: RUN.

Me: See you Saturday!

I put my phone away, knowing it'll take a day before someone adds her back into the chat. I stop walking and look over, feeling eyes on me, but it's all in my head when I see no one there. Turning, I walk with my head down, and the only thing I can see is Harlow and her smile. "She's out of your league," I mumble to myself, and for once, I look forward to going to my early class.

Three.

Harlow

The sound of knocking has me looking up from my book toward the closed door and then glance over at the clock beside my bed. It's 9:27 a.m. "Come in." I sit up in bed as the door creaks open, and Rachel comes in.

"I come with gifts." She holds up a cup of coffee in her hand, and I laugh. My roommates were quick to realize that any conversation with me would be minimal until I had my morning coffee.

"Thank you." I reach out to grab the cup, putting my hand on the hot mug and taking a deep inhale. "It's almost orgasmic, don't you think?" I take a sip, and it's like heaven on my tongue.

Rachel laughs and sits on the edge of the bed with her own cup of coffee in her hand. "I don't think you are having sex the right way if you think coffee is in the same category as having an orgasm."

I almost choke on my next sip as I start coughing and laughing at the same time. "I'll give you that," I say, putting the cup of coffee on my nightstand until I quit coughing.

"Anyway, I'm inviting you to a study session," she says, looking at me. "It's going to be the four of us. You remember those guys from last night?" The four of us decided to spend our Saturday low-key at a hole-in-the-wall bar. When we walked in, Lydia spotted a guy she knew from class, and we hung with him. A couple of his friends joined, and we all got to talking, but I took off after an hour, exhausted from the first week of school.

"Yeah," I say, grabbing the cup again to take another sip.

"Well, he and his roommates are hitting up the square coffee shop this afternoon, and I figured you would want to come." She takes a sip of her coffee. "One of his roommates, I think, is in the same program as you, so it might be worth it."

"Sure, what time?"

"I'm waiting for him to let me know." She gets up from the bed. "I'll go check in with Lydia and Victoria."

"Sounds good," I say as she turns and walks toward the door. "Thank you for the coffee." I hold up the cup.

It takes her an hour to come back and tell us that we are leaving at four. I nod at her and make notes on what I need to do. I grab my phone and scroll through Instagram, seeing the picture that my cousins took at the Sunday lunch. Out of everything I miss about home, Sunday lunch is at the top of the list. It was the day we all got together and just caught up with everyone. It's something I can't wait to share with my own family. I write a couple of comments before shutting it down, my heart aching just a touch, and I send out a text to my cousin group chat.

Me: Missing you guys.

I put the phone down and walk to the bathroom for a quick shower. Slipping on a pair of purple yoga pants and then a white sports bra, I turn back to the bathroom to comb my hair and braid it on the side before grabbing a white long-sleeved sweater that falls to the waist of the yoga pants. I take one more look at myself before I choose the white Adidas runners and pack my bag with the textbook and my computer. "Guys," I say, walking out of my room and looking to see if anyone is in the living room. I see no one there and then hear footsteps coming down the hall from one of the bedrooms.

Victoria comes out wearing joggers and a sweater, her hair piled on her head. "Ugh, I hate you," she moans. "How do you always look like you just stepped out of a fashion magazine?" I shake my head and laugh at her. "You don't even look tired." She walks into the kitchen and grabs a water bottle. "Like, how?"

"Well, I got home at midnight." I point at myself, then back at her. "You got home at six o'clock." She just smirks. "And from the looks of it, it doesn't look like you slept on someone's couch."

"I mean, I was on the couch." She takes a sip of

water, hiding her smile. "But we definitely didn't sleep."
I can't help but laugh at her. In the week we've lived
together, she seems to be the one with no expectations
from anyone, while also making sure you know not to
expect anything from her. She also has the softest heart
of everyone around.

Lydia and Rachel join us a couple of minutes later, and
the four of us head out. The sun is going down, and the
wind is picking up. "It's about that time," Rachel says,
and I look over at her as we walk down the sidewalk.

"What time is that?" I ask, confused.

"Change of season." Rachel takes a deep breath.
"Soon, when you walk out, it'll be crispy."

"She loves to say crispy," Victoria says when she stops
walking, and I look at the black door of the coffee shop.
Rachel steps up to the door and pulls it open, stepping
into the shop. I'm the last one in, and I look around, the
smell of coffee hitting my nose right away.

The three walls are all exposed brick, and I smile
when I think that it looks like home for a second. Small
tables are scattered around the place, pushed together as
students work in groups, and the long white counter is
located all the way in the back to make room for more
tables. My head turns to the other side when I feel the girls
walk away from me. My feet follow them as they walk
to the side of the room, where they sit on a long bench
against the wall. I see three guys get up, and suddenly
feeling eyes on me, I turn toward the back counter and
see him. My heart speeds up when our eyes finally meet,
and I try to hide my smile by looking down, but I look

up right away.

He just watches me, and I can see him laugh as he grabs his white cup of coffee and walks toward me. His black pants are loose on his legs but go tight on his ankles with a white T-shirt, his tanned arms on display. "Well, well, well, is someone stalking someone?" he says, and I can't help but laugh. I'm not going to lie and pretend that I didn't think of him during the last week and even last night when I was out. I secretly looked to see if maybe he was there, but I didn't see him.

"I don't know what you call stalking." I smirk at him, trying to make the smile on my face go away. Instead, I find myself smiling even bigger. "But I'm here for a study session." I point over at the tables that the guys are putting together.

My mouth flies open when I see an empty place at the end of the bench, and I see one of the guys from last night point toward us. "Isn't this a twist of fate?" he says to me and then walks over to the back bench sitting at the end, next to one of the guys. The girls have all sat down in the chairs facing the guys, leaving the chair beside him open for me.

I walk to the empty seat, trying to calm my nerves, but instead, they just pick up even faster. "Hi," I say to the rest of the guys at the table, trying to ignore the need to look over at him again. I met Jake, Chris, and Frankie last night, so they look at me and smile.

"I'm Travis," I hear him say from beside me as he introduces himself to the girls.

"You weren't there last night?" I hear Lydia ask. This

burning starts in my stomach, and I'm not sure why. I try to ignore the conversation as I open my bag and take out my things.

"No, I got back today," he replies and doesn't give anything else. I look over at him as he puts down the white cup. I move my chair just a touch to give us more room on the table and also to get away from him just a bit. My head is spinning, wanting to ask him where he was. Maybe he went to visit a girlfriend.

I open my laptop and put in my earbuds to block out the noise and focus on what I'm doing. I look down at the cursor, not sure, and then grab my book to read. Reaching into my bag for my pencil case to grab my highlighter, I see out of the corner of my eye that Travis sits with his back to the bench reading the same book as me. He looks up and smiles when he sees me looking. My leg starts to move up and down nervously. I finish reading a paragraph, and then my eyes glance over to him on their own to catch him looking at me, and I smile at him and then look back down again.

For over an hour, the two of us exchange little glances and smiles, and when I feel him move beside me, I think that he's leaving. Instead, he leaves his things and walks to the counter. I look over at the rest of the group, seeing four of them studying together while Lydia and Jake work in front of each other.

I take out my earbuds and lean down into my backpack to grab my wallet, turning when he sits down beside me again. "I hope you like coffee," he says, handing me a white cup, and I can't help the smile that fills my face.

"It's a latte." My hand grabs the cup, and our fingers graze each other.

"You're a godsend," I say, smelling the coffee before taking a sip of it. "So good." He laughs. "Thank you."

"You are very welcome," he states, leaning back on the bench and running his hand through his hair. "So tell me, Harlow." I raise my eyebrow. "Why do you want to be a vet?"

I shake my head. "Definitely not the question I thought you would ask." I wink at him, making him laugh, and the nerves leave me finally. "My family owns a couple of farms." I can't help but light up as I talk about it. "Generations of farmers in my family."

"That sounds very, very cool," he says. "So you have hands-on knowledge?"

I take another sip. "From when I was younger, all we did was ride horses. I think I rode a horse before I could even walk. I remember when I was eight, one of our prize horses had a foal. My father thought it was a great learning experience for me." I laugh, thinking back to it. "My mother didn't talk to him for a week after that, but I just remember being in awe of the whole situation." I shrug. "Besides, who doesn't love playing with puppies and kittens." I joke with him, and he nods his head. "What about you, Travis? Why do you want to be a vet?"

Four

Travis

I look at how her green eyes light up so bright as she talks about her family. The smile on her face makes the corners of her eyes crinkle. When my roommates messaged me about a study group, I was going to pass and just go home. But I knew I would just ignore my homework and crash if I went home, so I came. And boy, am I fucking happy I did. When the door opened and I looked at the girls coming in, my eyes found her right away. I couldn't believe my luck that she would be here. I knew I would see her again tomorrow in class, but seeing her tonight was just what I needed, and I didn't realize it until now.

The last hour has been a war in my head. Every single time I tried to look at her without getting caught, she would sense me looking at her, and she would catch me. But every single time I felt bad about it, I would look up and find her looking at me, too. I tried to hide the smile that came out sometimes, knowing she was feeling something toward me. At least that is what I was hoping.

"What about you, Travis?" she says, sitting back in her chair. "Why do you want to be a vet?" She brings her cup to her lips, and I wonder if I kissed her, if it would taste sweet because of the coffee or because of her.

I smile, looking down in my cup of coffee, and a pang of sadness fills my chest. "My dad." I inhale a deep breath and fight back the tears. I can see his bright smile in my head as if I saw it two days ago.

"Oh, your dad is a vet?" she asks with all the enthusiasm, and the lump in my throat grows. I take a couple of seconds before I can find the words.

"No. He was a lawyer." I laugh, hoping she doesn't catch the past tense.

"Was?" she asks, her voice going low as she looks at me, and I can see her eyes going just a touch darker.

"He passed away six months ago." I keep thinking that saying the words would hurt less than the last time I said it, but I'm reminded that it doesn't. Harlow sits up, leaning over, and her hand covers mine on my leg. She squeezes my hand under hers.

"I'm so, so sorry," she says, and her voice cracks. "I can't even imagine what it feels like." The softness of her voice melts a piece of me. Something in her voice tells me she means every single word of that sentence. You hear from everyone how sorry they are, you hear from friends near and far that they are thinking of you, but you know they're just words. Except for her. I honestly believe everything she is saying. She swallows as she blinks away tears. "I wouldn't have brought it up," she says, looking down.

"It's perfectly fine." I don't want her to feel bad for bringing it up. "You didn't know." I smile to make her feel better.

"He must be so proud of you," she says, and she lifts her hand that isn't holding mine to brush away the tear that comes out of her eye. She smiles, trying to be brave, and I just want to hug her for trying to make me feel better.

"I hope," I reply, squeezing her hand in mine. "He used to always say to me, 'Son, you need to be friends with five people. A doctor, a lawyer, a mechanic, an accountant, and a veterinarian.'"

She smiles. "My grandfather says the same thing. Except he also adds a plumber and electrician to that," she says, and I can't help but laugh.

"Yeah, I guess you can add those, too. But every time he said that, he kept telling me he didn't know a veterinarian. My mother would laugh at him and remind him we didn't have any pets." I smile, thinking back on the memory. "He kept saying that the reason we didn't have any pets was because he didn't know a vet." Her laughter fills the coffee shop, and it's a laugh you want to hear again. It's a laugh you hear, and all you want to do is laugh with her.

"How is your mom doing?" she asks, and I'm blown

away by her questions. "It must be hard for her."

I've just met her, and already she is asking stuff that not even my roommates have asked me. They were there when my dad died and gave me all the support they could, but I never sat down with them and discussed how I was doing or how my family was doing. It was something I kept to myself. It was my loss to handle. "She pretends that she is okay." I finally admit to someone besides my sisters. "But I think she's a little lost." The words hit me in the middle of my chest. "They were together for over twenty-five years. Then one day, he goes to work and doesn't come home. I think that is what hurts her the most. They never got to say goodbye." I shrug. "I mean, can you ever be ready for someone to die, even if they are sick?"

"No." She shakes her head. "Even if you had years and years to come to terms with the fact someone is going to die, you will never be ready for that moment. I can't even imagine how my mother would be," she says, letting go of my hand. The itch to grab her hand back comes over me, and I have to stop myself. "Do you have any brothers or sisters?"

"I have three sisters," I say, and she opens her mouth in glee.

"I wish I had a sister," she shares. "Instead, I have two brothers."

"How about I trade you a sister for a brother?" I bring the cup of coffee to my lips.

"Deal." She holds up her hand so we can shake on it. "Which one do you want?" she asks. "I have the cowboy or the military guy." She holds her hands, moving them from side to side as if she is weighing my options.

"Ohhh," I say, tapping my chin. "It depends on which sister you are going to take. Shelby, the oldest one who thinks she's always right." I smirk. "Clarabella, who just assumes she's always right. It's her way or the highway, and then Presley who sits back and just waits to clean up whatever mess it is that they made."

"They all sound amazing."

I laugh, shaking my head. "Trust me, they are not. I had to drive up there this weekend to put out the fire."

"Oh, no." Her eyes widen. "Hope everyone came out unscathed."

"You and me both." I take a sip of the coffee. "My mother was all in their business because, well, she has nothing else to do, so that started a fight."

"Oh, nothing quite like a family fight." She laughs. "My older brother, Quinn, and my father usually butt heads. But that has to do with work."

"What does he do?" I ask, wanting to know all about her.

"He actually has an equestrian therapy farm," she explains, and I can tell how proud she is of him. "He really helps with people who were abused mentally and physically."

"Holy shit, that sounds amazing. I bet he helps a lot of people."

"He does." She nods her head. "But when he started it, he wanted to do it on his own, and well, my father—"

"Wanted to give him money." She looks at me with

wide eyes.

"How did you know?" she asks, shocked that I guessed.

"My mother just did the same thing with my sisters," I say. "They are starting their own business called Happily Ever After Wedding Event Planning. They had this big dream of buying this run-down farmhouse with a barn and fixing up the house to be their office, and then the barn would be their venue. A one-stop-shop kind of thing."

"That sounds like so much fun," she says, and I literally could talk to her all night if she lets me. "Did they just decide to do this?"

"Yeah, I guess it started with my mother and her sister who did event planning until Mom stepped back when she had the kids, and then when my aunt was retiring, she gave my sisters all her contacts. My mother decided she would give them money, and they fought her, so she decided it was a good idea to go straight to the bank and withdraw their application for a loan."

I'm expecting her to be appalled Mom did that, but instead, she claps her hands. "Your mother and my father would have a field day. Then you throw in my grandfather, who would literally just go behind both of them and buy it in her name and be like, 'Oh, I bought you this' like if he picked up a pair of shoes and not a million-dollar business loan."

"I'm almost scared to have them meet." I see the guys start to put away their stuff.

"You ready?" Jake asks, and I want to shake my head. I look over at Harlow, who is looking at the girls following the guys as they put their things in their bags.

"I guess we should pack it up," she says, and I want to ask her to stay with me for a bit, but she picks up her bag and starts to fill it up.

I pack my own bag, and when she stands, I'm right behind her. The six of them start to walk toward the door, leaving us by ourselves. "Thank you," I say, putting my bag across my chest. She looks at me, confused. "For the talk."

"Thank you," she counters. "For sharing your family with me." She smiles. "Today was rough for me. I really missed my family, so hearing about yours made me miss mine just a touch less."

"I had a really great time," I say, walking with her toward the door. We both walk slowly, as if we don't want the night to end. Her hand grazes mine, and I have the need to slip my hand into hers, but the door opens, and one of her roommates comes in.

"Are you coming?" she asks Harlow, who just smiles and nods, looking back at me.

"See you tomorrow, Travis," she says and looks down shyly.

"See you tomorrow, Harlow," I say. She walks out of the coffee shop, and I watch her walk away from us with her friends and in the opposite direction of our place.

"Hey," Chris says, opening the door. "You coming?"

"Yeah." I walk out, turning my head toward where I know Harlow is. She takes one more look down the street, and when she sees me watching, she raises her hand and waves before disappearing around the corner.

Five

Harlow

"Okay, ladies," I say, walking out of my bedroom toward the kitchen. Music is playing from the speaker, and the orange and black lights are blinking around the little window. "Guys?" I say, turning to look toward the closed bedroom door. "Why am I always the one who is ready first?"

I shout down the hall, and Rachel pulls open her bedroom door. "Because you barely have to do anything to yourself," she huffs, and I laugh. "Like, look at you." She lifts her hand to point at me. "Where are the shorts?" I shake my head and walk into the kitchen and take out four shot glasses.

"The shorts have been replaced." I look down at the costume I decided to wear for Halloween. "With leggings." To be honest, the booty shorts were more like a thong, and there was no way in hell I was going out dressed like that. So I opted for my tightest pair of leggings, and even this is a little bit more exposed than I like.

She huffs, looking down at her own slutty nurse costume. The top button looks like it's going to pop open, and when it does, you better move out of the way or you might lose your eyeball. "Then that doesn't make you a slutty referee."

I move my hair to the back of my neck. The front of the shirt goes down into a deep vee, and it's two sizes too small. So my boobs look like they are trying to escape. "These puppies trying to escape means slutty to me. And it's so small"—I point at my vagina—"that the bodysuit is a full thong in the back." I point at my ass. "And the front at this point, I think it's just dental floss." She throws her head back and laughs. "It might have to be surgically removed at the end of the night."

"Well, I'm sure Travis will volunteer as tribute." She winks at me, and I just shake my head. It's been a full two months of us skating around each other, and I haven't been more confused about a situation in my life. It's like every time I flirt with him, he flirts back, but then the next day, it's like it never happened. I want to say it's just him, but I'm just as guilty, so I'm not sure if I want to go there. We've attended at least one study group a week, and we always end up sitting next to each other and studying together. The touches are the worst, and sometimes, I think it's all in my head, but then I catch him staring at me, making me second-guess everything.

A knock on the front door has Rachel grabbing the bowl of candy and opening it. "Happy Halloween." I hear the kids scream and rush over to the door to see them with their bags up. I smile at them and think back to the pictures I got about an hour ago from my mother and my nephew. He was dressed up as Spiderman, and you could see his two teeth in the front missing.

"I swear to God," Lydia says, coming into the kitchen after we close the door. "This gives new meaning to the word latex and spandex." I turn around, seeing her walk in wearing a black one-piece cat outfit. It even glistens in the dim light of the apartment, and her boobs look like they are pushed up to her chin. "All I have to say is whoever I go home with is going to think he's uncasing a sausage."

"I'm going on record for saying next year there will be no slutty in anyone's costume," I joke, walking back into the kitchen to pour the sweet tea shots. "We should go as Disney princesses."

"How is that going to get me laid?" Lydia asks when Victoria comes out of her room.

"I'm fine with this outfit," she says, laughing, and I just shake my head.

"It's tights and a corset top." I point at her.

"I have a whip and a top hat." She lifts her hand and slaps down the whip that her costume comes with. "And these pants are leather." It makes us all laugh. "And you can go as Ariel. She wore a shell bra and a mermaid tail."

"Ohh, I could," Lydia says. "Okay, fine. Next year,

it's princesses with a twist." She lifts her shot glass. "To a successful night."

I grab my own glass. "To a successful night," I repeat, and Rachel and Victoria follow. The shot goes down smooth, and it makes me miss home. "Let me make a couple of drinks," I say, turning to the little bar we have set up next to the coffee station. I start filling the mixer cup with ice and adding a mix of alcohol together.

"I love when she plays bartender," Rachel says, sitting down. "It's almost like you're a mixologist."

"Almost," I agree, shaking the mixer in my hand before pouring two drinks. "Taste this."

Rachel takes a sip. "All I'm missing is a beach chair and an umbrella," she states, passing the drink to Lydia, who oohs before passing it to Victoria, who finishes it off.

I make about four more drinks, and when we are all a bit tipsy, Victoria says, "Okay, picture time." We all squeeze in and take a picture. "Let's go prowl, girls," she suggests once she posts the picture to Instagram.

I grab my phone, tucking it in the front of my tights before walking over and putting the sweet tea away. "Just in case you savages escape before me and I come home and find you guys passed out."

"Ye have little faith in us," Rachel says, laughing.

"I went to the bathroom the other time and you guys took three shots in that time," I remind them as we walk down the steps.

"We would have had more had you not raced back," Victoria admits as we walk out the door.

The street is quiet as the lights to the homes are off. The only people on the streets are college kids as we make our way over to the local bar.

Victoria pulls open the door, and the noise from inside spills out into the street. I step in after her, holding the door open for Rachel and Lydia. I've seen it packed before, but nothing like this. The wooden bar is against one wall, the whole wall filled with bottles of booze, right in front of a mirror. The seven bartenders tonight all look like they are busy. The beer on tap lights up in the middle of the bar, and all the stools in front of the bar are taken. I look around, trying to convince myself that I'm not looking for him, but deep down, I know I am. The high-top tables are all taken, and people stand in the middle of what is the path to walk in and out. I follow Victoria through the crowd of people, trying not to step on anyone when I spot him in the corner with Jake, Chris, and Frankie.

My eyes are on him as he talks to a blonde beside him. They're both laughing, and something inside me burns. She puts her hands on his chest, an intimate move on her part, and he leans down and says something in her ear. When she looks up at him, you can tell she likes him, and I have to wonder if maybe they are seeing each other. The burning in my stomach comes on full force. I pretend it's the booze I drank on an empty stomach, but maybe it's just plain old jealousy.

"Hey!" I hear Jake shout at us, and I try to look away as fast as I can and then look back over at them. I avoid making eye contact with Travis. "Over here." He stands up on the rungs of the stool to wave us over.

"I'm going to go and get a drink," I say when I get close enough to the table to see that the girl is still standing next to him. "Anyone want anything?" I ask, looking around the table at the other three guys, then finally at him. He smiles at me, and his eyes light up, and I give him a tight smile.

"We got a couple of pitchers of beer coming," Frankie says, and I look at Rachel, who makes a face because she hates beer.

"I'll go get us something to drink," I say, wanting to get away from the table as fast as I can. I don't even wait for anyone else to answer before turning and walking to the bar. I make my way through the throngs of people until I see a spot open at the bar. I take a deep breath. *Are they dating?* I ask myself. I mean, it's not like we discussed anything like that for fear that he was seeing someone, and I didn't want to hear it.

I wait for the bartender to see me when I feel someone next to me, and when I turn to look, I'm shocked it's Travis. "Hey." He leans on the bar with one arm and looks at me. "Figured I'd help you carry the drinks," he says, and I look around to see if the girl followed him, but it's just him.

"Is your friend staying with us?" I want to kick myself for even asking him. "Did she want a drink?" He looks at me, confused. "I'll order one anyway, just in case."

"Who are you talking about?" he asks, and he really really doesn't know.

"The bunny?" I say, not even sure she was a bunny.

"Or I don't know what she was."

He smirks, which makes me just a touch pissed off. "Why don't you order your drink?"

I turn to look at him. "What are you doing here and not there?" I point over at the table where everyone else is and then put my hand on my hip.

"If you don't know already, I'm not doing it right," he says, and before I even ask him what the hell he's talking about, someone knocks into me, sending me into him. His one hand wraps around my waist, and my chest is pressed to his, and with him leaning on the bar, we are almost at the same height. My heart hammers in my chest as he looks into my eyes. "You look beautiful tonight," he says softly. "I mean, you look beautiful every day." There must be about fifty people around us. The sound of people laughing fills the room, but it's almost as if it's just the two of us. I feel his thumb rub up and down my back. "But today," he says and licks his lips, "it just takes the cake." He leans in, and my mouth goes dry when I think this is it, he's going to kiss me, but he moves his mouth to my ear. "You make me want to…" His voice makes my whole body shiver when his breath comes out heavy. "Head to the penalty box." And I can't help but throw my head back and laugh.

Six

Travis

" _You_ make me want to…" I say, my lips almost touching her ear, my hand at the base of her back pulling her even closer to me. I wonder if she could say what she really wants me to do. She has been driving me insane for the fucking last two months. It almost feels like I've been friend-zoned, but I'm not sure. I'm also afraid to step over the line with her and then ruin this amazing friendship that we've begun to have. But when she walked into the bar tonight, and I took one look at her, I was left with my tongue hanging out. I didn't even listen to what Katcy was telling me. All I knew was that I had to go and talk to her, but she avoided me and rushed away.

She is hands down the most beautiful woman I've

ever met, inside and out. But tonight, she was fucking smoking hot, and I knew it was time to make my move. I knew someone else would be waiting if I didn't, so I rushed after her, not leaving fate to chance. My heart speeds up so fast as I think of words to say to her. "Head to the penalty box." I close my eyes at how cheesy the line is, but I'm also confused on if it makes any fucking sense. She throws her head back, and her laughter fills the room.

"What can I get you?" the bartender asks. She turns in my arms, and I don't know if she stays there because she wants to or if it's because I haven't let her go. Either way, I'm going with it.

"I'll take a pitcher of marg." She leans in. "And four whiskey sours."

"That's a lot of alcohol," I say. She looks up at me, and I want to bend and kiss her lips, but I don't want to kiss her for the first time and rush through it.

The bartender comes back and puts the pitcher on the counter, and I finally have to let her go. "Can I have a tray?" she leans in and asks him, and he nods his head. She arranges everything on the tray and picks it up with ease.

"You ever need a job, let me know," the bartender says and winks at her, and I just glare at him. I literally just had my arms around her.

"Follow me," she says. I want to take the tray from her, but she is already moving ahead of me, so I put my hand on her hip as we walk through the crowd of people. I can see the guys giving her a second glance, and I fucking hate it.

"Okay," she says, putting the tray on the table. "We have some margaritas." She takes the pitcher off. "And we have some whiskey."

"Who drinks whiskey?" Frankie asks, scrunching his nose up.

"Only fine Southern folks do," Harlow says. "So none for you, city boy." I can't help but laugh at her as she sits down on a stool, and I stand next to her. She takes one of the whiskey glasses and brings it to her lips, taking it in one shot. "Okay, are we playing a game?" She looks around the table, and I can tell from her eyes that the liquor is getting to her.

"I want to play a game," Chris says, putting his hand up with his glass of beer. "Let's play seven minutes in heaven."

The girls shake their heads and laugh. "Why don't we play ABC animals," Harlow says, and we all look at her. "So I go first, and I choose an animal that starts with the letter A like armadillo and then the one who makes the worst sounding armadillo has to drink."

"What the fuck does an armadillo sound like?" Frankie says. "The only armadillo I've ever seen is Ross from *Friends*."

"I know what it sounds like." Rachel puts up her hand, and she proceeds to make the sound of a wounded cat, making everyone laugh.

"Almost," I finally say and make my own noise. The whole table laughs again, especially when it's Frankie's turn.

He loses his turn when he shouts out, "I'm a holiday armadillo!" He doesn't even wait to be announced the winner; he just drinks his glass of beer. By the end of the night, I don't think I've laughed as much as I have in the last hour and a half.

We've all lost at least one round. Some of us have lost more than we care to admit, and a couple of us have even argued our losses. "Okay, who is ready to head over to the house party that Chuck is throwing?" I look over at Harlow, who just looks at me, not sure what to say.

"I think I'm going to head home," she says while the girls look at her and moan.

"Fine, I'll come with," Rachel says, and I hold up my hand.

"I'm going to go also, so I'll make sure she gets home," I say, and Rachel just smiles as she and Lydia try to high-five each other but miss three times. I look over at Jake, who just nods at me, knowing he'll have to make sure they get home okay.

I look at Harlow, who just nods as we turn to walk out of the bar. The cold air hits me right away, and I look at Harlow, who just smiles at me. "You don't have to walk me," she says as she starts to walk toward her apartment.

"There is no way I would let you walk home by yourself," I finally say as we take our time walking down the sidewalk. "My father would haunt me."

"I can grab an Uber." She points behind her at the road. "You can go and join them."

"Harlow." I say her name as our feet move in sync, our hands grazing each other's. She looks over at me.

"This is exactly where I want to be." My pinky finger links with hers.

My eyes go to our hands as I try to calm my nerves. "So the blonde," she starts, and she smiles at me. "Is she someone you are seeing, or is she a friend?" I look at her, and I have no idea who she is talking about. "When we were walking into the bar, you were having a conversation with her."

"Katey?" I ask, not realizing this is an issue. "It's the first time I've seen her in over five months. We had classes with each other last semester."

"I don't know her name," she says. "I know she was about yay high." She motions with her free hand to her head. "Blonde hair, touched your chest." I try not to smile when she adds that part. "You leaned down and said something in her ear, and then she looked up at you like you hung all the stars in the sky and knew where Santa lived."

I can't help but laugh out loud when she says that. "I can tell you right now that I have nothing going on with anyone," I state, my stomach rising as if it's doing the wave. "I haven't for a while but especially not since I met you." She looks down, and I can see her try to hide her smile. She stops walking and beams up at me.

"This is me." She points over her shoulder at the house behind her.

I think about how I hate that this night is ending so soon. My heart speeds up in my chest. "What about you? Anyone back home that you are attached to?" I take the leap and ask her the big question.

She looks at me, her eyebrows pinching together, confused by my question. "You can't be serious? One, I wouldn't do that because I hate long-distance relationships, and two I wouldn't be trying to you know…" She just looks at me. In the darkness of the night, her eyes are a touch darker.

"You are not only beautiful but you are also kind and generous and…"

"Yes to all of that." Her smile fills her face, and she tilts her head back to look up at me, and my hand lets go of hers. I reach up with both my hands to hold her face in my palms. Her hands go to my hips, and here in the middle of the quiet street, I lean down and do what I've been dying to do since I bumped into her the first day I met her.

I kiss her softly, her eyes closing, and I'm about to let her go when she pushes herself against me, and her arms go around my neck. "Not so fast there," she says and tilts her head to the side, coming back with another kiss, but this one isn't as soft as the first one. This one, she kisses me, and then her tongue comes out. My hands move from her face into her hair as my tongue slides in with hers and I taste the whiskey on her. Her hands slide into the back of my hair as the kiss deepens. She makes me lose my mind completely with just a kiss. I kiss her lips softly as her eyes flutter open. "I should get going," I say, leaning in for just one more second and taking another kiss.

"Or you can stay over, and we can…" She puts her hand on my stomach, and my mouth waters to taste her again.

"Or I can go, and we can talk tomorrow," I say. When I have her for the first time, I don't want her to be tipsy. My hand slips into hers. "And then maybe we can."

"We can do that right now." She gets up on her tippy-toes and kisses under my chin. "Walk up those steps and…" She nips my neck.

I pull her close to me, not ready to say goodbye without one more kiss. "Go upstairs." I kiss her one more time, and then she turns and walks up the steps.

"If you want to come back," she says over her shoulder, "it's the second floor." She opens the door. "First room has my name on the door."

"You have your name on your door?" I ask.

"Lydia brought home a friend once, and he thought my room was hers and came in trying to do the helicopter with his penis." I can't help but laugh. "I threw my shoe at him, and he will never try that again." She lifts her hand. "But I won't say no if you try it."

"Good night, Harlow," I say, putting my hands in my back pockets to stop from going to her.

"Good night, Travis," she says and turns into the house. I wait a minute when I see a light come on. I don't move until the light goes back off and then turn to walk to my house. The whole time, I really fucking hope she remembers this kiss in the morning.

Seven

Harlow

"Good night, Harlow." I hear his voice, and my eyes flutter open. I take a second to blink the sleep away from my eyes before reaching over and grabbing my phone off the bedside table. "Eight forty-seven," I groan as I turn over to my other side, facing the wall and then looking at my phone as I open my Instagram app. My tongue feels like it's got little cotton balls on it.

The first picture that pops up is the picture we took at the bar last night. My eyes go straight to Travis, who stands beside me, and then all I can think about is our kiss. The kiss I've been dying to get for months. The kiss I've dreamed about. The kiss that just thinking about it gives me all the butterflies in the world. The kiss I would probably tell my cousins about. But what I wasn't expecting was the kiss that would end all fucking kisses. I felt it all the way down to my bones. My head kept spinning around and around as his tongue slipped in with mine. I kept telling myself it was the alcohol in me. I kept making one excuse after another. I hadn't been kissed in a long time, and he was a good kisser. I liked him. It was cold outside. It was only when I walked into the apartment and shut the door did I admit that this was the kiss I would be telling everyone in my life about. That kiss would ruin it for all other men.

I close down the phone when my heart gets a sudden little ping of regret that he didn't come in with me. Walking to the bathroom, I wash my face and brush my teeth before heading to the kitchen and making a coffee.

The coffee starts brewing when I walk over to the window in the corner and look out. The gray clouds in the sky make it a great day for staying in bed. I turn to walk back to the kitchen when the machine stops at the same time as one of the bedroom doors opens. My eyes go to the hallway, where I see Jake walking out with Lydia following him.

His shoes are in his hand as Lydia looks down, and when Jake's eyes land on me, he stops walking. "Hey," he greets, and my eyes just go wide.

"Morning," I say, looking over at Lydia, who just glares at me.

"Well, I'll be going," Jake says and turns toward Lydia. It looks like he's going to go in for a kiss when she puts her hand to his forehead and pushes him away.

"Go," she tells him, and he smirks at me, then walks

out of the apartment. When the door closes behind him, I look over at Lydia, who holds up her hand.

"What happened to the saying 'don't eat where you shit'?" I remind her when I said that Travis was cute. "Don't go there, I believe you said. It's not a great idea because he's part of your social circle. If you hook up with him, it'll be awkward the day after." I repeat all the things she told me.

"First of all." She holds up her finger. "It's don't shit where you eat," she corrects me, walking to the fridge and grabbing a water bottle. "And second of all, I know, I know." She brings the bottle of water to her lips and drinks half of it. I am not going to say that he left his mark on her neck because she hates hickeys. "But he was being cute, and I was drunk, and well, he's good with his mouth."

"I bet." I try to hide my smile as I walk to my coffee cup, grabbing it and pouring some milk into it.

"Whatever you are thinking." She points at me. "Stop thinking it."

"The only thing I was thinking is you are going to have to go seven to ten days without sex with anyone new." She looks at me, confused. "I mean, how else would you explain that hickey on your neck?"

Her hand flies to her neck, and she runs to the long mirror we have on the wall right next to the television. "That motherfucker." I snicker into my coffee, and she turns to glare at me. "I told him not to suck too hard."

"Isn't that something he would say?" I giggle at my own joke and walk toward my bedroom, leaving her looking at herself in the mirror as she tries to wash off the little red mark.

I get back into bed, grabbing my phone, when I hear a knock on the front door, and I laugh, knowing that it's probably Jake who came back asking for more. I'm about to call my parents when the knock on my door has me looking over.

"Yeah," I say softly, and my eyes widen when I see Travis opening my door. "Oh, my," I whisper, getting off my bed.

"Hey," he says, coming in, and he looks like he just woke up and ran his hands through his hair. His white long-sleeved shirt is pushed up to his elbows, his gray sweatpants are loose on his legs but tight around the ankles.

"Hey," I reply softly, and I can't help the smile that fills my face when I see him. My heart skips a literal fucking beat, and I contemplate going to him and giving him a kiss. One side of my head screams at me to go, while the other side of my head tells me not to move. "Um…"

He holds up his hand. "I need to say something," he says, and I can almost feel the tension in the room.

"Okay," I say, not sure why, but the way his tone is, I know that this conversation is one that I'm not going to be happy with. "Go ahead."

"Thank you," he says, looking down at his feet and then up again. "Last night." He looks at me, and I smile at him, remembering the best part of the night. "I spent the whole night replaying it over and over again in my head."

"Me, too," I say, and he just looks at me.

"I'm sorry I kissed you," he says, and the words feel like he just threw a bucket of ice water on me and not in any kind of refreshing way. He runs his hands through his hair again and holds his neck. My hands wring in front of me nervously, my heart feeling as if it's sinking in my chest. "Even though I loved kissing you." His voice trembles. "I don't want to ruin our friendship."

"What if it doesn't ruin our friendship?" I finally say, looking at him. "What if we don't let it ruin our friendship?"

"You mean a lot to me," he says, and this time, I groan.

"That is so much worse than it's not you, it's me." I try to make a joke out of it while I chase away the tears.

"It's so not that," he says. "You." He points at me. "You literally are a dream come true, and I just don't want to push anything on you." He looks down. "I know that you were drinking last night, and I would hate for you to think I took advantage of that. I never ever."

"What if I want you to kiss me again?" I ask, and his hand falls from his neck. "Like if I told you right now that I want you to kiss me when there is no alcohol in my system, and I'm refreshed, and it's the day after. Would you kiss me?" I take a step toward him. "Because if truth be told, I've been waiting for you to kiss me for a really long time." I stand in front of him, and I can see his chest is rising and falling. I take a leap of faith and put my hands on his chest. "And if I'm really honest…" I look down nervously. "I wasn't drunk at all. But for memory's sake, I think we should share another kiss before we make the final decision." I take the final step to him, making our chests flush against each other. "I mean, if we aren't going to even try, I'd like to make sure it's what I remembered."

"Harlow." I'm not sure if it's a question or a plea, but I move my hands up on his chest toward his neck.

"I feel a full reenactment is mandatory at this time." I stop talking when his mouth falls on mine. His tongue slides into my mouth, and I realize I was wrong last night. Because today, with his tongue twirling with mine, is the best kiss I've ever had. His hands go to my waist as he grips my hips, pulling me closer to him. I moan when I feel his cock erect, and the sudden need to have him on top of me is almost carnal. The need to jump on him and wrap my legs around his waist fills my head.

I move my hands down his shoulders toward his arms and slide to the front of his shirt, bunching it up in my hands. The kiss goes from soft to a needy kiss, and then he steps away from me. The both of us are panting as he looks at me. "That was…"

"That was insane." The words come out of my mouth like word vomit as my hand comes up to touch my lips. "Thank God I asked for a rematch because that"—I point at where we were just kissing—"that is so much better than last night."

"It was, wasn't it?" He shakes his head almost in disbelief. "It wasn't supposed to be so good."

"I mean, if we are good at kissing, can you imagine what else we are good at?" I wiggle my eyebrows at him.

"Get dressed," he tells me, and I just look at him. "I'm not going to go to second base without taking you out on a date."

"It's nine o'clock in the morning," I remind him.

"We can go for breakfast." He runs his hands through his hair. "And then we can maybe go for a walk."

I look at him and peel the shirt off me, leaving me standing in the middle of the room with my tits out. "Or," I say, my heart beating and my stomach flip-flopping like a fish out of water, tossing my shirt to the side, "we can pretend every single time we met for coffee was a date, so technically, we are way ahead of the dating game, but way behind in the let's-get-naked game." He just looks at me and doesn't say a word. Shit, maybe this was a bad idea. The nervousness in my head turns to mortification, and I really wish I wasn't standing here topless. I'm about to turn around and hope the floor opens up and swallows me when in one smooth motion, he reaches behind him and pulls his shirt over his head. I stare at him with my mouth open. His whole chest is defined, and you see every single muscle he has. "Holy shit." The words come out before I can stop them.

"I like going to the gym." He smirks. "It's like therapy to me."

"Well, if we are taking votes," I say, holding up my hand, walking toward him, I can see the outline of his cock pushing against his pants. I use my index finger to run down the middle of his chest. "I approve."

"Harlow." He says my name when my finger gets to the waist of his pants. "Are you sure about this?"

I look up at him and lick my lips. "Only thing that I'm sure of right now is that I need you to get me naked."

He swoops down and wraps an arm around my waist, picking me up. My legs automatically wrap around his waist as he walks me toward my bed. "Well, then, let's get you naked."

Eight

Travis

"Well, then, let's get you naked." I carry her to her bed. I was going to take her out and wine and dine her. Instead, she took off her top, leaving me fucking speechless because one, she is fucking perfect, and two, my cock has never been so hard in my life.

I put a knee on her bed and then lower her on her back, her legs still wrapped around my waist while I lean down and kiss her. My tongue comes out to play with hers, round and round in a circle, and my hands move on their own when I cup her tits. She lets go of my mouth to moan out my name. "Travis," she says softly.

My head moves without thinking as I take one perfectly pebbled pink nipple into my mouth. My teeth come down to nibble on it before sucking it back into my mouth. Her hips rise, and she tries to ride my covered dick. "Fuck," I curse, taking the other nipple into my mouth. I feel her hands moving down my chest, and my stomach goes in with her touch as she slips her small hand into my pants. When her hands find my cock, I close my eyes for a second and don't move.

Her legs fall to the sides, and I move, lying down next to her. "Yes," she pants. "I can get better access like this." I lean forward, kissing her lips with my hand on her hip as she fists my cock. I sit up, pulling my cock out of her reach, and she groans, "Why did you do that?"

"Because I want you naked," I admit, reaching for her shorts and pulling them down, seeing that she isn't even wearing panties. Her pussy has a tiny landing strip right on top. "Now this," I say, my fingers moving between her pussy lips. "This is fucking heaven." I slide one of my fingers inside her, her legs open wide for me.

I move in and out twice before she sits up and pulls my pants down. "We should both be naked," she says, and my finger slides out of her. I take off my pants and get back into bed with her, facing her. She moans as she comes in for a kiss while her hand jerks my cock. Her tongue slides into my mouth while I move my hand down to slide my fingers back into her again. Her hand moves at the same speed as mine as we torture each other. She lets my mouth go when I feel her squeezing my fingers. "Oh, God." Her head flies back, and I lean in and take one of her pebbled nipples in my mouth, and she finally comes on my fingers. Her hand stops midjerk on my cock, and I know that had she continued, I would have come on her hand. I move my head lower down her chest, kissing her stomach, my fingers still fucking her when I get to her landing strip and give it a soft kiss. My tongue slides out as I trail down to her clit, her wetness hitting my tongue as I flick it. "No," she says, and I look up at her, stopping. "Sensitive," she says, panting. While I look into her eyes, I suck her clit into my mouth. Her head falls to the side as she comes again, and my fingers fuck her until her legs fall to the sides. "Jesus," she says, looking at me. "That was."

"It was." I smirk, taking my fingers out of her and licking them clean.

"Condom," she says as she watches, and I look at her with big eyes.

"I don't," I start to say when she leans over and opens the side drawer table.

"My cousins bought me a box as a joke," she shares, and I look at her. "I guess the joke's on them."

I grab the condom and tear it open. I'm about to put it on me when her hand grabs the base of my cock, and her mouth slides down on it. I stop midway as I close my eyes and take in the wetness of her mouth. "I don't know what I'm doing," she says. "So tell me if I'm doing this wrong." She swallows my cock again, trying to get it as deep as she can. Her hand joins her mouth, and when I feel my balls start to get tight, I push her away. "Was that not good?" she asks, and I shake my head, squeezing my cock with my hand to stop before I come on her face.

"I was going to come," I say.

"Isn't that the point?" she says, and I cover my cock

with the condom. She lies on her back, opening her legs.

I crawl between her legs. "That's the point, but I'd much rather do it like this." Sliding my cock up and down her slit, I then slowly enter her. I watch her close her eyes as I push all the way in her, my balls hitting her ass. We both groan, and she lifts her legs to my shoulders. "More?" I ask, and she nods her head. I pull out until the tip and slam into her, and this time, I have to close my eyes because it feels so fucking good. "So tight." My hips start moving faster, the sound of my balls hitting her ass fills the room.

"Travis." She moans my name. One of her hands plays with her nipple while the other one moves down between her legs. "Faster," she begs me. "Right there." My cock pounds into her as hard as I can go, and her pussy gets tighter and tighter. "Yes," she says out loud. "Yes," she repeats every single time I bury myself in her. "I'm going to." Her eyes close, and she lifts her hips up and comes all over my cock. I can't stop myself this time, when my balls get tight, as I slam into her holding her hips in place, but she rotates them anyway as she comes again.

"Fuck," I pant out, rolling to the side of her. My cock slips out of her as I lie on my back, my arm flinging onto my chest. "I think." I close my eyes, trying to get my panting under control.

"I think we need to do that again," she says from beside me. When my head turns to look at her, she explains, "That has got to be a mistake."

My eyebrows pull together, and she must see the

confused look on my face. "There is no way that the sex was this good." She shakes her head, putting her hands to her head. "Like poof. Mind blown."

I can't help but laugh, and she turns to look at me. "So when can we do round two to make sure that it was as good as I think it was? Or was it just me?"

Turning on my side, I say honestly, "It wasn't just you. I thought that the kiss was out of this world and now this." I point at us. "It's almost like it's not real."

"Oh, it's real," she says, kissing me. "And the minute your cock wakes up, and I ride you, I'll let you pinch me just to make sure it's real." She winks at me, and my cock wakes up, but I know that I have to get away from her and take off the condom.

"Bathroom?" I ask. She points at the door in the corner of the room, and I walk into the bathroom, not closing the door. Taking the condom off and turning on the water, I wet a rag.

"Should I start without you?" she shouts. I poke my head out of the door, and she's in the middle of the bed with her legs spread, waiting for me. My cock goes hard in exactly one second.

"Don't you dare start without me," I say, rushing out of the bathroom and diving straight for her pussy. I lick up her slit and flick her clit, and she moans. She runs her hand through my hair and then pulls my face closer to her pussy as she moves her hips side to side. "You are going to be the death of me." I look up at her right before biting down on her clit.

We spend the whole day licking, sucking, and making

sure the last time was as good as we thought it was. Every single time I thought we couldn't top it, she proved me wrong. "I'm going to need food," I say after I come down her throat for the second time. "And definitely water. I think I'm dehydrated."

She rolls off the bed, and I watch her perfect ass walk over to the little fridge she has in the corner as she takes out a bottle of water. "Here, drink this, and I'll get dressed. We can go somewhere to eat."

"You want to go out?" I ask her, grabbing the water bottle from her and finishing it in one go.

"I don't want to go out, but if we stay in this room, we'll just keep having sex." She smirks. "Not that I'm complaining." She walks over to her tall dresser, taking out a thong and a bra. "You just going to watch me get dressed?"

"That was the plan," I say, my cock needing to rest but then seeing her bend over gets me to half-mast again.

"Get up and put that away until later." She points at my cock, and I get up, grabbing my boxers and pants. We walk out of the room ten minutes later, and I stop when I come face-to-face with all three girls. Rachel sits on the couch while Victoria and Lydia stand in the kitchen.

"Hey," I say, trying not to be embarrassed.

"Hey," Rachel replies, rolling her lips. "I'd ask you how you are doing…" she starts.

"But from the moans and groans of the past six hours, I'm going to go out on a limb," Lydia starts to say, bringing the bottle of water to her lips to hide the smile. "You are really good."

"Oh, he was," Harlow says, slipping her hand in mine as she looks up at me, the smile on her face spreading from ear to ear.

"Trust me, we know," Victoria says, and I just shake my head. "At one point, I thought you were going to bust the wall."

"It wasn't that bad," I finally say out loud.

"At one point, I think I needed a cigarette," Lydia jokes. "And I don't smoke." She looks at Harlow. "And you, all Miss Innocent Harder Faster," she mimics Harlow "A lady in the streets and a freak in the bed." I can't help but laugh.

"Okay," Harlow says, pulling me out the door. "You are one to talk. We had to throw out the last couch because you had sex on it."

"We could have steam cleaned it." She rolls her eyes. "How was I supposed to know you guys would catch us?"

"It was noon," Rachel says, sitting on what must be the brand-new couch.

"On a Sunday," Victoria reminds her. "How could we not catch you?"

"This sounds like fun," I say. "But I got to get my girl fed." I pull her out of the apartment, and she laughs. "What's so funny?"

"Your girl fed." She repeats the words as we walk down the stairs.

"What's funny about that?" I ask, and she just chuckles. "Are you not my girl?" I ask, and the pit of my stomach burns. "I assumed after that…" I point back at the house when we walk down the steps and are standing outside. "That you were definitely my girl."

I don't move from the spot, and she turns to me, and she is more beautiful than she was before. She puts her hands on my chest. "You want me to be your girl?" She tilts her head back, and my hands come up to hold her hips.

"You can say that," I say nervously, leaning down and kissing her lips. My body wakes up as if she is the beating of my heart.

"Okay." She smirks at me, kissing my neck where my heart beats. "I'll be your girl."

Nine

Harlow

"What do you mean, you aren't coming home for the summer?" my father says, his face coming into the phone. "The last time we saw you was Christmas." I'm in the middle of my bed on my weekly FaceTime call with my parents.

"You see me weekly," I remind him. "I can't say no to this job," I tell them. "It's interning at the emergency vet clinic in the city. Do you know how much experience that will give me?" I shake my head. "You told me to apply for it." When I got the application form in class, I didn't know if I should apply or not.

"What about Travis? Is he staying?" my mother asks, and I smile.

"Are you still with that guy?" my father groans, and I

can't help but laugh.

"Yes, he's staying, too. We both were chosen," I answer, thinking about how nervous we both were to get it and then nervous about if one of us got it and not the other. "And I'm very much still with Travis." I don't tell them that we are almost living together and barely spend a night apart from each other. They don't need to know this. "Besides, you said he was a good guy." I point at my father. They haven't officially met, but one day, he FaceTimed me, and Travis was here, so I introduced them.

"That was before I knew he was your boyfriend." My father groans the last word. "Who dates a girl without asking their father's permission?"

I can't help but laugh while my mother rolls her eyes. "It's not marriage, honey." She puts her hand on his arm.

"I will remind you," I start to say. "Reed knocked up Hazel, and they weren't even dating."

"He married her," my father counters.

"Six years later." I laugh. "Anyway, I have to go now. Travis is taking me out on a date. I will call you guys next week," I confirm, blowing kisses to them before I get off the bed and walk over to the closet.

"What does one wear for a six-month date?" I ask myself, looking in and seeing what I should wear. He didn't even give me hints; he just said be ready to go at six.

I walk back to the bed and call him. "Hey, baby," he says softly when he picks up the phone. He left me this morning to go work out with a kiss on my neck.

"Hi. Listen, I know you want to surprise me and all," I start to say, and he laughs.

"You hate surprises," he reminds me.

"I don't hate surprises." He knows me sometimes better than I know myself, and it's both wonderful and scary all at the same time. "I just choose to know things before they happen. Anyway," I huff out, going back to the closet. "What should I wear? Is it casual or white-glove service?"

"Okay, one," he says. "I would never do white-glove service and not tell you."

"So, casual," I say, and he laughs.

"It's casual," he confirms.

"Casual pants or casual skirt?" I ask, and he groans.

"Anything you wear will be perfect, just like you," he says, and I can hear my cousins' fake vomit.

"See you in twenty," he says, and I shake my head, hanging up the phone. I grab my long floral skirt that hugs my hips, then goes loose all the way to my ankles and grab a tight white top that reaches just above my belly button.

I'm standing in the bathroom when I hear my door open, and I see him. "Ohh, you look nice," he says, standing behind me with his hands on my hips when he leans down and kisses my neck. His hands move to the front as he hugs me to him.

"I figured that I'd go with a long skirt so if we have sex in the car again, I can be somewhat covered." I watch his face in the mirror. "You know because last time security caught us."

"Don't remind me." He shakes his head. "We almost got a ticket for indecent exposure."

"It would serve you well. I told you to wait until we got home." His face looks at me through the mirror in shock.

"You literally turned in the passenger seat and opened your legs and said, 'Do I look wet?'" I roll my lips. "I almost crashed the car."

"It was a legitimate question," I say, and he just shakes his head. "Okay, let's go. Before you fake a fight with me just to have make-up sex."

We walk out of the apartment and down the stairs. He opens the car door for me, and I wish I could say that he does it only sometimes, but he does it every single time. He opens my door for me, he pulls out my chair, he waits for me to eat. "Thank you," I say, kissing his lips and then getting in.

I watch him walk around the car, and my heart still skips a beat every single time I see him, and trust me, I've seen every single inch of him. I hold his hand when he pulls away from the apartment and looks out the window. "How far is this place?" I ask, trying not to ask too many questions.

"Not too far, about forty minutes," he replies, and I look over at him.

"So, not in the city." I tilt my head to the side, and he just shakes his head.

"You are the worst," he says, turning up the music louder so I don't ask any questions. It's more than an hour before he parks in a gravel parking lot.

"Oooh," I say, looking around and seeing trees everywhere. "We've never been here," I state, and he smirks at me, getting out of the car and walking to the trunk.

I get out and walk around to meet him in the back as he takes out a big picnic basket and then grabs another bag. "Are we having a picnic?" I ask him, putting my hand to my mouth.

"You said that you never had one and how romantic it could be," he reminds me, and I lean up and kiss his lips. "Now follow me," he says, and I hold his forearm as we walk onto the grass.

All I see are trees everywhere, and I can hear the soft sound of a stream coming when we make our way around the bend. I see willow trees everywhere and the creek running down in front of it. "This is magical," I say, looking up as I hear a bird flying by.

"So, you approve?" he says, stopping near the creek under two big willow trees. I can't help the big smile on my face as I nod at him. "Good. Now, go over there." He points at me. "And let me set up."

"I can help you," I offer, and he shakes his head and points toward the creek.

"And don't peek either," he warns me as I walk down to the creek. The urge to look over my shoulder is huge. But five minutes later, he calls my name, and when I turn around, I'm stunned.

The blanket is open in the middle with the picnic basket at the corner. Platters of food are in front of it, all covered. A bouquet of sunflowers is at another corner with a bottle of champagne and two glasses. Two pillows are at another corner. "I hope this is okay," he says, and I have no words.

"You did all this?" I ask, looking to see that he has a platter of fruit, another of cakes, another of sandwiches, and then one more of cheese.

"I want to say yes." He sits down in the middle of the blanket, pulling me down on it with him. "But my sisters did help me, and well, my mother." I shake my head. I have yet to meet his family in person, but we have met through FaceTime. "I hope it's okay."

"It is," I confirm, and then I see the soft little candles he has put around the blanket for when the sun goes down. "This is more than okay." I sit with my legs to the side. He leans over and grabs the bottle of champagne and pops the cork, moving it off the blanket when it starts to bubble over, making me laugh. "Very smooth," I say as he hands me a glass of champagne and then grabs the bottle of water for himself, pouring it into the other glass.

"To us." He holds the glass of water up, and I can't even try not to smile.

"To us," I say, clinking my glass with his and then taking a sip. I can't help but look around again. "I can't believe you did all this." I lean forward, giving him a soft kiss on his lips. "It's just perfect."

"No." He shakes his head. "You are perfect." I can't even control the butterflies in my stomach. Instead, I finish off the glass of champagne. Putting the glass down beside the food, I move toward him.

I get on my knees, lifting my dress, when I move my

leg over to straddle him. I hold his face in my hands and say the words that I've been biting my tongue to say for the past five months. "I love you." I look into his eyes when I say the words and then see his mouth open, and I put my finger on it. "You don't have to say it back. I just wanted you to know that these past six months with you have been more than I could ever imagine." I lean forward and kiss him softly.

His hands rub my back. "Promise me something." He says the words so softly, and I can hear the sounds of crickets in the distance.

"I will promise you anything," I say, knowing that he could ask me anything, and the answer will always be yes.

"Promise me that you'll be there by my side on the happiest day of my life."

My fingers push back the hair on his forehead as the image of me walking down the aisle to him fills my mind. "I promise," I assure him.

"Good," he says, kissing me softly. My heart speeds up so fast in my chest I think I'm going to throw up from all this happiness. I don't think it can get better than this, and then it does when he says the words I've been dying to hear. "I love you, Harlow."

Ten

Travis

"I'm so nervous I think I'm going to throw up," Harlow says from beside me, sitting in the passenger seat.

My hand is stretched over the console to rest on her lap. "Would you relax? It's going to be fine."

"It's a big deal," she says. "Meeting the whole family is always a big deal." We are on our way home for my cousin's wedding. She's already met my sisters and my mother, but this weekend, she'll meet all of them.

"I met all of your family," I remind her. "I thought your father was going to shoot me at least once that weekend."

She throws her head back and laughs. "He was just making sure you stayed on your side of the house."

"He put an alarm on my bedroom door. Every time I

got up to go to the bathroom, the alarm was saying 'door one opened.'" I shake my head as she rolls her eyes.

"It was one day, and my mother made him take it off." She lifts my hand and brings it to her lips. We've been together for a year and a half, and it's been a dream. After we spent the summer interning at the emergency clinic, we each got part-time jobs there. We were together all the time. Although this semester was a tricky one, our class schedule was all opposite of each other, so our shifts at the clinic were split. There would be days we wouldn't be able to see each other, and I hated it.

"Well, lucky for us, we are staying at a hotel this weekend," I say, and she shakes her head.

"Did you tell your mom yet?" she asks, rolling her lips, knowing full well that my mother will not be happy about that little part.

"I will," I say, turning down on my street. "Tonight after dinner when I say goodbye." I pull into the driveway. "Also, it's good to note I'm going to be blaming you." I get out of the car before she chews my ass, and I'm not even on her side of the car yet before the front door opens and my mother comes out.

"Hi!" she shouts from the top of the porch and waves her hand at us. "Just in time, I just took the pie out of the oven." I wait for Harlow to get out of the car to join me and slip my hand in hers.

"Hi, Mom," I say, walking up the step and kissing her on the cheek.

"Hey, honey," she says, smiling at me. "Harlow, looking beautiful as always." She pushes me out of the way to kiss Harlow's cheek.

"Thank you so much for having me," Harlow says, and every single time I look at her, I fall more and more in love with her.

"Travis, why don't you go get the bags out of the car, and the girls will go and wait in the kitchen?" my mother says.

"Yes, Travis, why don't you do that?" Harlow says, knowing full well we aren't staying here. The last time we stayed here, she refused to have sex with the fear that my mother would hear. It was a long four days, and by the time we got on the highway, I had to pull over.

"Why don't I do it later?" I say, ignoring the look Harlow is giving me. "Is the pie warm?"

"Probably too hot to eat just this moment," Harlow says, and I glare at her. "So it's the perfect time to get the bags."

Thankfully, another car comes down the driveway, and I'm saved. I look over and see that it's Shelby. I lean over. "Tonight, I'm going to make you pay for that," I whisper in Harlow's ear.

"With your mouth or your fingers?" She winks at me. "Either way, I win." She kisses my neck and then greets my sister.

"Did you bring me the dress?" Shelby comes up the steps and takes off her glasses, putting them on top of her head.

"Nice to see you, Shelby," I say, putting my arm around Harlow.

"I'm not talking to you." She looks at me. "And you

know why."

I look at her, shocked. "What did I do now?"

"That's enough, you two," my mother says as Shelby glares at me, and I stare at her with my mouth hanging open.

"By the way," Shelby says, "Suzanne from the hotel says that everything is set for you when you arrive." I glare at her.

"What hotel?" my mother asks.

"Oh, you didn't tell Mom?" Shelby says, and I want to push her shoulder and hope she falls down, but I did that when I was eight, and I got the spanking of my life. "Travis is staying at the hotel."

"What?" my mother says out loud in a gasp.

"Let's eat pie," Harlow says, clapping her hands together. "I'm a little hungry."

My mother looks at Harlow, who walks up the steps and asks her if she can have water. My mother will never be rude and say no, so she turns and walks into the house with Harlow.

"Who hurt you as a child?" I ask, and the question makes her laugh as she punches my arm and walks into the house. "But seriously, why are you pissed at me?"

"Oh, I'm not," she says over her shoulder. "Just keeping you on your toes." She throws her head back and laughs.

"Why couldn't I have a brother?" I look up at the sky, shaking my head, and then walk into the house, hoping my mother forgot about us staying at the hotel. She did not.

"THERE YOU ARE." I look over my shoulder and see my best friend, Bennett, walking toward me. His tie is to the side, and I know that he hates wearing suits. I'm at the bar waiting to get something to drink. He stops next to me and slaps my shoulder. "I fucking hate wearing a suit."

I laugh at him, turning back and leaning on the bar. He's in law school and he better get used to wearing suits, "The key is to leave the top shirt button open."

"It is," he says. "It's this whole restriction." He motions with his arms, trying to cross them together. "It's like a straitjacket."

I can't help but laugh. We have been best friends since we met on the first day of kindergarten. The both of us cried the whole day, so we kind of sat together being miserable until dismissal. "Saw your girl when I walked in. She's a beauty," he says to me, holding up his hand and ordering a beer, when the guy drops my own beer down in front of me.

"I've never hit you before," I say, putting the beer to my mouth and taking a pull. "I would hate to do it now." I look around, spotting her right away as she stands with my three sisters, each of them with a wineglass in their hand. The light pink dress she is wearing molds her figure, and I can't wait to tear it off her. My cock gets hard just thinking about it. She must feel me looking at her because her eyes find mine, and she smiles at me.

He just laughs at me. "Relax there." He holds up his hand. "I'm not after your woman."

"Good to know," I say, turning back to him. "You look like shit," I say, and he laughs.

"Fucking finals," he says, shaking his head, and I close my eyes.

"Don't remind me." I take another pull of the beer.

"When are you done?" he asks, and I look over at him.

"Four weeks," I say. "I have my board certification exam, and then it's done." I look up at the ceiling. "It's been a crazy four years."

"Did you decide what you are doing after?" he asks the loaded question, and I look over at Harlow.

"No clue," I say. "I've never really brought it up." My stomach burns when I think about actually having this conversation.

"I mean, you can always do long distance," he offers, and I shake my head.

"Fuck no." I shake my head. "Long distance never works for anyone, and it just makes everyone resentful of the other. I'll never do long distance."

"I think that you really need to discuss this with her," he tells me, and I know he's right, the beer starting to burn in my stomach. I nod at him, turning and not seeing her.

"I'll see you later," I say, and he gives me a chin up before I walk away and look for her.

I stop when I see a couple of people I didn't say hello to, and then I see her talking to one of my mother's friends. Zigzagging through people to get to her, I hear the conversation as soon as I start to get close.

"So, what will you do after graduation?" Maureen asks her.

"Well," she says, looking down nervously. "Probably going to head back to the farm." Her whole face lights up when she says it. "My dream was always to open a practice there." My stomach sinks when I hear her say the words. "But I have to pass the exam first and then go from there."

"That sounds lovely," Ruby says. "I bet your parents are going to be happy you are home."

"Yes," she says softly. "They are." She brings the glass of wine to her lips and looks up and sees me. "Hi," she greets, and I smile at her, the whole time my stomach burns more and more.

"Hi," I say softly and then look around the room, not sure what to say or where to look. "Having fun?" I ask her awkwardly, and she just looks at me strangely.

"Are you okay?" She chuckles as Ruby and Maureen slowly walk toward the bar.

"Yeah, just tired," I lie to her. "Dreading going back home. It's going to be hell the next four weeks."

"You'll be fine. You are acing all your classes, and I'm not going to say this again. You might even beat me." She tilts her head back, and when she does this, I know she wants me to kiss her lips. I lean down and kiss her lips quickly, and that just makes me feel more like an ass.

"Time will tell," I say, bringing the beer to my lips, ignoring the pressure filling my chest. "Time will tell."

Eleven

Harlow

I look down at the textbook, the words not even registering in my head. The last two days have been so weird I can't even explain it if I wanted to. Everything was fine until the night of the wedding, and then he started acting very differently. I look over and see that it's almost five, and I know he's leaving the clinic. I pick up the phone and call him, expecting him to answer right away. Instead, it goes to voice mail. I hang up the phone and text him.

Me: Hey, want to study together?

I press send and look down, waiting for the three dots to come up, and when they do, my heart speeds up faster than before.

Travis: Already had plans to study with the boys. I'll

call you later.

"What the fuck?" I say, looking down at the phone. I let my anger get the best of me and text him.

Me: Let me know when you have time. We need to talk.

I wait for his reply, and when he doesn't answer, I throw on my jacket and go over to his place. The whole time my heart is pounding against my chest so fast it's almost as if I've run to his house instead of walked at a brisk pace. I keep going over everything in my head, trying to pinpoint if I did or said anything wrong. I walk up the stairs or better yet pounce up the steps.

I knock on the door and hear the sound of the boys on the other side. Usually, I would just walk in, but I am not sure about anything anymore. The door swings open, and Jake looks at me with a smile. "Why the hell did you knock?" He moves out of the way so I walk in and look around the room, not seeing Travis there.

"Is he here?" I ask, and Jake points at his bedroom. I walk toward his bedroom and knock on the door before entering. Which is stupid, to say the least, so I walk in and he's sitting in the middle of his bed, and he just looks at me, shocked I'm here. "Hey," I say, closing the door.

"Hey," he replies, putting the book down and getting up. "I didn't know you were coming."

I can't wait anymore. "What's going on?" I ask him, not moving from my spot, and the burning rolls up from my back to my neck. "Like, is there something going on that I don't know about?"

"I don't know what you're talking about," he denies,

and he's not even convinced himself.

"Something is bothering you." I point at him, and I have to think that this is the first time I've walked into a room with him, and he hasn't kissed me. He hasn't even attempted to kiss me.

"Nothing is bothering me." He runs his hands through his hair. "I'm just thinking, is all."

"Would you care to share what you are thinking about?" I ask him, wringing my hands together.

"I think that the next couple of weeks are going to be hard," he starts to say, putting his hands on his hips, and I know he does this when he's nervous, "And then I'm going to go home."

"Okay?" I say, my eyes never leaving him. "What are you saying?"

"I'm not saying anything, Harlow. I'm just pointing out the facts," he says, his voice rising just a bit, and it's so unusual for him. Usually, I'm the one raising my voice, and he stays calm. "In a couple of weeks, we will be finished with school, and then I'm going home. And maybe we should think about that." His voice trails off.

It's then it hits me, just like cold water hits you on a blistering hot day in the desert. "Are you breaking up with me?" I say, the pain in my chest creeping up. I stand here stiff as stone, my legs feeling like they are stuck to the floor, my shoulders feeling like they're pushing me down.

"I'm not saying that," he says. "I'm just saying that..." He throws up his hands. "I don't want a long-distance relationship," he says. "You have your plans, and I have mine."

I swallow, the stinging of tears rushing to my eyes as my nose starts to burn. "You made this decision without even talking to me about it," I say, my voice never wavering, and I am even surprised by it. My whole body is one nerve away from shaking like a leaf.

"What is there to talk about?" he says, and all I can do is look at him.

I shake my head. "Nothing." I stare at this man who I fell in love with, the man who held me when I was cold. The man who used to make me smile just by walking into a room. The man who would leave me little Post-it notes on my computer to tell me he loved me. The man who destroyed one of my lipsticks to write I love you on my mirror. The man who I thought I would spend forever with. The man who just like that, without even a second thought, broke my heart so willingly. "You're right; there is nothing to talk about." I turn, walking out of the room with my head down, one tear slipping out and then rolling down my cheek. I walk down the steps and then hear him calling my name.

"Harlow, wait," he says, and I make the stupid mistake of looking back.

"Goodbye, Travis," I say right before I run down the rest of the stairs. The phone in my pocket rings right away, and I know it's him. It stops ringing, and then the notification of a text message comes through.

Travis: Can you let me know when you get home?

I laugh bitterly as the tears run down my face freely. I press the little 'I' button on the corner of the screen, and then his name pops up, Travis, my love, along with all the pictures we've shared. The last picture he sent to me we took before the wedding. Him leaning in and kissing my neck while I laughed as I took the picture. I press the info button, and then with shaking hands, I click on block this caller.

I then call my father, who answers right away. "Hey, Dad," I say, trying to make my voice sound normal.

"Hey, honey," he says. "How're you doing?"

"Good, good," I say. "I was just wondering if the job offer was still on the table?" I ask him, and he laughs.

"Of course, it is," he says softly. "Anytime you want it."

"Great, I'll take it," I say, looking over my shoulder at the house I just ran out of. The lump in my throat is making it hard to swallow.

"That's great. What changed your mind?" he asks, because two weeks ago he called and gave me the job opportunity, and I turned him down, knowing I would likely stay in the city next to Travis.

"Just had a change of heart is all," I say, not ready to talk about what just happened. "Hey, do you think you can come down and help me pack up my stuff?"

"Sure can," he says. "Just name the time and place."

"I'll text you later," I say, taking a deep breath, and I hang up. "I'm going home," I say to the universe, not sure what the universe has in store for me.

FOUR YEARS LATER.

"You have mail," my secretary, Donna, says, and I just nod at her, grabbing the pile of letters on the counter.

"Thank you." I look down at the stack of envelopes in my hand, and the big white square one catches my attention.

"Looks like a wedding invitation," she says when I look to see who it's from. My heart stops in my chest. My hands drop everything else while I run my finger under the little sticker at the end.

Pulling out the white card, I can't move. Everything around me feels like it's spinning when I read the words.

You are cordially invited to the wedding of

Travis Baker & Jennifer Garner

Things are starting to settle down again, and the wedding season will be upon us before we even know it.

It's always an exciting and magical time.

It's even extra special this year because Travis is getting married.

Only time will tell if he actually walks down the aisle.

I wouldn't bet on it.

Dearest Love,

Nothing says spring like wedding season. The flowers, the champagne, the wedding guests. Surrounded by all the people you love. Sigh...the romance, it's my favorite time of year.

Travis will soon be walking down the aisle. Or will he?

It seems a couple of orders were placed by mistake, or were they? It also looks like an invitation was sent out that wasn't supposed to be sent out.

Will they get their happily ever after, or was he always meant for someone else?

Time will tell!

XOXO

NM

Twelve

Harlow

"So what's the verdict?" my brother, Quinn, asks as soon as I walk back out of the stall and into the hallway. I use the back of my forearm to wipe the sweat away from my forehead. My hands are dusty and dirty from being in the stall.

"Why yes, I'll take a bottle of water." I side-eye him as I walk toward the sink in the corner, washing off my hands, and then heading straight to the kitchen at the end of the long concrete pathway. I pass the empty office that I used to help out in when I was a teenager, going over to the fridge and grabbing a water bottle. Opening the bottle, I down half of it before turning back to him. "God, that feels good."

"Can you not be such a pain in the ass?" Quinn huffs

as he stands there in his blue jeans and white shirt, all put together with his cowboy boots. He puts his hands on his hips as he glares at me.

"I can," I say, putting the bottle on the counter next to me and leaning back on it. Crossing my arms over my chest, I then cross my feet at the ankles. My own boots are dusty and dirty. My scrubs that were clean now have some blood on them. "But then, what fun would that be?" I try not to smile, but when he groans, I can't help the laugh that escapes me.

"I swear to all the saints in the world." He looks up at the ceiling. "Can you be professional for once?"

I stand. "One, me coming to see you on a Friday afternoon at three is fucking professional, especially since I don't do calls on Friday." I point at him. "But since you made Grandpa call me like a pussy-ass bitch, I came out."

"One, I didn't make anyone call you." He puts up one finger. "And two, he was just here, so he said he would do me a favor."

I roll my eyes, knowing full well that my grandfather took matters into his own hands, regardless of if my brother called me or not. "Yeah, yeah," I say, huffing out. "Anyway, he's got mud fever."

"Shit," he swears, shaking his head.

"It's not bad. Got to clean it a couple of times and keep it dry," I say, grabbing my jacket. "I'll swing by tomorrow to see how he's doing."

He nods at me as I walk out of the barn, my eyes squinting as the sun hits my face. I take a second to lift my face and feel the heat before walking over to my pickup as I make my way back to my practice.

The sounds of gravel crunching under my tires as I come to a stop. The trees all around block most of the sun from coming in, so it's cooler. My boots also crunch when I walk toward the front stairs.

I've always had a vision of what my practice would look like, and when I showed my father, he made it happen. When it was time to discuss how I would pay him, he scoffed and informed me that it would just come to me when he died. I shake my head, thinking about it. Whenever they wanted to give you something or pay for something, they always brought up them dying.

I wanted the house to look like a log cabin, and when you walked in, the reception area was in the middle of the room with four rooms all around. Each room for a different type of animal. Behind those four rooms was where I did most of my work. The operating room was there, along with all the crates where we housed the pets we kept overnight. I can't help the smile that comes to my face when I stand at the door and see my logo, H.B. Animal Veterinarian. I turn the brass handle to the door and walk in. The bell on top of me rings, making Donna, the receptionist, look up from her desk. Donna has been with me since day two when I started, and she came in with her cat. I am not going to lie, I was overwhelmed with the phone ringing, and then it was all just so much at once. She smiled at me, sat in the chair, and has been with me ever since. She makes sure everything is neat and organized, so I get to do what I love best, which is work with the animals.

"Hey," she greets, and I look around to see that no one is waiting for me. The two wooden benches under the front windows are empty.

"Is this a dream?" I ask, trying not to get too excited. "Is there no one here?" I am even tempted not to walk in, afraid I'm going to hear a bark from one of the rooms with the closed doors.

She leans back in her chair. "You're welcome," she says, and I look at her. "I made sure that I booked you this afternoon off." My mouth hangs open. "You are going on forty-five days in a row of work."

"Forty-seven." I walk to the counter. "But hey, who's counting?" I lean on the counter. "I love my job." I close my eyes, and I swear I could probably fall asleep sitting in a chair.

"You have mail." Donna points at the stack of letters that sit at the end of the counter. I just nod at her, grabbing the pile of letters. Looking down at the first one, I then slowly move my finger to flip to the second.

"Thank you." I keep flipping one after another. The big white square one catches my attention. I stop and see my name addressed on the front of it. Dr. Harlow Barnes.

"Looks like a wedding invitation," Donna says, and I turn it. My heart stops in my chest, and I'm finding it so hard to breathe. My hands drop everything else while I run my finger under the little sticker at the end.

Pulling out the white card, I can't move. My breaths come out almost in pants, and I feel as if I'm having an out-of-body experience when I see the words written at the top of the white card in purple writing.

You are cordially invited to the wedding of

Travis Baker & Jennifer Garner

My feet automatically move across the floor toward my office. "Are you all right?" Donna asks, and I mechanically nod my head up and down.

"You can take off." My voice comes out without cracking, and I'm even shocked. The lump forms in my throat as I close the door behind me. My eyes never leave the top of the invitation. "He's getting married," I say the words out loud, the pain in my chest throbbing. "Oh my God." I grab my cell phone and call my cousin, Amelia, who answers after one ring.

"Hello," she says, and I can hear her kids in the background.

"Hey," I reply, and my voice cracks finally. "You will never guess what I just got." I blink away the tears, but one of them escapes and runs down my cheek. "You'll never guess," I say, sniffling, and I can hear a door close in the background, and it goes quiet.

"Where are you?" she huffs, and I can hear her moving fast and then the slam of a car door.

I close my eyes, listening to her start the car. "I'm in my office." I lean back in my chair, my eyes still closed.

"I'll be there in five." She disconnects, and I'm not sure I would be able to move anyway.

The phone drops from my hand, and I wonder if this is really happening or if it's a bad dream. It has to be a bad dream. Why in the world would this happen? I pick up my phone and text Rachel.

Me: Did you get something in the mail today?

I don't know how fast she will get back to me. In the past four years, the four of us have kept in touch. We usually see each other every couple of years, but I've kept in touch with Rachel almost monthly.

My phone rings in my hand, and I look down to see it's Rachel. "Hello," I answer, putting it on speakerphone.

"Please tell me you did not get a wedding invitation to his wedding!" she shrieks out. I can just imagine her face right now, and I laugh but it comes out with a sob. "Jesus Christ, why the fuck would he invite you to his wedding?"

"I have no idea," I say. "The last time I saw him was when he broke up with me," I lie. The actual last time I saw him was the day before I left to come home. I stupidly took one more walk to his place and saw him walking out. His head was down, and he had a hat on his head. Sunglasses hid his eyes. My heart sank to my feet, and I turned around and cried the rest of the way home.

"Lydia just texted that she got the invitation also," Rachel says. "And from what she is saying, so did Victoria."

"I just don't understand it," I finally say out loud. "Why the fuck would he invite me to his wedding?"

"I have no idea," she says, huffing out and then laughing. "But I know that if there is ever a time for some sweet tea, it's now."

"That sounds like a great idea." I look up at the ceiling when the door slams. "I have to go. I'll call you back later," I say and disconnect when my office door flies open.

"What happened?" Amelia asks, standing in front of me, and it looks like she's wearing pjs.

"What are you wearing?" I ask, and she looks down at herself.

"It's been a day," she states, coming in, and I laugh.

"You think your day is going bad," I say, picking up the white square paper in front of me and handing it to her. "I win."

She reaches out her hand to grab the white paper, and I let it go. Her eyes go to the top, and I know the minute she sees his name because they widen, and she looks back at me. "Shut the front door!" she shouts, and all I can do is nod my head. "Unbelievable. Who does this?"

"I have no idea," I say honestly, getting up and walking over to the cabinet that I keep the sweet tea in. "Rachel and the girls also got the invitations." I twist open the top and take a swig, then look over at her, offering her the bottle. She just shakes her head, and I take another gulp of it. "Why the fuck would he invite me to his wedding?" I look over at her and wait for her to answer.

"Oh, I thought you were asking the question and then were going to answer it yourself," she says, going to the couch in the corner and sitting on it. "Well, let's look at this."

"Yes, please, let's look at this," I say sarcastically, taking another swig of the bottle, the heat rising up in my body. I know that this is the sign when I should stop taking shots. It's the telltale sign that nothing good is going to come if I continue. "He breaks up with me two weeks before I have to write my exam." I hold up my finger. "And then." I take a swig and look at her. "I don't know if there is anything else after that."

"You dated for two years," Amelia points out, and I glare at her. "This is a huge deal."

"You don't think I know this," I retort, my voice going higher. The nerves in my body start, and my feet move on their own, pacing back and forth. "It's Travis." Saying his name feels foreign to me, yet feels like coming back home. "He was my everything." I take another sip of the tea. "I was going to…" I stop talking, knowing that this walk down memory lane will help no one.

"You were going to marry him." She fills in for me.

"I mean, if he would have asked, yes, I would have," I admit to her. "But apparently, Jennifer is the one for him."

"Well, imagine his surprise when you put down that you aren't going," Amelia says, and I look over at her. "You aren't going."

"I promised." The words come out in a whisper. "I promised that I would be there at the happiest day of his life."

Her mouth opens. "Well, promises can be broken." She stands up. "You are not going. That would be crazy. How does he even introduce you? Honey, this is Harlow. We went out in college?" She shakes her head. "It's not a good idea." She grabs the bottle from me. "And neither is drinking this shit when you're mad. You'll make bad decisions."

"You aren't even wearing a bra." I point at her, and

she gasps and covers her nipples.

"I rushed over here," she huffs. "Because I thought you were in need."

"I am in need," I confirm to her. "I'm in need of a date to go to my ex-boyfriend's wedding!" I yell.

"I'm going home," she announces. "Are you coming?"

"Did you make dinner?" I ask, and she glares at me.

"I haven't put on a bra. You think I made dinner?" she says with her teeth clenched.

"Gosh, just asking," I say and start to walk out of the office with her. "If you want, I can cook."

"The last time you tried to cook, the fire department had to come to your house." She looks over her shoulder at me.

"That was because I forgot I put the pot on the stove and then went to take a bath." I stop moving. "I'll meet you there," I say, turning around and walking back into my office.

I grab the white envelope and take it out. The pen is in my hand next as I click off the "will attend" with my name "Harlow Barnes." Sealing it back in the envelope, I toss it in the mailbox at the corner. "It'll be fine," I say as I open the mailbox and place the envelope in it. "I'll go and fulfill my promise, and then we can all move on." I close the lid and let go of the breath in me. "And I'll never see him again."

Thirteen

Travis

"Would you be quiet?" I hear someone whisper, and my eyes spring open. I take a minute to look around and see if I was dreaming or if it was actually coming from someplace in my house. "We should make coffee." I hear another whisper, and I look over and see that it's almost seven o'clock. The sun from outside is slowly trying to creep in from the blinds. My head turns toward the bedroom door as I listen to make sure.

"Oh, we should maybe make him something to eat." I close my eyes, blinking away the sleep, before sitting up in bed, and tossing the top cover to the side. Sliding out of bed, I tiptoe toward the front door while I hear another whisper. I stand in the doorway, making sure I recognize the voices before I walk out.

"We should have brought doughnuts or something." I shake my head and look out of the bedroom, seeing my three sisters all huddled at the front door. "You go and get him." Presley pushes Shelby toward the stairs, and if I hadn't just awoken from a deep sleep, I would laugh at the three of them.

"What the hell are you guys doing here?" I say, stepping out of my bedroom and looking down over the railing. The sound of all three of my sisters yelling fills the house. They all look up at me, huddled together.

"Jesus fucking Christ," Shelby, my oldest sister, says, putting her hand to her chest. "You gave me a fucking heart attack." Her black hair is tied up on top of her head, and she wears black yoga pants with a white shirt. Her blue eyes glare at me as if I did something wrong.

"Why the hell are you sneaking into my house?" I put my hand on the wooden banister and look down at them.

"We aren't sneaking." Clarabella shakes her head. "Who sneaks in by using a key?" She holds up the key she got from under the mat outside.

"You are lucky that I didn't come down with the baseball bat I have in the bedroom." I look at each of them.

"One." My youngest sister, Presley, puts up a manicured finger. "You suck at baseball," she reminds me. "You lost the game for us last year, and two"—she puts up another finger—"go get dressed. I'm about to throw up my croissant I just ate."

"I'm in my boxers," I say, looking down at myself. "And you are in my house. Imagine if I was naked." I throw my hands up, and my voice goes louder. The three of them all grimace with the fact that I could have been naked. "And two, I did not lose that game. It was the three of you thinking you can each catch a ball and fall into each other." I point at the three of them, all of them rolling their eyes.

"Go get dressed. We'll start the coffee," Shelby says, walking into the house and toward the kitchen.

I shake my head and walk back into my bedroom, going straight for the bathroom. I wash my face and run my hands through my hair before grabbing my blue sweatpants and going back downstairs. The smell of coffee fills the whole house. "Okay," Shelby says. "Rock-paper-scissors on who gets to say."

"No way," Presley says. "You're the oldest." She points at her, and I walk into the kitchen. The three of them stop talking as soon as they see me standing here.

"What the hell is going on?" I look at my sisters as they each look at each other, neither of them wanting to talk. Walking to the coffee machine, I pour myself a cup of steaming hot coffee. I don't bother with the milk when I turn and lean back on the counter. "Okay, go." I take another gulp.

"Okay, don't freak out," Clarabella starts. "But the fridges at the venue stopped working."

I look at them, not sure what she is saying as she walks out of the kitchen and goes to the living room, sitting on the L-shaped gray couch. "Okay, and...?" I look at Shelby.

"All the food for the wedding is spoiled." She says

the words, and I close my eyes. This is definitely not something you want to hear on your wedding day.

"But the good news," Clarabella says, "is that we already called our supplier, and from what he said, he should be able to get us most of the stuff."

"Most of the stuff," I repeat. "What about the rest of it?"

"Well, that is going to be our problem," Shelby says. "All you have to worry about is showing up on time."

"God, I'm starving," Clarabella announces, going to the fridge and opening it. "Why don't we have a nice family breakfast before our brother finally ties the knot?" She smiles.

"Oh, we should have brought champagne," Presley says from the couch. "We did not put our best foot forward." She lies down on the couch. "I can't believe you are giving away this couch."

I don't say anything. Instead, I look around at the brown boxes stacked all over the place. Jennifer's things were delivered over a month ago and have yet to be unboxed. Every single time we had plans to unpack, something would come up. I walk over to the couch and sit down, looking around at the bare walls. All the things I had hanging I took down to make Jennifer feel more at home. "I swear you guys will be married five years, and I have a feeling these boxes will still be here," Presley says quietly from beside me.

"We've been busy," I remind her. "I was the only vet at the practice for over a month. I worked seven days a week." When I passed the exam, I stayed at the emergency clinic. They hired me full-time, and I can't tell you how much I loved it. But I knew that there was no way I would be able to move up, so two years after that, I got the opportunity to open a practice near my hometown with two other vets.

The three of us never expected it to become as big as it did. We were so in demand that we outgrew the little place we rented after six months and bought our own land and built it to our liking. "Michelle had her baby early, and Roy broke his foot. What did you want from me?"

"You've been engaged for six months, and she has yet to move in," Presley states, pointing at all the boxes starting to collect dust.

"She had a lease, and she couldn't break it," I repeat the same thing I've been telling my mother and anyone else who asked about why she wasn't living with me. "And she didn't want to leave her roommate high and dry."

"I just find it crazy that you are marrying someone you haven't even lived with." She sits up. "It's insane to me. What if you get on her nerves, or she gets on yours?"

I take another gulp of coffee, hoping she doesn't see that I have had the conversation with myself over and over again. "It'll be fine. It's a learning curve."

"A learning curve." She gets up and laughs. "A learning curve is getting bangs. Moving in with someone is a huge deal."

"Aren't you supposed to be calming me down on my wedding day and telling me that everything is going to be okay, instead of making me second-guess it?" I ask her, and she just shrugs.

"Fine." She rolls her eyes. "It's a great idea that you didn't live with each other and the longest you spent in the same house at one time is two weeks because you were both on vacation and stuck on an island."

I pfft out and laugh all at the same time nervously. "She stays over all the time," I say, and she puts her hands on her hips.

"I bet you one hundred dollars that she doesn't even have a toothbrush here." She puts out her hand for me to smack it.

"Mom said I'm not allowed to take any money from you," I say, refusing to admit that she is right, and also it goes to say I also don't have one at her place.

"Presley," Shelby calls her. "You are in charge of making toast." Shelby then looks at me. "You"—she points at me—"over easy or scrambled?"

"Either is good," I reply as Presley walks into the kitchen to help my sisters with breakfast.

Today is my wedding day, I think to myself, leaning over and putting my coffee cup on the little table that will soon be leaving. Married, I let the word sink in. It feels like just yesterday we met, and now we are getting married. The nerves start to kick in my stomach. The feeling slowly climbs up, and the pressure starts in my chest.

"Come and eat," Clarabella calls from the kitchen over her shoulder. I grab my cup, getting up and zigzagging toward the kitchen. Grabbing one of the plates on the counter, I fill it up with eggs, bacon, and sausage.

I walk over to the little dinette table I have off to the side, pulling out a chair. My sisters join me a minute later. "Your last meal as a single person," Clarabella says, sighing.

"Can we not make it sound like I'm having my last meal before I'm executed?" I say, grabbing my fork, and the three of them laugh.

"You ready for today?" Shelby asks as she takes a bite of her toast.

"The question I should be asking is are you guys ready for today?" I look at them. When it came to planning the wedding, I left them in charge of it because they were the professionals after all. I had no idea what I was doing, and if a decision needed to be made, they called Jennifer.

"Everything is going to be perfect," Clarabella claims. "I double-checked everything last night before I went home." She smiles at me, and then her phone rings in her hand.

"Private caller," she says, swiping on the phone. "Hello," she answers, and I can see it happen all before my eyes. "What are you talking about?" Her face goes white as she looks at my sister. "Oh my God, we will be right there." The way her voice sounds, you know that it's not good. She's already out of her seat, and so are we when she looks at me. "Don't freak out," she says, and I don't know if she is telling me this or herself. It really feels like it's the calm before the storm because as soon as she says the words, chaos erupts: "The kitchen is on fire."

Fourteen

Harlow

"Okay, kiddo." I look over at my thirteen-year-old niece, Sofia. "Give me a hug. I'll be gone this weekend." We spent the whole day shopping together and then had dinner before I brought her back. It was one of the best days I've had in a while.

Sofia walks to me and gives me a hug, turning and walking to her room on her tippy-toes. My brother, Reed, and Hazel just had their third child a month ago, and well, he came into the world showing them why they shouldn't have another child.

"Are you really going to that wedding?" Reed looks at me as I walk to the kitchen. I pull open the fridge, grabbing a bottle of water, and then walk over to the island.

"What am I supposed to do?" I pull out the stool and sit down next to him. "I made a promise, and a promise is a promise." A fucking promise that I've been regretting ever since I got his wedding initiation in the mail a month ago.

"I don't think you need to keep a promise you made to an ex-boyfriend," Hazel says. "An ex-boyfriend you still love."

I roll my eyes at her. "I don't still love him." I take another sip of water, hoping that she doesn't see the bullshit written all over my face. "Besides, I got an invitation. If I don't show up, he's going to know it bothers me." I push off the counter, the anger coming back to me because who the fuck invites their ex anything to their wedding? "I'll go to the wedding, show my face, smile, and wish him well." I give them the same smile I'm going to give him. My hands are balled into fists beside me. "See? Fine." I turn on my heels and storm out of the house. Slamming the front door behind me, I stop and close my eyes, hoping to hell I didn't wake the baby.

Getting in my truck, it takes me three minutes to get home. Grabbing all the bags in my hand, I walk up the four front steps, and the phone rings from my back pocket. I reach around to grab the phone, and two bags fall out of my hand at the same time my phone falls out of my hand onto the welcome mat. "Fuck," I huff out, pushing the hair away from my face and seeing that it's Rachel.

"Hello," I greet, putting the phone to my ear and pressing it with my shoulder as I open the front door.

"Hey," Rachel says. "I'm just calling to ask what time you are arriving tomorrow?"

"I'm leaving home at eight, so I should be getting to the hotel at around noon." I walk past the living room that leads to the kitchen and straight to my bedroom. "What about you?"

"I should be getting there at the same time," she says. It gets quiet, and I stop midstep.

"What's the matter?" I ask her, and she huffs.

"Do you really want to do this?" she asks, and I sit on the bed, the bag falling from my hand.

"It's closure," I finally say. "Seeing him again will be closure."

"Nobody would think less of you if you opted out," Rachel reassures me.

"I'm going to go to that wedding, wish them well, and then maybe—just maybe—get drunk in my room."

She laughs. "Fine, I'll be right there."

I smile, and we hang up with the plans to text each other when we get there. I pack two dresses, not sure which one I'm going to wear, and when I slide into bed, I lie awake most of the night. Memories of the first time I met him come back, and if I close my eyes tight enough, I can still hear the way he used to say my name. I give up and get out of bed at six and decide to hit the road and take my time going there.

I stop twice on the way, and when I pull up to the hotel, my stomach starts to flip-flop like a fish that just got out of the water. Check-in goes off without a hitch, and I'm thankful I didn't see anyone. I know that we are all staying at the same hotel, and I know I'm going to have to face the music at one point, but now isn't the time I want to do it. Pushing open the door, I see it's a standard room with one king bed and a desk in the corner of the room. I text Rachel as soon as I get into the room.

Me: I'm here and in room 227

I put the phone beside me, walking over to the window and looking out. The last time I stayed in this hotel was when he brought me back home for his cousin's wedding. I put my hand to my stomach, ignoring the pain in the middle of my chest. "I need a shower and then a nap."

The nap lasts a full forty-five minutes before the alarm rings, followed by a text from Rachel that she is on her way up. A minute later, the knock on the door comes. I pull open the door and smile when I see her. "Hi," I say when she walks in, and she gives me a hug.

"I come bearing gifts," she announces, holding up the brown paper bag. I close the door behind her when she walks over to the desk. She pulls out a bottle of champagne and another bottle of orange juice. "Mimosas for everyone."

I laugh and shake my head. "I don't know if it's a good idea to drink before the wedding."

Rachel just shakes her head. "If there is ever a good time to drink before a wedding, it's when it's your ex's." She grabs one of the glasses from the little tray on the desk next to the ice bucket. "Trust me, I googled." She holds out a glass for me.

"I mean, if Google said it." I walk to her. "Thank you." I grab the glass from her as she does her own drink.

"To closure." She smiles at me, and I have to blink away the tears threatening to come.

"To closure," I toast softly and take a sip of the drink. "What room are you in?"

"Right next door." She points at the wall that separates us. "The car will be here in an hour."

"I already took my shower," I say. "All I have to do is put my makeup and the dress on."

"Okay, well, I'm going to go shower," Rachel says, pouring more champagne into her cup. "And then I'll come back." I nod at her. "It's going to be fine."

"Piece of cake." I fake it, and she walks out of the room. I finish the mimosa and walk back to the bathroom to do my makeup.

I comb my hair and then blow-dry it, the whole time wondering if me going is really that good of an idea. The man I love is marrying someone else. I shake my head. No, the man I used to love is marrying someone else. I don't love him anymore. In fact, when it comes down to it, I don't even believe in love anymore.

I mean, who would believe in love when the only person you've ever loved breaks your heart and throws away everything you had. The hurt is still there four years later. The wound has been healed, but the hurt and the pain are something I will never forget. It's also something that I never ever want to go through again. Which is why I never got involved with anyone after that. I did date, occasionally, but I had this wall up around my heart, and nothing was tearing it down.

Going through the motions of leaving my hair down

with soft curls and then putting on light makeup, I walk over to the closet and open the door seeing the two dresses hanging. Grabbing the green dress, I slip into it. The silk is smooth on my body as I slide my arm through the one sleeve and then zip it up at the side. The elastic on the sleeve makes it puff out just a touch.

Walking over to the mirror, I take a deep breath in and then exhale when I look at myself in the mirror. I don't even have a chance because the knock on the door interrupts me.

When I pull open the door, Rachel stands there in her purple dress that is tight until her knees. "Oh my God," she says when she looks at me. "Are you wearing that?"

I look down. "I have another option, but…"

"You look fantastic," she declares, and I walk back toward the mirror and take myself in. The one-sleeved green satin dress is an eye-catcher for sure, especially with my tan. It hugs my hips and falls mid thigh. There is a big bow on my hip that makes it elegant and sleek, the two sashes falling to the hem of the dress. "If he wasn't going to be green with envy before, he definitely will now."

I laugh. "I don't think so." I walk to the bed and slip on my nude high-heel sandals. One strap around my toes and another around my ankle. "Are you ready?" I ask, and she nods her head.

"The question is, are you ready?" She points at me.

"I don't think I'll ever be ready," I mumble, grabbing my suede clutch purse. "But the car is here." I look at the notification on my phone when I'm putting it away.

We walk down the carpeted hallway, neither of us saying anything. Even when the driver opens the door for us. I look out the back of the car, trying to push the memories back into the little black box I stored them in. A box that was sealed shut until I got the wedding invitation.

We pull up to the venue, and I look around the parking lot as people are slowly starting to arrive. Getting out, I take a look around and see that it really has changed since I've last been here. His sisters are no doubt killing it with their wedding business.

I walk and look up, seeing someone smile at me, and I smile back awkwardly, wondering if we met the last time I was here. I put my hand to my stomach, and the anger starts to fill my body.

"What kind of masochist invites the girl he used to love to his wedding?" I look over at Rachel, and her eyes widen. "Think about it? If I would get married, do you think I would send him an invitation?"

She's about to answer me when I hear someone call my name and turn to see Jake and Frankie coming toward us, both of them in a suit. "Oh my God," Jake says, leaning down and kissing my cheek. "Aren't you a sight for sore eyes?"

"There is nothing wrong with your eyes." I point at him. "How are you?" I move toward Frankie and kiss his cheek while Jake says hello to Rachel.

"Not too bad," Jake replies. "Where are Lydia and Victoria?"

I stand here with my clutch in my hand in front of

me, and I can feel my body start to fill with nerves again. "They should be here soon. What about Chris?"

"He arrives any minute, and he's coming straight here," Frankie explains. "This is crazy," he says and then looks at me, and I feel so awkward being here now. I know in my head I was adamant about coming, but maybe, just maybe, I should have said no.

"We should get inside," Jake says and holds out his hand for us to walk up the steps toward the ceremony.

My heart beats so hard in my chest I don't even know how I'm breathing, let alone functioning. "Here goes nothing," I mumble when the doors open, and I step in.

Fifteen

Travis

"How do I look?" I turn around to look at my best friend, Bennett, who stands beside me. The collar of my shirt feels like it's getting tighter and tighter. I put my finger between my collar and my neck. The tan linen suit was supposed to be light and airy, but it suddenly feels like a weighted blanket pushing my shoulders down.

"You look like you are being carted off to the middle of town where they are going to hang you." He tries not to laugh. "Almost like you have a noose around your neck." He wears the same suit as me, except his tie is in his jacket pocket for now. He promised he would put it on right before we walked down the aisle. Since kindergarten, the two of us have been best friends, and when we got into high school, we did everything together. We tried out for the same sports teams, were in almost the same classes. Even though we went to different colleges, I knew that I could count on him for everything. Now that we are back living in our hometown, it is just like before we left.

"You're a dick." I shake my head and look around the ceremony space, standing to the side. My sisters really outdid themselves. Gold folding chairs fill what used to be a run-down barn that they restored and made into a church. The back of the barn has floor-to-ceiling windows letting in all the natural light. An arch in front of the chairs looks like vines wrapped together with white roses stuck into them. Soft candles float in vases all down the aisle with vines wrapped around them. "This shit is too tight." I take a second to look around the room and see my mother at the front of the ceremony space, greeting some of the guests she knows. The smile on her face looks fake and stressed, but that could just be because the fire department deemed the kitchen unusable two hours ago. She tries to look calm, cool, and collected, but the meltdown she had this morning was anything but cool. People are coming in, and some have even taken a seat to wait for the main event.

The doors open again, and I suddenly feel a shift move in the space. My eyes go to the door, and everything stops inside me. I blink my eyes ten times to see if I'm dreaming this. "Oh my God," Bennett says from beside me, and what sounds like a herd of horses running through the field fills my ears. I feel like my body is detaching from my bones. "Is that who I think it is?" My hand falls from my neck as if it weighs a thousand pounds. "That can't be," Bennett still beside me, and then I see Jake and Frankie with her. "Why the hell would you invite her?" He was the only person I confided in when I broke up with Harlow. He was the one who drove during the middle of the night to get to me and make sure I was okay. I was not. The minute she walked out of the room, I felt my heart shatter to a million pieces. The pain was as if I was being stabbed over and over again. It was practically unbearable. I kept staring at my phone, waiting for her to call me back, but nothing, and after two days of sending her messages, I found out that she blocked me.

"I didn't," are the only two words that come out of me. My eyes don't move from her as she laughs at something Jake is saying, and I want to throat punch him. "What the fuck?"

"So, it's not just my eyes," Bennett says from beside me, and I force my eyes away from her and then turn to him. The shock on his face is apparent when he puts his hand over his mouth. "I can't believe you invited her." He looks back at her, and even though my head tells me not to look over at her, I do it anyway. It's even worse than before. I feel as if someone just kicked me in the balls, and my stomach has been pushed to my throat. She's even more beautiful than she was four years ago. I shake my head and look around.

"Shelby," I say when I see her off to the side hidden in one of the rooms, and I storm over to her. Bennett follows me. "Shelby," I say when I step in the room and see that my sisters are all huddled and look like they are in the middle of a serious situation.

"Oh, hey," Clarabella says, trying not to show how much she's panicking, but you can see her eyes move around the room.

"Can one of you explain why the fuck you sent an invitation to Harlow?" My voice goes from low to high, and Bennett jumps back to close the door. I turn back to my sisters, lowering my voice into a hiss. "Who the fuck invited Harlow to my wedding?"

"I told you that I was inviting your friend group from college." Shelby points out to me. "I wanted to go over the list with you, and what did you tell me?" She glares at me. "I don't care, just invite whoever, go over it with Mom, so I did."

"Harlow?" Presley says. "Like Harlow, 'the love of his life' Harlow?" She looks at Shelby and then at me while I glare at her. "I mean, not your whole life." She puts her hands up. "The love of his life before Jennifer." She laughs nervously.

"Nice save there," Bennett quips, and she gives him the finger with a sweet smile.

"Okay, the question everyone needs to be asking is why is she here?" Clarabella asks, walking over to the door and opening it, and sticking her head out. She comes back in with her eyes wide. "Damn, not only is she here, that dress." I hold up my hand, and I'm biting so hard on my teeth I think that my teeth might actually shatter in my mouth.

"Clarabella." I growl her name through said clenched teeth.

"I'm just asking." She puts her hands up. "Is she here

to object to the wedding?"

"I will kill someone," Shelby says. "There is no one objecting to anything. This fucking wedding is already a wedding that if you weren't my brother, I would say to reschedule, but." She smiles, and I can see it's fake. "We are going to make the best of it."

"What the hell does that mean?" I say to her, and she looks at my sisters, and neither of them wants to say it. "Guys, would you please?"

"Okay, well, the kitchen situation is somewhat handled," Shelby starts to say. "If only Clarabella would call Luke and beg him to cater it."

"I would rather get my asshole bleached with lesions." She folds her arms over her chest.

"What is wrong with you?" Bennett looks at her.

"One, he broke up with best friend." She holds up her hand.

"Ex-best friend," Presley corrects her. "Your ex-best friend."

"Whatever, it's girl code." She throws her hands up to the ceiling.

"Wasn't she cheating on him, and that is why you stopped talking to him?" Presley asks her.

"It doesn't matter. He's cocky and arrogant, and I don't want to call him. You call him," she tells Shelby.

"He knows you," Shelby counters. "And if this was my part of the business, I would totally bury my pride and call him."

"You're an asshole," Clarabella declares. "And I'm going to do it." She takes her phone out of her pocket.

"For Travis and Harlow." She corrects herself, "Jennifer." She looks at me, grimacing, knowing she fucked up. "It's just, I saw her, and it's like Harlow and Travis." She throws her hands up in the air. "I'm going to go and call Luke," she says, walking out of the room and closing the door behind her.

I hang my head down, my head spinning, and I walk over to the couch in the room and sit down. Running my hands through my hair. "I can't believe you invited her." I look up, defeated, at Shelby. "I can't believe she is here." I say the words out loud instead of to myself. It's been four years; I've gotten over her. Or at least I thought I did until I actually saw her again. Fuck, I played this scene out in my head over and over again for the last four years. Well, not this scene at my wedding but when I would see her again. It did not go the way I thought it would, not even close.

Shelby comes over and sits next to me, and I see Bennett walk back out of the room. "I was just as shocked as you were when I got her response back." I turn to her, my mouth opening.

"Do you think that would have been a better time to tell me that she was coming, not when she walked into the church?" I ask her, and she rolls her eyes.

"I got reinforcement," Bennett says, walking back into the room with a bottle of scotch. "It's going to be okay," he assures me, opening the bottle and handing it to me. "Just take a gulp."

"Do not take a gulp," Presley snaps. "That's going to be gross, and we won't be able to serve it." She runs to the closet and comes back with shot glasses. "Have at it."

"Thank you," Bennett says, pouring a shot, and I don't even wait for him to finish pouring his own before I swallow down the amber liquid. It burns all the way down to my stomach, and I hold out the glass for another one. He looks at Shelby, and she nods her head, and he pours me another one. "I don't think that you should have any more after that."

"Oh my God," Presley says. "Imagine you say her name while you are exchanging vows?" She puts both hands to her cheeks, and Shelby gasps and jumps up from her seat beside me.

"What is wrong with you? Why would you put that out into the universe?" she huffs at her, and then the door opens and all of our eyes go to Clarabella, who stands there.

"So, good news," she says, but from how she looks, there has to be some bad also. "Luke said to leave everything to him, and he'll figure it out."

"Thank God," Shelby says from beside me.

"And bad news," Clarabella continues talking and then stops when the sound of sirens starts coming closer and closer. "We have a slight problem."

Sixteen

Travis

"What the hell is happening?" I look at Clarabella.

"Jennifer is having an allergic reaction to something, and we don't know what," Clarabella starts to say, and we all rush toward the bridal suite. "We think it's the funeral flowers."

"Funeral flowers?" Bennett asks them as we walk down the stairs.

"We got the wrong flowers," Presley states as she follows us. "Instead of the wedding flowers, we got funeral flowers. We didn't want to tell you because, well, how much can go wrong with one wedding?"

"Isn't it like a three-strikes-and-you're-out kind of thing?" Bennett asks, and Presley slaps his shoulder. "I'm just asking, how do I know? There was the fridge." He holds up one finger. "The fire, and now this. Oh, and we forgot that Harlow showed up, so it's really four strikes."

"It's going to be fine," Clarabella reassures me. "We just had to call the ambulance because, well, her throat started to get scratchy, and then well." We all stop and look at her. "Her face blew up."

"You," Shelby says. "Stay here." She looks at Bennett. "You keep him here. It's bad luck to see the bride before the wedding."

"Trust me, this isn't what is going to bring bad luck to this wedding," Bennett counters, and all my sisters glare at him. He holds up his hands. "Fine, I'll man the station. Jeez, you try to make a joke and everyone wants to jump down your throat."

My sisters run into the room at the same time as the ambulance technicians come in through the back door. "Excuse us," they say and go into the room. I can hear the commotion in the room, and all I can do is pace in front of the door.

"This is crazy." I run my hand through my hair and hold my neck, the tension coming all through my body.

"Look at the bright side," Bennett says. "How many people can be like, on my wedding day…"

I shake my head and stop moving when the doors open, and Jennifer is rushed past me on a gurney.

"What is going on?" I ask, running next to her, and I can't see her face.

"We have to get her to the hospital. She's having a severe allergic reaction," one of the EMTs says, and everything is happening so fast I don't have a minute to think.

"Oh my God." I run out toward the ambulance and see them placing the gurney inside. One of the ambulance technicians looks at me.

"I assume you are the groom. Are you coming with us?" he asks, and I nod my head, and he moves to the side to give me a chance to get up. I put my foot on the step and get into the ambulance.

"Let us know," Shelby starts to say when the ambulance technician closes the back door. The ambulance takes off a second later.

"Jennifer," I say, getting to her side, and she looks over at me, and I try not to freak out. Her lips are swollen ten times their size. One of her eyes is sealed shut. The other one is slowly going to close. "Are you okay?" I hold her hand in mine and try not to show her how freaked out I am.

"My throat is scratchy," she says and tries to clear her throat.

"Did you guys give her an EpiPen?" I look over at the technician, who just nods his head.

"We are four minutes out," he says. "And we already gave her one."

"Well, it's clearly not working," I point out, looking over at Jennifer, who is wearing a white satin pjs set. Her black hair is half curled, and she has makeup on one side.

"Is she allergic to any medications?" he asks, and I have to admit that I have no idea. The phone buzzes in my pocket, and I ignore it.

"Not that I know of," I say and then look back at

Jennifer, who shakes her head. I bury away the voice in my head asking me how I didn't know she was allergic to anything.

The ambulance comes to a stop, the back door opens, and they whisk her out. I keep up with them. They usher her into the room, and the doctor comes in. I stand in the corner out of the way, while they are talking about what they gave her. The doctor orders epinephrine. "She's going into anaphylactic shock." He injects her right away and then looks over at me. "Why don't you step out?"

I put my hand on my head, and the nurse comes over to me. "She's going to be fine," she says to me with a smile. "Why don't you go get something to drink?" she says. I look over at Jennifer, who lies with her head back, while the doctor checks something else and is telling the other nurse to get him something.

I walk over to Jennifer and put my hand in hers. "I'll go and get you some water." She groans, and I just look over at the nurse who smiles at me. The phone vibrates again in my back pocket, and I walk out of the room. I close my eyes as soon as I get in the hallway and then put my head back. The phone buzzes again in my back pocket, and I'm one second away from throwing it against the wall.

Taking a deep breath, I head down the hallway and away from her door before I take my phone out of my pocket and find that my phone has five missed FaceTime calls and then texts from everyone.

Mom: Do you want me to come to the hospital?
Shelby: Any news?

Mom: I'm going to keep everyone calm here. Jennifer's mother is a mess.

Clarabella: Let me know if you are okay.

Bennett: Don't worry about anything here!!!!

I'm about to answer Bennett when the phone rings again, and I see that it's my sister Shelby FaceTiming me. I press the connect button. "Why the hell would we say that the waitstaff got into an accident?" She glares at Clarabella, who just shrugs. "The last thing he needs is to hear more bad news."

"Hi," I say, interrupting them, and they both look back at the phone with their eyes wide.

"How is she?" Shelby comes back to me, and I see people walking around behind her, and then I see her moving out of the room.

"The doctor is in with her now," I start to say.

"Listen, don't worry about anything over here," Shelby assures me. "Everyone is waiting, and if anything, we can do the ceremony during the reception. Which will give the service staff enough time to get here."

I close my eyes and lean back against the wall. "Can one thing go right today?" I ask her, and she just stares at me.

"This is just a hiccup," she says softly, and I see her sit on the couch. "It's a bump in the road."

"It's a meteor that crashed into earth," I correct her.

"And the aliens are invading us," Clarabella says, and Shelby just glares at her.

"It's not that bad. I've seen worse." She rolls her eyes.

"Have you really?" I ask, and she doesn't answer.

"Didn't think so."

I look up and see the doctor coming out of the room. "Doctor is here. Let me call you back. Tell everyone the news."

I disconnect and walk toward him as he stands outside of her door and writes on her chart. "How is she?" I ask when I get close enough, and he looks toward me.

"She is going to make a full recovery," he says. "I strongly suggest that she has an allergy test done as soon as possible." He closes the chart. "She's good to go in a bit."

"Thank you," I say and walk back into the room. I look over at her as she lies on the bed with her head back on the pillow. Making my way to her, I see that her lips are already starting to go down. Her one eye opens, and she sees me. "Hi," I say softly, sitting on the bed beside her. "How are you doing?"

"Awful," she says, and I see a tear escape from the eye that is still sealed shut. "I can't get married."

I reach out and touch her hand. "We don't have to get married today." I smile at her, and she pulls her hand away from me.

"I don't mean today," she says and then looks down and then up at me. "I don't want to marry you."

I stare at her in shock. "I'm sorry, what?"

"I almost died today." She sits up in the middle of the bed. "Do you know what went through my head the whole time?"

"I have no idea," I say, looking at her, and it dawns on me that this news is not destroying me.

"The thought that we would be together for the rest of my life." I look at her, and if this wasn't happening to me, I might just burst out laughing. "Like, don't get me wrong, you are amazing."

"I don't know if that is supposed to make me feel better or not," I say, and my collar feels like it's going to strangle me, so I loosen the knot on the tie and then undo the top button of the shirt.

"You are amazing," she says, reaching out to put her hand on mine. "But I don't know if I love you like that." I just look at her, not sure what to say. "The last two weeks, I've been going over this in my head." She blinks as the swollen eye starts to open a little bit. "I've been wondering, is this really what I want."

I get up, taking off my jacket. "You think maybe we could have discussed this before we had a whole venue full of people?"

"Oh, come on, Travis," she says. "You can't honestly say that you really wanted to get married in the first place."

"Well, I showed up," I retort because I'm not really sure I wanted to get married in the first place. Especially after today. "Why didn't you say anything before today?"

"I didn't really know," she says softly. "And then today when I was getting my makeup done and then my throat started to get all scratchy, and I was thinking about what we were going to do. It just…" I shake my head. "I think I'm in love with Jackie." She wrings her hands together.

"Jackie?" I ask, shocked, like a bomb just went off.

"Jackie, like your roommate Jackie?"

With tears in her eyes and rolling down her cheeks, she nods her head. "I know that it's wrong." She wipes a tear away. "And my uber religious parents are going to condemn me to hell but..."

I hold up a hand. "So you're telling me that you're gay?"

"I don't know," she admits. "I've never done anything about it. I know that the thought of not being with her makes my heart hurt."

"Is this why you never wanted to move in with me?" I ask her, thinking of all the times she made excuses. It wasn't the right time. Things were too busy. Heck, she slept over at my house a max of four times.

"I don't even know if she feels the same way about me," she says. "But I can't marry you if I feel this way."

"I don't know what to say," I answer her.

"Do you love me?" she asks.

"Yes," I answer her honestly, and she tilts her head to the side.

"Like full-on completely love me?" She points at herself. "Give your life away for my love?" I know the answer, my head knows the answer, my heart definitely knows the answer. But I can't say it out loud. Seeing Harlow walk into the church today just made everything so crystal clear. I thought I was in love with Jennifer. But I was fooling myself. There was no one I could have loved as much as I did Harlow. No one even came close to completing me like she did. For the last four years, I have fooled myself into thinking that she didn't exist.

Yet one fucking look at her, and I was right back there. Instead, I take a deep inhale and then exhale. "Exactly. I mean, think about it; you didn't even propose. It came up one day when we were having lunch with your family, and your mother asked if we were going to get married, and we just said yeah. It was more along the lines of well, we are dating, so we might as well take the next step. Neither of us dared to back out, but now, after almost dying, I can't marry you."

"What do you want to tell people?" I ask her, knowing that I'm going to have to call my sisters.

"I don't care. You can blame me." She shrugs. "But whatever you do, you need to do it now. There are two hundred people expected to attend the reception." She moves to get out of bed, and I stop her.

"I'll take care of this," I say. "You stay here." I turn, walking out of the room, stopping. "I'll send Jackie," I add, and she smiles at me.

"You really are amazing," she says to me, and I turn and walk out of the room thinking about what the fuck I'm going to tell two hundred people.

Seventeen

Harlow

"*I* wonder what the hell is going on?" Rachel leans over to me and mumbles. "It looks like chickens running around without their heads." I look up from my chair and see that his sisters are trying to remain calm, but you can tell in their faces that something terrible just happened. It doesn't help that an ambulance left a short while ago, and they announced that there had been a delay.

"It's a wedding," I state. "Things always go wrong at weddings."

"How many weddings have you been to?" Victoria asks, leaning over Rachel. "I've been to five in the last four months and this is the first time it's been this chaotic."

"I was at one last weekend," Lydia shares. "It was

nothing like this."

"You should go and ask if everything is okay," Victoria suggests.

I gasp. "Why the hell would I go?" I look around, and ever since I walked into the ceremony space, I've done my best to keep my head down and avoid any eye contact that I would have with anyone. I walked with my back almost against the wall and then sat down in the closest seat I could find. My heart was in my throat the whole time and I prayed to all the saints in the world that I wouldn't throw up everywhere.

"You know them, maybe they will tell you why an ambulance was here," Lydia says.

"I'm going to get a drink," Rachel states and looks down at me. "And you're coming because maybe with you they will give me something."

"Ohh," Lydia says. "I'll take a drink."

"Me, too," Victoria adds, and I look back at Rachel, who just gives me a look.

"It's too late. You're already here. You think no one is going to see you?" I roll my eyes at her and get up. "Fine. But get the drink and then get back."

"Do you think the ambulance was here because she found out you were here and then tried to stab him?" Lydia jokes, and she can't help but throw her head back and laugh, but the space is so open, and no one else is laughing, so all eyes come to us.

I take a second to look around, and I see his mom first. She looks at me in shock. Trust me, I know this is weird, I want to say to her, but all I can do is smile at her while holding up my hand and waving at her.

She leaves whoever she is talking to and starts to come over to me. My heart hammers in my chest as I walk out into the pathway beside the chairs. "Oh my word!" she exclaims when she gets close enough. "I can't believe it." She smiles at me, and I don't know what I expected, but it wasn't the big hug she gives me. "Harlow." She says my name, and I fight back the tears that are threatening to come out. She lets go of me and steps back. "I can't believe it's you." She holds one of my hands in hers. She has always been kind to me, and I wondered what he told his family. I mean, I wasn't that close to them that they would've reached out to me, but I did still follow them on social media. "You look stunning."

"Thank you, Deborah." I'm finally able to speak. "You look great." I smile at her, and she does in her light gray lace top, matched with a dark gray satin skirt that goes down to the floor.

"What have you been up to?" she asks as she moves me away from the chairs and toward two red barn doors that lead into what is the reception area. The doors were closed when we walked in, but then they slowly opened an inch at a time. I refused to look inside because I wasn't sure if I would be able to keep myself composed. This whole day has been draining, and I have regretted coming every single second. But I am here, and I am not going to back down.

"Nothing much. I have my practice back home." My chest fills with pride. "Everything is great." I stop walking when I see his sisters coming toward us. Deborah's face goes white, and her eyes widen.

"I swear to everything," she says between clenched teeth. "If there is one more thing that you have to tell me." I look at his sisters, who have frazzled looks on their faces.

"Well, the waitstaff just got into an accident, and well, we have no one to help serve," Shelby says.

"What can I do to help?" The words come, and it doesn't even register in my brain that I said them aloud.

"We couldn't ask you," Clarabella says, shaking her head and then looking over at the door that just slammed shut. "Ugh, he's here." I look over at the man who just walked in. He wears jeans and a T-shirt, his black hair pushed back as his eyes search the room, and then when he sees her, he stops. "I'll be right back."

"Be nice to him," Shelby hisses when she walks away and flips the bird behind her head. I roll my lips because Deborah looks like she's about to throttle them all.

"Why can't you three just get along?" She smiles as she says it, but she hisses it out. "This is a fucking catastrophe." She waves at someone she knows. "We need to get some food and drinks served."

"Already on that," Shelby says. "I've got Bennett tending bar."

"I can help him." Again, my mouth gets me in trouble before my head tells me to shut the fuck up.

"Are you sure?" Presley looks at me. "You don't have to."

"It's more than okay." I smile as my stomach dips and then rises again. "Just show me where the bar is."

"I will," Presley says. "You." She points at Shelby. "Get those guys." She points at Jake, Frankie, and Chris. "To pass around some finger foods." Then she points at her mother. "You stay freaking calm and mingle."

"What the hell am I supposed to say is happening?" Deborah asks, the whole time smiling.

"You'll think of something," Shelby says. "You always do."

"Come with me," Presley says, motioning with her head. I follow her to the big doors that were half open, and I step in and stop walking the minute I take it all in. The exposed beams have tuille hanging from it. Long wooden tables are set up everywhere with brown folding chairs and cream-colored cushions. Cream-colored runners on all the tables with glass vases with floating candles in each of them. A big dance floor is in the middle with big lanterns hanging from the ceiling with green vines all around it.

"It's so romantic," I say, putting my hand to my stomach.

"Thank you," she says. "They left it up to us, so we hope they love it." I look at her, shocked and surprised that they didn't have a say in this. "The bar is over there." She points at the long wooden bar in the back corner. "I'll go and tell them that they can come and get drinks," she says, looking down and then up. "Are you sure you're okay doing this?"

"What, you never had the ex-girlfriend show up to a wedding?" I joke, and she laughs now.

"Not that I know of, and if they did, no one said

anything," Presley replies. "It's good to see you."

"It's good to see you, too." I point at the bar. "I'm going to go and tend the bar."

She nods at me as she rushes back out the doors that we came in, and when I get close to the bar, Bennett turns around and stops when he sees me. "Well, well well," he says, trying to hide his smile. "Fancy seeing you here."

I walk around the bar, chuckling. "It's not that weird," I say to him, and his eyebrows pinch together. "Okay, fine, it's weird as fuck, but I'm here, and I might as well help."

He puts his arm around my shoulder, just like he did the first time he met me. "It's good to see you," he admits, and I wrap my arm around his waist. "Shocking but good to see you." I throw my head back and laugh.

"It's good seeing you, too," I say as I look over and see people now trickling into the space. "It looks like the party is starting."

"Well, let's hope the bride and groom get here soon," he says, and I want to ask him what he's talking about, but I don't have time when ten people head straight for us. "Think you can keep up with me?"

I shake my head. "You forgot that I used to work at my cousin's bar." I look around to see where everything is kept. "This is going to be a piece of cake." I lean on the bar. "Bet you I can serve five people before you."

"Oh." He points at me. "It's on." He slips off his jacket and rolls up his sleeves, and I can't help but slap my hands together and laugh.

I turn toward the people in front of the bar and start

serving them. It takes me a couple of minutes to see that the bottles are placed alphabetically, which Bennett doesn't seem to get, and when I serve the tenth person, he's still serving his fourth.

I look around to see that the room is almost filled up as the bridesmaids all stand by the door, looking for the bride. I walk up to Bennett. "Can I ask what is going on?" I turn to look at everyone mingling.

"Bride's face swelled up," he shares, and I can't help the way my mouth opens in shock, and my eyes are probably the size of saucers. "She was allergic to something."

"Oh my God," I say, and then I turn my head, and I see him. Everything in me stops: my heart, my mind, my breathing. It all stops. The only thing that moves are my eyes when I follow him. I forced myself to erase all of his pictures from my phone. I forced myself to block him on all social media sites. I forced myself to forget what he even looked like, but my heart still remembered. His hair is a touch longer, and his five o'clock shadow is coming in strong. My fingers move, thinking back to how it used to pinch me when I grabbed his face in my hands right before I kissed him.

He walks with his jacket in one hand, the collar of his shirt open, and his sleeves rolled up to the elbows. His chest looks like he got bigger, and so do his arms. I see him search the room for someone, and he finds her and walks over to her. She looks like she is one of the bridesmaids. He walks over to her; she gets up from her chair when she sees him. He leans down and says something to her, and I can hear his voice in my head, the way he used to say my name. The woman looks at him, shocked, and then rushes out.

Travis watches her leave and then puts his head down. He's even better looking than he was in my memories. He is even hotter than he was when he was younger. He's a man now, and it shows. My mouth gets dry when I see him look up and then make his way to the bar. I'm about to tell Bennett that I'm going to leave when the inevitable happens.

His eyes meet mine, my whole body shivers from his look, and then he throws his head back and laughs. "Of course, you would be behind the bar."

Eighteen

Travis

My eyes meet hers, and my heart fucking soars. Everything I was feeling on the way here is gone with one look at her. I can't help but put my head back to laugh at the irony of what today is. My fucking wedding day, and she walks into the church. "Of course, you would be behind the bar." I sit on one of the stools by the bar and look over at Bennett, who just gives me a chin up. I'm sure he's dying to ask me all the questions, but he's giving me a chance to catch my bearings.

"I figured this is the only place where I could help." I can smell her from this side of the bar, and it takes me back to all those times we would go to the bar, and I would sit on a stool, and she would stand between my legs. My mind goes back to one of the last times it happened.

Sitting on a stool when she walked in, her eyes scanned the room before she found me. She smiled and then made her way through the crowd of people. I turned on the stool as she placed her bag in the middle of the feet of the stool. "Hi." I smiled at her, and she leaned in and kissed my lips.

My hands went straight to her hips, and she turned and looked at the bar. "What are we having?" she said and placed her back to my front, and that is where she stood all night long. One hand on my leg while she talked to people, with one of my hands on her hip. I would lean in and bury my face in her neck, and I felt at peace.

I hear whispers all around me, and I'm back to my wedding venue. I watch Harlow as she walks down the bar. Now grabbing a glass, she walks over and takes the bottle of scotch down, fills it two fingers in, and puts it in front of me.

I shake my head because she knows me, also because how fucking crazy is it that she's here. I grab the glass and down it in one shot. The burning follows all the way to my stomach. "Another one?" she asks, and I nod my head, knowing that shit is going to hit the fan in a matter of minutes.

She leans over and pours another two fingers, and I smile at her and take the glass, laughing at the irony of this. I down it again and then look over at Bennett, who just stands there waiting for whatever I am going to say. "Wedding is off," I say to him, and he just puts his hand in front of his mouth. I don't look at Harlow, I can't, and when I get up, my sisters are at my side. I hold up my hand to stop them from talking and walk over to the stage.

I grab the microphone and turn it on. I tap it once to see if there is a sound that comes on. I look out at the people who have gathered now and see Jake, Frankie, and Chris standing by the door, and they just chin up to me. I look over toward my mother, who looks like she's about to storm the stage as she stands with my sisters. "Testing, one two three," I say as my voice fills the venue. "Hi, everyone." I lift my hand awkwardly. "First off, I'd like to thank you all for coming," I say, looking around and seeing that Jennifer's parents aren't here. No doubt they took off with Jackie to see her. "I want to thank my sisters for everything they did to make this day special." I look over to them and know that they are all standing together now, glaring at me for something that they will be sure to tell me as soon as I step down. "With that said," I continue. "We have to announce that the wedding is off." There are gasps all over the room, especially from my mother, who is now glaring at me also. "Thank you to everyone for coming out, and I invite you to make full use of the bar." I point over to the bar where the guys have now made their way, along with Rachel, Victoria, and Lydia. "And if I'm not mistaken, there is also some food coming." I look at my sisters. "I hope." I turn the mic off and walk down the steps, and my sisters are the first ones to pounce on me.

Shelby says, looking around, "Um, where is Jennifer?"

"At the hospital," I state, and I try to walk past her

and toward the bar because something tells me I should have another drink. It might not be a great idea given that people will want to try to talk to me, but whatever.

"So, is this wedding postponed?" Clarabella is the one with the big enough balls to ask me.

"No," I confirm, shaking my head. "Definitely canceled." I look up at the ceiling and can feel the pounding headache coming on. Or maybe it's the booze.

"Fuck," Presley curses. "Incoming." She tries to give me a warning, but it's not enough time when my mother steps in front of them.

"Excuse me," she says, looking around to see if there is anyone within earshot so she knows whether or not she can curse me out or not. Luckily for everyone, they are too busy whispering to each other, no doubt making up different stories. "Where is Jennifer?" She doesn't even give me time to answer. "Can we not get the minister and get married at the hospital?" She looks around, searching for the minister.

"Um, the minister never showed," Shelby says, and I can't help but laugh. If there were ever signs to say not to get married, this was the signs of all signs.

"Of course." I shake my head. "I want to know what did go right?"

"It's fine," Clarabella says. "I'm ordained, so I would have been able to jump in."

"Well, then good thing it's not happening," I say, and I try to walk away from them, but I can't move.

"Just a minute, young man," my mother says, and my sisters laugh and then stop when my mother gives them that look.

"Young man?" Shelby is the one who can't keep her face straight. "He's almost thirty. We have to drop the young."

"Why aren't you going back to the hospital with her?" My mother asks the question indirectly. She cocks one hip and waits for my answer.

"Because, Mom, we broke up," I explain, and Bennett shows up out of nowhere.

"Sorry to interrupt," he says, handing me a glass with scotch in it. "Thought you might need this." He looks around at the group. "To help with this." His hand does a circle of the group. "I'll have another brought to you right away."

"More than you can ever know," I mumble and finish off the drink. He turns and walks away, going back to the bar. "Bottom line is it's over and…" I don't know what else I was going to say. The burning of my stomach is now replaced with warm heat. "Turns out she didn't want to get married." I leave out the part that she didn't want to marry me and that she was in love with Jackie. That's not for me to share.

"I'll get the guests taken care of," Shelby announces.

"I'll check with the kitchen and have the food come out in bite sizes instead of plated," Clarabella says.

"I'll check with the music and see if we can get it going," Presley adds.

The three of them go in different directions, and it's just my mother and me. "Are you okay?" she asks, her voice soft.

"Actually." I look down at the empty glass in my hand. "I am." I look over, seeing that most people have stayed. "Better now than later, right?"

"She wasn't the one," my mother says now, and I look at her and see her dabbing the corners of her eyes. "When it's the right one, you'll know." My mother looks over at the bar. "Maybe the right one was at the wrong time."

I look over at the bar. "Or maybe she was the right one all along, and I was stupid and scared she wouldn't pick me."

"Only one way to find out." She comes to me and kisses my cheek. "Truth be told, you might still be stupid and scared."

"Not sure about scared," I joke with her. "Definitely still stupid." I look back over at Harlow and see her moving behind the bar as if she does this all the time. I wonder how she's been. I wonder if she is happy. I wonder so many fucking things, and all I can do is stand here staring at her. But there is no mistaking that she still takes my breath away and makes me feel things I thought were gone forever.

"I'm proud of you." She cups my cheek. "Now, I shall go and mingle."

She walks away from me, and I have to say that that went better than I could ever imagine it going, like tenfold. I walk toward the bar and see my college friends all huddled on one side. I get closer, and the guys look up at me, and one of them just hands me their drink, and I take it without caring what it is. "Well, this is nice," I say, and I laugh.

"Listen, if you wanted to see us so bad," Frankie starts, taking a pull of his beer. "All you had to do was ask. You didn't have to go out of your way and pretend to get married."

I throw my head back, and I laugh at him. "Guilty," I say, taking a gulp of the drink. I look to the side and see ten people now running in, all wearing black with white dress shirts. Two guys come over and walk behind the bar.

"I think this means I'm fired," Harlow declares and walks over to the sink to wash her hands. I follow her every move. I don't think it sank in that she's really here. She walks over to Bennett now. "Good job," she says, holding up her hand for him to give her a high five. "But I still won."

"I didn't know where any of the bottles were," he whines to her retreating back. "We should have a rematch."

She shakes her head and walks out from behind the bar. Rachel whispers something into her ear, and she smiles and nods her head. "Okay, people," Jake says. "We know the drill." He looks over at the bartender. "We will take nine shots of tequila." The bartender nods at him and pours nine shots, and then he looks at all of us. "It's time to play monkey business."

Everyone now groans and then laughs. "Got to bring it back old-school," I say, looking over at Harlow, who made up the game.

"If there is ever a time for monkey business," Harlow says and turns to hand me a shot. I laugh because she always had a way to make me feel better. If I had a crappy day at school, she would order my favorite food. If I got a bad result back, she would turn off all the lights in the room, and we would play touchy-feely, as she called it, trying to find each other. That's Harlow, that is who she is. That is who I pushed away and forced myself to believe that I did it so she didn't have to choose me over her family. I pushed her away because I was scared that she would sacrifice everything that she wanted for me, and then she would end up resenting me. I pushed her away, scared that in the end, she wouldn't pick me. "It's definitely now. Who wants to start?"

Nineteen

Harlow

"Tomcat," Bennett says, and everyone laughs at him. "It's an animal."

"No, it's not," Presley says from her spot beside him. We moved from the bar to a table when the music started. People slowly started to leave, and now it was just our table left. We've been playing this game for the last hour, and the drinks have been flowing. The tension of me being here is gone, or at least it doesn't bother me now because I have booze flowing through my system.

Sitting at the table between Rachel and Victoria, it's definitely different from when we did this before. Especially since I used to either sit beside Travis or on top of him. Now he is facing me, and I am having a hard time not looking over at him. I would, of course, have to look over at him when it was his time during the game, but when it wasn't, I would sneak looks over at him and hope he would miss me. A couple of times, I caught him looking and just smiled at him. My whole body was on high alert as if it was waiting for his touch. When he came to the bar and I handed him a drink, it was to make myself not reach out for him. It was what I always did. I had to tell myself that it was the past and he was with someone now. It was hard for me to swallow, but I did it for him. I did it because I promised him that I would be here and I was a woman of my word. I mean, I also promised to kick him in the balls the next time I would see him, so there is a promise that I don't know if I will keep.

His voice when he said it was canceled, I thought I wasn't hearing him correctly. I thought it was a mistake, and then he announced it, and I had all the questions in the world. What the hell was happening? Where was the bride? Who changed their mind? All the questions yet knew that he owed me nothing.

"I'm going to the bathroom," I say, standing up, the room spins, and then I sit down and laugh. I look around the table to see if anyone is watching and find his eyes on me. His eyes are a touch lighter than they were when he walked in. His side smirk makes my stomach flip and flop, and then the feeling goes a touch lower to a specific area he definitely made happy daily. It's the smirk that I used to reach up and touch with my index finger right before I leaned in and kissed his lips.

"What is that smirk about?" I wrapped my arms

around his neck as he placed his hands on my hips. His hands always were on my hips, where he squeezed me and pulled me toward him.

He would lift one of his hands and push my hair to the back of my shoulder so he could lean in and whisper in my ear. "Because I know what I'm going to be doing to you after we leave here." I would throw my head back and laugh, and he would take the opportunity to lean in and kiss my neck while he wrapped his arms around my waist, and I would be stuck to him.

"You are fortunate that I like you," I would say to him, and that would make him laugh, giving me the opportunity to kiss his neck and slip my hands into the back of his hair. "I like you a lot." His eyes would come back to mine. "I love you, Harlow," he would say, and no matter where we were or how loud it was, I could always hear those words clear as day. It would fill my whole body; it would make me feel complete. It would make my heart full in my chest. It was a feeling I thought would never go away.

I blink away the memory. "Okay, take two," I say, getting up, putting my hands on the table to steady myself, and when I don't wobble, I want to give myself a high five. Instead, I giggle to myself.

"I'll come with you," Shelby says, getting up. "I need to pee also."

We walk side by side through the tables and into the bathroom, and I stand here in shock. "Oh my God." I look around the square room that has all exposed red bricks. Wooden beams are exposed on the ceiling, with a crystal chandelier hanging down.

Five white sinks are along one of the walls, but what gets me is the big white bench right in front of a mirror that fills most of the wall, but it's the thick gold antique frame. "This is gorgeous." I walk to the edge and touch the intricate lines with my fingers, tracing the tiny flowers.

"It's the perfect place for a selfie," Shelby suggests, taking her phone out of her pocket. "Sit down," she says, motioning to the seat in front of it, and I do. "Face the mirror," she instructs me, and I follow her lead. "Put your legs to the side." I laugh when she says this. "Smile."

I smile into the mirror, and then she shows me the picture. "Damn, if you ever give up being a vet." She laughs when she walks into one of the stalls while I hold her phone in my hand. "You could be a model."

I can't help but laugh at that. "Thanks"—I shake my head—"but no, thanks. I'm happy doing what I'm doing."

I look up at the stall when I hear the toilet flush, and then she walks out going to the sink. "You know," she says. "I'm not going to lie. I was shocked when I got your response." I get up from the bench and go to her as she turns the water off and then takes one of the white hand towels and dries her hands.

"I made him a promise I would be there on the happiest day of his life," I share with her, looking down and then blinking away the tears from that memory. "And I am a woman of my word." I look back at her, smiling. "For the most part."

"There is a reason that you came today." She grabs the phone from me. "I have no idea what it is, but it's the universe telling you something."

I shake my head. "It's probably the universe telling me I should have let sleeping dogs lie," I say, walking into the stall and going to the bathroom.

When I walk out, she is sitting on the bench, and she watches me while I wash my hands. "I don't think that Jennifer was the one for him," she confides, and I stop my hands from rinsing under the water. "I know it's a shitty thing to say, and I am not going to talk bad about her, but I just didn't think that they loved each other." I turn off the water, trying to get my heart to calm down at this news. "I mean, I think he loved her but I don't think he was in love with her."

I grab a towel and dry my hands. "Your brother wouldn't marry anyone that he didn't love. I might not know the man he is today." The burning now comes to fill my stomach. "But the man he was wouldn't ask someone to marry him if he didn't love her."

"I think, that before you leave"—she puts the phone back into her pocket—"I would have a talk with my brother. At least to clear some things up."

I shake my head. "Nothing to clear up. We were two young kids who dated ages ago." I don't believe the words coming out of my mouth and I have a strong feeling that neither does Shelby. "We've moved on. The end." I put the towel into the basket at the side.

She shakes her head. "You really should at least clear the air."

"There is no air to clear." I put my hand to my stomach. "I came here to wish a friend well, and tomorrow I'll be going back to my life, and he will continue with his."

"Okay," she says, not sounding convinced at all. "Shall we get back to the party?"

I pull open the door, and I hear the song "Hey Girl" come on, and I laugh when I hear the song start. I clap my hands when I get close to the table, and the girls look up at me. I take a glance at Travis, smile, and he brings his cup to his lips.

"Oh, now we start," Rachel says, taking the shot in front of her. "I lose this round." She takes another shot. "Time to line dance." She points at me, going to the dance floor. "Let's see if I remember this."

She starts to move her feet, and she stumbles a bit. Everyone from the table is now on the dance floor. "Harlow," Shelby says. "Go in front, and we will follow you."

I laugh as I walk to the front and then start to move my feet, but with the heels, it's hurting my feet, so I bend and untie the straps around my ankles and then start over. I look over at the DJ. "Can we start over?" He nods his head and starts the song again. "Okay, so you are going to walk right foot, left foot, shake shake." I shimmy my hips. "Shimmy shimmy." I move my hips from side to side. "And then triple step back. Repeating the steps again."

"I'm sorry," Frankie says. "You lost me at shimmy."

"Yeah, can you shimmy shimmy again?" Jake jokes, clapping his hands.

"Or we can change the song," Travis suggests. "Put on another song."

"Yes," Rachel says. "Put the 'Cha-Cha Slide.'"

The DJ puts the song on, and everyone is moving at their own speed. No one is following anyone, and then the song goes into Usher, and now we are all dancing to our own beat. I walk back to the table to grab a drink, and so does Bennett. "It's good to see you," he says, smiling at me.

"Is that the booze talking?" I ask him, grabbing a glass of water and downing it.

"Could be a bit of both," he confesses and takes a shot of tequila. The song changes to a slow one, and he holds out his hand to me. "May I have this dance?"

I bat my eyes at him. "Why, I would be honored." He drags me to the dance floor and puts his hand around my waist and holds my hand up.

We move side to side and then bump into Presley and Travis. "Yeah, this is wrong," Bennett says, letting me go and then grabbing Presley's hand. "Now this." He wraps his arms around her. "This is so much better." He moves away from us, leaving Travis and me just standing here.

I shake my head. "That would be weird," I say to him, and he nods his head.

"Let's get a drink," he offers and holds out his hand for me to lead the way, and I can feel his hand at the bottom of my back as he follows me to the bar.

"Two glasses of scotch." He holds up two fingers and sits on the stool beside me. I lean on the bar instead of sitting.

The bartender comes back in record time, putting the two glasses down on two white napkins. "You know what I didn't expect today?" he asks, bringing his glass to his mouth.

"Not to get married?" I say, picking up my own glass and bringing it to my lips while he chuckles. The liquid is cool against my tongue yet burns all the way down. My eyes never leave his, and I see the little lines at the side of his eyes that weren't there before. He's older now, and I wonder if his lips taste like scotch. I wonder if I kissed him, would it be just like it was back then? I move my eyes away from him, scared that he will be able to read my thoughts.

"That." He points at me, putting his glass down. "And." He looks at his glass and then at me. "Seeing you."

Twenty

Travis

"You know what I didn't expect today?" I sit on the stool holding the glass of scotch in my hand, taking a sip and then placing it down. She leans against the bar in front of me.

"Not to get married?" She picks up her glass, bringing it to her plump lips, and I can't help the chuckle that comes out of me. She was always sassy and funny. She looks at me, and I can't help but think about how it would be four years ago. For one, she wouldn't be this far away from me, and two, my mouth would be on hers. She looks away from me, and I wonder if it's because she's seen what I've been thinking. Seeing her today has thrown me off-kilter. My life in black and white is now littered with color, and I know it is because of her.

"That." I point at her, putting my glass down on the bar. "And." I look at the amber liquid in the glass and then look back at her. "Seeing you," I say honestly.

She throws her head back and laughs, and it makes my stomach tighten. It was a sound I buried away in my mind somewhere, and now it's back out. When we were together, I would always do something that would make her laugh just so I could hear it. "Well, I got an invitation," she says, and now it's my turn to laugh, and she just looks at me.

"You can thank my sisters for that," I admit it to her, and her eyes widen and her mouth hangs open.

"Are you saying that you wouldn't have invited me?" She has a serious face, and I suddenly feel like a dick for bringing it up when her mouth slowly forms a smile. Now it's her turn to chuckle while she brings her glass of scotch to her mouth. She takes a sip, and I want to suck her lower lip into my mouth right before my tongue slides into her mouth. "So if I invited you to my wedding," she says, and the knot in my stomach feels like it's turning and twisting. "You wouldn't come?"

I grab the glass of scotch, downing the rest of it as a lump grows in my throat, and the anger starts to form and spreads from my toes all the way to the tip of my head. "Are you getting married anytime soon?" Everything in me stops while I wait for her to answer the question. For four years, I pretended I was fine. For four years, I let myself only think of her on special days, like the day we met, her birthday, and until this day, no one knows why Halloween was always my most hated holiday.

She finishes her own scotch and then places the glass down. The bartender comes over and refills the glasses. "Can I have water also?" He nods at her and then comes back with a bottle of water. "What did you ask?" She looks at me, and it takes everything I have not to reach out and tuck the strand of her hair behind her ear.

"I asked if you were getting married anytime soon," I repeat the question, and this time my hand holds the glass of scotch harder than I did before as my heartbeat fills my ears.

"Nope." She shakes her head, taking a pull of her water bottle. She dabs her lips with a napkin. "Not anytime soon, that is." She looks around the venue now.

"Haven't met the one?" I ask her, taking another long pull of scotch.

"Thought I did." She turns from me, looking at the dance floor away from me. "Didn't work out."

I want to ask her who the guy was. I want to ask her if I was that guy. I want to ask her everything. I want to know everything. "How did you meet Jennifer?"

"Work," I say, and she just nods. "She was watching her friend's cat for the weekend, and the cat ate her birth control pills."

She nods, not sure what to say. "Are you dating?"

"Not at the moment," she replies, and I'm pretty sure I'm a glutton for punishment at this point.

"How long were you two dating?" She turns to look at the bar as she spins the glass of scotch in her hand.

"About a year," I say, and her head just nods. "Did you open the practice like you wanted to?"

"I did." She smiles, and it makes what I did feel just a touch better. Breaking up with her so that she could open her practice was the hardest thing I've ever had to do.

"Bet your dad is happy you're home." I get up and lean against the bar. The sound of people on the dance floor clapping has me turning my head to look and see what is going on.

"Is he doing the Worm?" Harlow tilts her head toward my side to see what is going on. She is right in front of me, and I can feel her heat on my arm as she leans in. "Oh my God." She puts her hand on my arm, laughing. "He's doing the full Worm." I look at the dance floor and see that Jake is now doing the Worm from one end of the dance floor to the other, and then he tries to go back while everyone cheers him on.

He gets up and high-fives Frankie, who takes off his jacket and looks like he's about to get on the dance floor. "They are insane," I state, not moving because I'm afraid she's going to let go of my arm.

I look to the side and see that Shelby is talking to a guy dressed in a black suit with a hat under his arm. She looks around the room, and when she finds me, she comes straight for me. "Okay, so your car is here." I look at her, and Harlow's hand falls off my arm.

My skin still tingles from where she had her hand on me. "My car?" I ask, confused.

"Did you listen to anything we spoke about at the wedding meetings?" she hisses out. "Like anything?"

"One"—I hold up my finger—"we didn't have one."

"Well, I'm sure I mentioned it." She tries to remember

and then flips her hands. "It was supposed to whisk you guys away like a glass carriage. But what now is more like a pumpkin since you were ditched on your wedding day. It's going to take you away," Shelby says and flaps her arms like a bird. "You need to be outside in five minutes."

"Oh, are we going to throw rice and stuff?" Harlow asks, clapping her hands and laughing. She gasps. "Blow balloons?"

"You mean bubbles," Shelby corrects, and she laughs even harder now.

"If there was a bride, I'd say sure," Shelby says, then points at me. "But since he's a lone wolf, he gets nothing."

"You know what you should have done," Harlow shares, and whatever she is thinking is really funny to her because she can't stop laughing. Her laughter is infectious because now Shelby starts to laugh with her. "You should have married yourself," she finally says, and Shelby howls in laughter.

"I'm going to go and tell the driver if you aren't there in five minutes that he can leave." She turns and walks toward the kitchen.

"What are you going to do?" She looks over at me with the loaded question.

"Want to get out of here?" I ask her, knowing that I'm putting myself out there to be crushed. But I also know that if I didn't ask her, I would end up regretting not taking the chance. She just looks at me. "I mean, how many times can you say you rode in a limo with a jilted groom?"

"I don't think anyone has ever done that," she points out. "But we should ask your sisters. They would know for sure."

"Or," I say with a smirk. "You could be the first, Harlow." I finish the scotch and stand. "Besides, I don't want the night to end just yet."

She spins the glass of scotch in her hand and brings it to her lips. "You think that's a good idea?" She looks at me, waiting for my answer as she finishes the drink.

"Probably not." I shake my head. "But the universe brought us together again."

"I don't think we can blame the universe for this," she quips. "It was the wedding invitation that did it."

"Whatever it was," I say. "I'm not ready to say goodbye just yet." If she says no, I'm going to walk out and tell the driver to leave. I put my hands in my pockets instead of reaching out and dragging her out of here. "So what do you say?"

"Fine," she agrees. "I have to get my shoes." She points down to her bare feet. Her toenails are painted cherry red.

"I have to get my jacket and talk to my sisters. I'll meet you there." I point at the door that Shelby went into.

"Okay," she says and walks away from me. I take a second to watch her walk back to the table.

I turn and walk around the bar, grabbing a bottle of scotch and two glasses. "Put it on my tab," I tell the bartender, who laughs as he wipes down the bar and picks up the two empty glasses we left. I look around, spotting Presley talking to someone, and when she looks over at me carrying the bottle, she holds up her finger to the girl. It takes her a second before she comes over to me.

"What the hell are you doing?" she asks, pointing at the bottle and two glasses.

"My car is here, and I'm going to take off," I explain, and she cocks her hip while folding her arms over her chest.

"You think you are going to go get drunk in the car?" she asks. "How old are you, eighteen?"

"I'm actually older than you and"—I look down and then up—"I'm going to take off."

"Alone?" she asks, tapping her foot, and I just glare at her. "Oh my God, are you leaving with Harlow?"

"Mind your business," I advise. "And focus on the fact that you and Bennett have been playing cat and mouse." I point at her, and she shrieks out. "Have a good night."

"Asshole," she hisses, and then I walk away laughing, going to the spot where I told Harlow to meet me. I stand here looking around the room and spot her at the table with Rachel.

"Fuck, she's beautiful," I say to myself. "Don't fuck it up!" my head shouts back.

Twenty One

Harlow

I walk over to the table. My head is screaming at me that this is a bad idea. Sitting on the chair, I slip my feet back in my heels, and bend to tie the strap around my ankle. "Hey," Rachel says, sitting down in the empty chair beside me. She has sweat on the corner of her forehead, and she grabs a glass of water and downs it. Her chest is heaving from dancing so much. "God, that was fun," she says breathlessly.

"I'm not going to lie." I grab the other shoe and start putting it on. "I thought you were going to go toe to toe with the Worm." She throws her head back and laughs. I sit up, grabbing my purse.

"Are you leaving?" she asks with her eyebrows pushed together. I try to put on my poker face, but if anyone else knows me besides Travis, it's Rachel.

"I'm going to get out of here," I share, avoiding her eyes while I look up at the room and see that Travis is waiting beside the door, where he told me to meet him. His eyes find mine, and he motions with his head that he's heading out. He turns and walks out of the room.

"Are you sure about this?" Rachel asks, and I turn to her and see her looking at me. I stare at her, turn back to look at our friends on the dance floor, and then back again to the doorway that is now empty.

"Nope." I shake my head. "Not even a little bit," I lie to her. "This whole day, I haven't been sure about anything."

"I mean, weddings are all about regrets, right?" She laughs. "How many people do things at weddings that they wouldn't do anywhere else? Like, sex in the coatroom. Or sex in the bathroom."

"Or sex with the best man," I add in. "Or during a drunk speech."

"Yes." She points at me. "And how many people can say they banged the groom on his wedding day and wasn't the bride?"

I gasp. "I'm not banging anyone," I refute, and even my head yells liar.

"Oh, please." She rolls her eyes. "You guys are like two magnets." One hand is in a fist while the other hand slaps it.

"We're friends." I look back at the table, grabbing a glass of water. "I mean, we were friends," I add in. "He was my best friend."

"Hey," she huffs, and I laugh.

"He was my best guy friend." I put my arm around her and bring her to me.

"I bet he regrets it," she says softly. I shake my head, and my arm drops from her.

"I can't go there," I say, getting up. "It's in the past, and that is where it is going to stay. He's going to give me a lift to my hotel."

"Well, have fun." She smiles at me. "I'll call you in the morning." I lean down and kiss her cheek. "Don't do anything I wouldn't do," she snickers, and then I shake my head.

I debate going to say goodbye to everyone else, but then it might draw attention to me and the fact I'm leaving with Travis. Walking with my head down to avoid eye contact with anyone, I walk into the room and then see Clarabella and a man close to each other. They spring apart when I walk into the hallway. "I'm sorry." I hold up my hand. "I was just leaving." I point at the brown door at the end of the hallway with the Exit sign on it.

"Leaving?" Clarabella quizzes, folding her arms over her chest, cocking her hip. "Isn't that interesting?"

Playing dumb, I just smirk. "It's been a long day." *And the alcohol is just enough that I would do something but not something I regret,* I want to add in.

"Oh, I bet it has." She smiles. "Chances are it's going to be even longer." She motions to the brown door. "See you tomorrow, Harlow."

"Nice seeing you, Clarabella." I nod at her. "And you have fun with your friend." I point at the guy who stands there in jeans and a white shirt. His tatted arms look like they're going to make the shirt split.

She glares at me, and I try to hide the smile when I turn to walk out of the room. The darkness hits me right away, along with the thick humidity. A white limo is right in front of the stairs leading down. He leans on the back of the car, waiting for me. He smiles when he sees me. "I thought you changed your mind," he says when I walk down the four steps as he holds out his hand to help me walk.

"Just saying goodbye." The butterflies start in my stomach, and I'm blaming the booze. He opens the back door and waits for me to get in. I put one leg in and scoot over to the other side, giving him room to sit. He comes in and closes the door, and I can't help but laugh. "Oh, my," I say, looking at the wedding decorations that are hanging from the back window.

"Just wait until he moves the car," Travis says, and I look at him as the car starts moving, and I can hear cans dinging. I get up, looking out the back window, and see five strings of cans following us. "Does it say just married?"

"It did," he says. "Shelby took a Sharpie and crossed off just and put almost." I throw my head back and laugh.

He reaches for the bottle of scotch I saw him holding. He turns the top, and then it pops with the cork. I grab a glass and keep it for him as he fills them both. He puts the scotch back and takes one of the glasses. Our fingers graze each other, and my nipples perk up at his touch. *"Hussy."* My head screams at me at the same time as I answer back, *"Fuck off."*

"To Jackie." He holds up the glass, and I click my glass with his. He takes a sip of his scotch.

"Who is Jackie?" I ask him, taking a sip of the scotch and then wondering if this is even a good idea.

"Jackie," he says, leaning back against the seat, exhaling. "Is Jennifer's roommate and her best friend." I hold the glass in my lap as he turns toward me now. "And also the one who Jennifer is in love with." My mouth hangs open. "Yeah, that's about what I did when she told me."

"So, she's gay?" I ask him, and I'm trying my best not to laugh at him.

"She isn't sure," he admits, looking down into his glass of scotch. "But she is sure that she doesn't want to be married." He chuckles. "At least to me, that is."

I sit here shocked, and I have so many questions to ask. "I," I start to say. "Um, did you not suspect?" I ask him and then hold up my hand. "Sorry, it's not my place." The butterflies that started have moved to knots that are beginning to move up to my throat.

"It's fine," he assures me, taking another sip, maybe for courage. "What Jennifer and I had," he says, and it's safe to say that I don't even want to know. "It wasn't what we had."

I shake my head. "You don't have to say that," I finally say and take my own sip of scotch, hoping it stops me from talking. "What we had. It was a long time ago." I blink and look over at him.

He just looks at me, not saying anything and the car

comes to a stop. "Where are we?" I look around and see the white building.

"Well"—he puts his glass down and grabs mine—"it's a surprise." He opens the car door and steps out. His hand comes into the car to help me out, and I slip my hand in his, stepping out of the vehicle. The sounds of crickets now fills the area as we stand in the empty gravel parking lot.

"Where are we?" I repeat, looking around. I don't even see a sign or anything.

"You'll see," he says as he walks backward and pulls me with him. His smile lights up his face, and I am totally out of my mind. I should just end the night now and have the car take me back to my hotel room.

He pulls open the two glass doors, and I hear the sounds of pins being knocked down. "You did not," I say, looking around and then seeing the bowling lanes. I shake my head, thinking back to how he used to take me bowling once a week. No matter what time it was, he would drag me to the bowling alley every Friday night.

I look around and see that there are about four people here. Stopping at the blue counter that is filled with bowling shoes. "What can I do for you?" she asks and then takes in our outfits.

"We will take two games," he says, pulling out his wallet. "Two pairs of shoes, and we need to buy one pair of socks." He points at me. "Also a pitcher of beer."

"Two hot dogs with that and a basket of fries," I add in. "If we are going to bowl, we might as well do it the right way." I smile at him.

The girl hands me a pair of white folded socks and a pair of size seven shoes. "These shoes complete my outfit," I say, looking down at the light white and blue shoes. "I might not return them," I joke, and the girl just stares at me. "Tough crowd," I mumble and step aside while Travis gets his shoes.

"Lane ten." She points at the end of the lane, and I see it's dark. "It's disco bowling."

"Oh, fun," I say, walking toward the lane and dumping my purse and shoes there before walking back to Travis. I pick up the pitcher of beer with the red Solo cups while Travis brings the food.

I put the pitcher down at the little table on the side with four seats. I pour two glasses and then walk over to the shoes, taking off my heels, sliding the thick white socks on. "Should I do my socks up or down?" I ask him, laughing at myself while I put on the shoes.

"Only you could make bowling shoes stylish," he says to me, and I shake my head, walking over to the machine and putting our names in it.

"I will have you know." I look over at him as he comes over with the food, putting it down in front of me. "I haven't played in four years."

"Well, then I guess we are starting off the same," he tells me as he picks up the hot dog and takes a bite out of it.

"You love bowling." I grab my own hot dog and bite into it.

"Yeah, I stopped," he says, taking another bite. "It wasn't the same without you," he admits for the first time as he brings up the past, making me speechless. "Nothing was the same without you."

Twenty-Two

Travis

"Yeah, I stopped," I admit, taking another bite of the hot dog. "It wasn't the same without you." My head is telling me to shut the fuck up while my mouth has verbal diarrhea, and there is nothing I can do about it. "Nothing was the same without you." She looks at me and then looks down at her lap, and I see her eyes blinking away the tears, and I want to kick myself. "Okay, enough of this chitchat," I say, putting my hot dog down. "It's time to bowl."

She smiles and then looks at me. "Let's bowl, let's bowl, let's rock and roll." She gets up from her seat, puts her hot dog down, and then picks up the red Solo cup and takes a sip of the beer. "Hey, come on, let's get the show on the road." I groan out. "You knew it was coming."

She laughs, picking up a pink ball. Every single time we used to go bowling, she would bust out the *Grease 2* soundtrack. "We're gonna rock. We're gonna roll."

She points at me, and I shake my head but say the words anyway. "We're gonna bop. We're gonna bowl." She laughs again, and just because, she laughs. "We're gonna score tonight." She turns and takes her place. "God, I hate that movie."

"You fucking lie," she throws over her shoulder, and she looks so fucking beautiful she takes my fucking breath away. She starts to count out loud. "One." She takes a step. "Two." She takes another step and then another. I can hear her counting when she releases the ball, and all I can watch is the way her ass fills out that fucking dress. She knocks down four pins and then turns around. "That was a warm-up." She comes back and takes another sip of beer. If it was four years ago, I would run my hand up the back of her leg, and she would bend down and kiss me. She would hold my face in her hands, and her whole face would light up with a smile while she leaned down and kissed me. And I would love every fucking second of it. "Okay, get ready for the spare," she says, holding the ball beside her, and I have to laugh at what my wedding night is turning out to be. She starts counting the steps, and the ball ends up hitting one more pin. "Shit," she swears, turning and walking toward me, sitting next to me and grabbing her hot dog. "You're up." I get up, walking over to the balls to take my turn.

"Ready to get smoked?" I say the same words I said all those years ago. This time without slipping my tongue into her mouth. Which is totally a different experience, especially since I can almost taste the kiss again.

She holds up her hand. "Blah, blah, blah." She smirks at me, taking a fry and dipping it in ketchup. "Let's see what you got." I grab the ball and hold it up in front of me, looking at the pins, and I shoot it down the middle and knock most of the pins down. "Bullshit." I look over my shoulder at her, and she flips me the bird. "I think you lied about bowling."

I stand here in the middle of the alley and put my hands on my hips. "I don't lie." She folds her arms over her chest, raising her eyebrows. "Fine, I lied once." I hold up my hand, thinking back to when we started dating, and she decided to cook me a homemade meal. She worked on it for hours, and I mean hours, and the thing was so bad. It was overcooked, burned, half soggy, and tasted like garbage. I don't even know what it was supposed to be, But I ate it and said it was good because that is what you did when the woman you loved just slaved over a hot stove. The only one who blew it for me was Frankie. When he tasted a bite of it, he ran straight to the kitchen sink and threw up. "And that doesn't count because you forgave me."

"I had no choice but to forgive you," she huffs at me, her voice going louder. "You ate garbage."

"It wasn't that bad," I say, and she tilts her head to the side. "Fine, it was the worst meal of my life."

"Thank you," she says, dipping her fry in ketchup and tossing it in her mouth. "For finally admitting it to me."

I sit back down next to her. "So tell me, Harlow." I

take a french fry and dip it. "What have you been doing for the last four years?"

"Well"—she puts down her hot dog—"I've been traveling the world." She starts to laugh, and I know she's joking. "Not really much. Went back home and opened a practice. Worked every single day at all hours of the day. Busted my ass to be the best in the area."

"Which you succeeded in, no doubt." I get up and walk over to the balls. "I say this to anyone who asks, you were always the best." And I'm not lying either. Even when we were working together, she was better than me.

"My practice started with one little room in Quinn's barn," she shares. "And then it just got to be a bit too busy. Since then, I have a practice that has expanded three times." She smiles, and she should because I know that she must have worked her ass off. "I finally decided that the one-woman show is just too much for me. I've hired a new guy who just graduated a couple of weeks ago. He interned with me, so he knows how I work, and he's actually really good. Which is why I could be here this weekend."

"You don't get time off?" I ask her, wanting to know it all.

"Not usually." She gets up and walks over to the balls. "No rest for the wicked."

"You are a lot of things, Harlow," I state, looking into her eyes. "Wicked isn't one of them." I want to say she's the most loyal person I know. I mean, she attended my fucking wedding because she made me a promise.

A promise that I made her make, thinking she would be there on all my best days. A promise that every single time I have one of the best days, she was the person I always thought of at the end of the night. Until it got so hard, and I forced myself to stop.

She picks up the pink ball again. "If you think you can say sweet things to me to throw me off my game." She shakes her head. "Think again."

After two balls, she finally knocks down nine pins. "I can feel it." She sits down while I get up, taking a drink of my beer. "The next one is going to be a strike."

"Is that so?" I ask her, grabbing a ball, and when I finally let it go, I get a strike. I stand here in the middle of the lane, turn around, putting both my hands up by my head. "You called it."

She flips me the bird, making me laugh. "I don't know why you are flipping me off."

"So seriously, when is the last time you went bowling?" she asks, standing up and walking toward the balls. I don't move out of the way. Instead, I stand next to her. My hand is itching to hold her hip. My fingers also twitch to pull the sash of the bow down and see if the dress opens up.

"Four years ago," I tell the truth. I leave out that every time Jennifer asked me to go, I would bow out at the last minute. I just couldn't do it.

She picks up her pink ball and holds it up. "There are two things I hate in life." She walks over to the middle of the lane and holds up the ball. "One, surprise." I laugh because I already knew that. "And two, losing." She takes four steps before she lets go of the ball, and it looks like it's going to be a strike, but the two back pins stay up. "Fuck," she hisses out, turning and going back to get another ball. "What about you?" she asks, bowling the other ball, and it ends up in the gutter. "What have you been up to?"

She stands in front of me, waiting for me to answer. Her green eyes glisten in the almost dark lane. "After I graduated, I stayed on with the emergency clinic for two years. Then I ventured out on my own and opened a practice here with two other people," I say.

"That's amazing," she says. "It must be so good to have to share the responsibility with the other two." She walks over to the chair and sits down, drinking some beer. "So jealous." I walk back to the chair instead of taking my turn. "What do you do in your spare time?" she asks, and I wonder if she's as interested in finding out everything about me as I am with her.

"I don't really have spare time," I admit to her, taking my glass of beer and finishing it. "I'm the only one without a family, so I work most weekends, and I'm on call for the holidays." As soon as I say the words, I feel a little bit of emptiness inside me that I didn't know was there. "What about you?"

"I wish I could say that I'm out galivanting, but the truth is I barely have spare time, and when I do, I usually spend it with Sofia." She smiles at me, and even when we were dating, she used to call her all the time. I used to tease her during her FaceTimes with her. "She's a teenager now." She beams. "Thirteen going on thirty."

"Thirteen." I shake my head. "I remember her when she had two missing teeth in the front." We both laugh.

"It's funny that I don't see myself as older, but then I look at my nieces and nephews, and I'm like, how did they grow up?" she says, and I can hear a hint of regret in her voice also. She fills me in about her family, and hearing her speak, I know that regardless of how much it hurt when I let her go, taking her away from her family would have been too much for her, and I couldn't do that to her.

I'm about to say something when the lady from the front counter comes to us. "Sorry, folks, but we are closing up." She looks over at the screen and sees that we've been here for over an hour and have played two frames.

"Of course," Harlow says, walking over to the other chair and taking off the shoes and socks.

"Looks like I won," I say once I take off my shoes and look up at the scoreboard.

"Um, I don't think so," she says, standing up and taking the shoes in her hand. "It's incomplete."

"But I have more points than you." I point at the board.

"But I could have had five strikes and won." She cocks her hip to the side. "Or you could have had four gutter balls," she scoffs. "Anything could have happened."

"Fine," I give in. "But rematch." I hold out my hand, and she laughs.

"Fine, rematch." She puts her hand in mine to shake it, and it's as if a lightning zap has been put in my veins.

An electric shock, and my whole body lights up in ways it hasn't before.

She drops my hand, and we turn to walk out. My hand comes out to hold hers, but then I catch myself and place it on her lower back. "I haven't had this much fun in a while," she says to me when we walk out and toward the waiting car. She looks up at the stars. "I almost don't want this night to end." She looks at me, and her eyes widen. "I mean, you must be dying for this day to end so you can forget about it."

I smile and look down. "It doesn't have to end," I say the words that I might regret if she turns me down, "at least not yet anyway."

Twenty-Three

Harlow

*H*e smiles at me and looks down at his feet. The need to reach out and run my hands through his hair is overwhelming. Even more overwhelming than me being a hussy and trying to sway my hips while I bowled. "It doesn't have to end," He says the words almost in a whisper, his eyes full of mischief. "At least not yet anyway."

I smirk at him. "What else do you have in mind?" I ask, and he throws his head back and laughs.

"I have no idea," he admits. "But we can improvise." He opens the car door to the limo, and I get in. I hear him talking to the driver, but I can't make out the words. I put my head back on the seat; it's whirling from everything that has happened today. Or maybe it's the booze. Either way, I don't want tonight to end. Talking to him about what he has been doing and indirectly asking about his life with Jennifer, I found out that he wasn't as happy as I thought he would be. Not once did he mention her or their life, and from the sound of it, he worked just as much as I did. Every time he sat next to me and his leg touched mine, I would feel goose bumps start to form and would hope that he wouldn't comment on it. I already had the excuse that I was cold, hoping he wouldn't see me lying. When I feel the car bounce, I open my eyes, looking out the window into the darkness.

"Where are we going?" I ask when the door shuts, and I hear the driver get into the car.

"You'll see," he says. I look out the window and remember the time he brought me here or around here and I made him that promise.

I got on my knees, lifted my dress, and moved my leg over to straddle him. I held his face in my hands and said the words that I'd bitten my tongue on for the past five months. "I love you." I looked into his eyes when I said the words and then saw his mouth open, and I put my finger on it. "You don't have to say it back. I just wanted you to know that these past six months with you have been more than I could ever imagine." I leaned forward and kissed him softly.

His hands rubbed up my back. "Promise me something." He said the words so softly.

"I will promise you anything," I said, knowing that he could have asked me anything and the answer would always be yes.

"Promise me that you'll be there by my side on the happiest day of my life."

My fingers pushed back the hair on his forehead as the image of me walking down the aisle to him filled my mind. "I promise," I assured him.

"Good," he said and kissed me softly. My heart sped up so fast in my chest I thought I was going to throw up from all this happiness. I didn't think it could have gotten better than this, and then it did when he said the words I'd been dying to hear. "I love you, Harlow."

The car comes to a stop, and I look out the window at this little cabin. "What in the world?" I say when my door opens, and the driver is there to help me out.

The lights from the front door illuminate the five steps leading to a brown door. Looking to the side of the house, I see the soft lights coming out of four big long windows. The light is showing all around, and when I take a few steps to the side, I see that you can see right through to the other side of the house. It has a whole rustic feel to it. I look up and see the balcony on the second floor that sits right on top of the front door. "Let's go." He grabs my hand, pulls me up the steps, and opens the door. His fingers are now linked with mine, and my eyes are so fixated on our hands together I don't even notice him open the door.

I take a step in, and I'm in shock when I see rose petals scattered on the floor everywhere, leading to a side toward the stairs and another toward the open room with the windows. "Oh my God," I say as he walks into the house a bit, and I see the red heart balloons floating in the living room. An L-shaped couch faces a coffee table covered in vases of red roses. The room where all the windows are is almost all covered in rose petals and balloons. He lets my hand go as he walks over to the table that has a silver bucket with a champagne bottle. Right next to a silver tray with two crystal glasses are two bowls on another silver tray of strawberries, one covered with chocolate and the other plain.

"What the fuck is all this?" he says, and I have to look at him, not sure what he means as I take a minute to look around and see that there are crystal vases filled with water and floating candles placed on every single step leading to upstairs. Travis walks to the table, his walking is a bit off, and all I can do is laugh and put my hand to my mouth, missing my face. "I told them this was off-limits." He grabs the bottle of champagne out of the silver bucket. The bottle is leaking water everywhere, and he couldn't care less. He leans down and grabs the bowl. "Can't forget these," he says to me, laughing, and I walk over, putting my purse on the edge of the table, but it falls right off, making us both laugh out loud and picking up the other bowl. "Follow me." He smirks at me, nudging me with his head, and his eyes light up so bright I'm mesmerized and walk over to the staircase.

"Don't do it!" my head yells at me as my stomach flutters and the heat starts to rise up my neck from the nerves that are filling my body. *"Just call it a night and go."* But my feet are already following him up the stairs. The glow of the candles helps lead the way as we stop at the top of the stairs. It's just a one-bedroom open-concept

loft style. The king-size bed is in the middle of the room but is up on a raised platform. A four-poster bed at that, with white sheets draped around the top. Rose petals in the shape of a heart are in the middle of the bed with Mr. & Mrs. pillows. I stand beside him, swaying from side to side as I try to get myself balanced. "Is this weird?" I say the words out loud, hoping that he tells me that we should just call it a night. I look around to see the rose petals are scattered everywhere. There isn't a piece of floor that isn't covered with at least one rose petal. In the corner of the room beside the bed is a deep white tub that can fit more than two people. I step into the room just a bit more, but my balance is a bit off, and I see that the tub is filled with water and rose petals, candles floating on the top. "If this is weird." I look back at him. "I can go." He just stands there taking in the room, and then shakes his head.

"After today," he says, looking back at me, "you being here isn't the weirdest thing that has happened to me." He walks over to me and hands me the bowl of strawberries that he is carrying in his hand. "Hold these." I look down at his hand that is reaching out, trying to focus on grabbing the bowl from him. I giggle while I take it from him, and then he turns back, walking toward the bed. I stand here nervously, wondering what he is going to do. I watch with bated breath and a fit of nervous giggles as he walks over to the bed and grabs the cover by the corner, and he rips it off. The rose petals that were perfectly placed in the middle of the bed fly everywhere. "This way." He slurs a bit, walking to the door in the middle of the room and opening it. I follow him toward the door and step onto the balcony into the dark night. A breeze runs through me, and I shiver. "Thank God." He looks around and puts the cover down on the wooden balcony floor. He kicks off his shoes and walks to the middle of the blanket. "Come on." He motions with his head, and I put the bowls down to take off my shoes.

When I step out onto the wood, it's cooler on my feet than I thought it would be. I try to tiptoe toward the cover, and my foot sinks into it. It feels like I'm walking on a cloud. "I don't think this cover is meant to be on this balcony." I laugh, unsure of myself.

He sits down on one side of the blanket and then pats the side beside him. "Make yourself at home."

I walk to the spot that he just patted and go down on one knee and then the other, trying to gracefully sit without my feet flying out from under me and avoid suddenly being on my back with my legs up in the air. I almost celebrate out loud when I sit down next to him without a disaster. I curl my feet to the side of me, but my knees are close to him, touching his leg. He takes off the tin foil around the cork and then twists the little wire around it, and then he pops the cork. Champagne flies out, and he quickly moves his hand to the side so it can spill off the cover. "I hope you didn't put your credit card down for a deposit," I joke with him, and he brings the bottle to his lips and takes a sip.

"I know the owner," he assures me, handing me the bottle. I try not to think about how his lips just touched the top of the bottle when I bring it to my lips. The cold sweet, bubbly champagne hits my lips and then my tongue. I really shouldn't be drinking anything else tonight, but my buzz says otherwise.

"This is a good one," I say, handing it back to him, and our fingers graze when he takes it. The little way my stomach rises and then falls makes me look up at the sky. The stars are twinkling like little diamonds, the sound of crickets fills the area, and if you close your eyes, it sounds just like home.

"Only the best," he says, and I look over at him as he sits down with his legs extended in front of him. "For the mister." He laughs, shaking his head. He brings the bottle to his lips and takes three gulps, and then hands it back to me. Our fingers graze each other again, and this time they linger longer, and my heartbeat starts to speed up faster and faster. I try to control my breathing and also the way my head is starting to spin, and I wonder if it's from the booze or being with him.

"Good to know," I say, putting the bottle against my lips again while Travis grabs a strawberry and bites it.

"Strawberry and champagne," he says, looking up at the stars. "Who knew that combination was good."

I put the bottle down on the cover and then take my hand off it. I can see it falling to the side as soon as my fingers are not touching it, and we both spring into action before it spills all over the cover, and it would have mostly fallen on him. "Ooh," I say, rushing to get it at the same time as his hands come out to stop it also. His hands cover mine as he catches the bottle at the same time as me, but it spills half out onto the blanket, and he picks it up, my hand still wrapped around the bottle. "Crisis averted," I say, looking down at our hands touching. My breathing is coming out in pants, and I really hope it's not echoing in the silent night. I make the stupid mistake of looking up at him, and he's suddenly a lot closer than I thought he was. So close I can feel his breath on my face, so close that I can smell his cologne. So close that I'm afraid to move away from him. "Travis." I say his name in a whisper, and it happens in slow motion, or maybe it's just the fog of what is happening.

His hands leave mine and come up to hold my face. "Harlow." I see his lips moving to say my name, and before I know what is happening, his lips are on mine. I don't know if I'm the one who moans, or he is the one, or if it's the both of us. But my mouth opens for his, and here in the middle of the night under the stars, I finally get the kiss that I've thought about for the last four years.

Twenty-Four

Travis

I rush to make sure the bottle doesn't spill beside me, and my hands fall on hers. The heat from her hands runs through me. My whole chest contracts in a way that only she can do. It's only ever done that with her. I thought that after her, it was all in my head, but the minute my eyes fell on her, everything became clear. "It's you. It's always been you." My hands fly off hers, and I grab her face in mine, and my heart speeds up so fast it sounds like a herd of bulls running through the streets in Spain. Her name leaves my lips right before I pull her to me and kiss her lips.

I moan into her mouth when I slip my tongue into her mouth. If there were ever fireworks for a kiss, there should be some. Actually, every single fucking time I've kissed her, I've felt fireworks go off. My hands move from her face to her hair as I tilt her head to the side, and the kiss deepens. My tongue goes around and around in a circle as if I can never get enough, and now that I've tasted her again, I will never go without her.

She pants, letting go of my lips, and my whole body stops moving. My heart stops beating, and it's like I turned to stone. My eyes search hers to see if the kiss had the same effect on her as it did on me. "Wait," she says, and my hands won't let her go, from fear that I'll never be able to touch her again. I really should have waited for her to make a move. I should have told her flat out that I wanted to kiss her, but it all happened so fast. "I want to," she says, turning and putting the bottle on the other side. It falls on its side, but she doesn't even notice when she turns back to me. Fuck, she's stunning. "Where were we?" she asks with a smirk. "If I remember well, your tongue was." I don't wait for her to tell me where my tongue was since I remember exactly where it was.

"It was right here." I smile right before claiming her lips again. This time she turns in my arms, and our lips slip apart.

"Sorry," she says as her hands pull up her dress even more, and she throws her legs over me. "That's better." Her hands come up to my face as she pulls me to her. My hands fall out of her hair and take their place at her hips. They fit in my hands perfectly. Her tongue comes out as she licks my lower lip before sliding into my mouth. Her hand leaves my face and runs through my hair. My hands move from her hips to her ass as I squeeze, and she sits fully on my cock. My cock is harder than it's ever been, and she grinds on me.

"Fuck," I hiss out, leaving her lips, her head falls back, leaving her neck bare for me. My arms wrap around her, pulling her to me as my tongue comes out and traces down her neck before I nip at her and suck in. Her hands pull my hair, so my head goes back, and she attacks my lips. Her tongue is fighting with mine. The soft kisses of before are gone, and the both of us are needy. Her hands go from my hair to my shoulders and then to my chest, where she bunches the shirt in her fists. She moves her head from side to side, trying to get the kiss deeper as she grinds back and forth on my cock. "Torture." I let go of her lips, panting out. "It's fucking torture." And her mouth attacks my neck and slowly moves up toward my ear as she nips the lobe at the same time. She pulls the shirt out of my pants. I place my hands behind me, leaning back to give her access to me.

Her fingers go to my buttons, her eyes on me the whole time. She fumbles with a couple of buttons, and at this point, I'm ready to just tear my shirt off me. When she finally gets to the last button, she lets the shirt slide to the side. "I did it." She smiles proudly, and I raise one hand to her head and pull her to me to kiss her again. Her tongue slides against mine, her chest goes flush with mine, the satin from the dress feels smooth. I sit up straight, and my other hand goes to her hip. My hand slips to her shoulder, and my fingers trace down her arm to hold her other hip. She moans into my mouth when my hands move up the sides of her rib cage and then cup her tits. She tilts her hips up the length of my covered cock, and it's my turn to moan into her mouth. I can feel her nipples through her dress, and my mouth waters to taste them. I push down the one side of the dress with no sleeve, leave her mouth, and bend my head to take her nipple into my mouth. She arches her back when I twirl my tongue around her nipple, biting down on it. "Travis," she moans, and my hand pinches the other covered nipple. My mouth goes to it, and I bite it through her satin dress. She moves her hand to the side of her, and I hear the sound of a zipper, and before I know it, her arm with the sleeve is being moved down, and her dress falls to her waist. I look into her eyes before kissing her again. Now our naked chests are pressed together as she tries to push me down on my back.

"Not yet." I chuckle. "You'll get me on my back soon," I say, wrapping my arm around her waist and turning her to her back.

"This works, too." She smirks as she wraps her legs around my hips, her hands coming out to push my shirt off my shoulders. "You got bigger," she says of my arms. "And more defined." She uses her index finger to run down one of my pecs. She isn't wrong. When I wasn't working, I would spend time in the gym. I get on my knees, taking off the shirt, and her legs fall from my hips when she sits up, and I look down at her, pushing her hair away from her face, leaning down, and kissing her lips. She smiles at me when I leave her lips as she leans in and bites my pec right beside my nipple.

I hiss out, and she laughs. Lying back down, my eyes

travel from her beautiful face down to her neck, and I fall forward on her, but my hands catch me before I squash her. My head bends, and I suck in her neck on the right spot and she moans. Her hands are on my sides, and I swear my stomach sinks in from her touch, making me shiver. My tongue comes out, and I trail down to her nipple, teasing it with the tip of my tongue before sucking it into my mouth. Her hands go to the back of my head, and when I look up, I see that she's watching me. With my eyes on hers, I move to the other breast and do the same thing. I suck right next to her nipple and see the spot becoming red as I trail kisses to her stomach. I push away from her and kneel with my back straight in the middle of her legs. "There is one thing," I say, running my hands from her ankles all the way up to her thighs. Soft goose bumps form when I get close to her pussy. "One thing I'm dying to do."

"Is there?" She puts one hand behind her head. "If it makes you feel better, there is also one thing I'm dying for you to do." She smirks at me.

"Is that so?" My finger inches higher on her inner thigh. "I wonder if what I'm dying to do." I can feel the heat coming from between her legs, and my hand disappears under her skirt. "Is the same thing you are dying for me to do."

My fingertips graze the lace of her panties. I can feel them wet already when she lifts her hips up off the floor. "Let me give you a hint." Her hands go to her hips as she pulls her dress up to around her waist. Her green lace panties are the exact color of her dress. "I'd like your mouth," she says, putting her hips down. "Right here." She moves her panties to the side, and she doesn't have to ask me twice. My head dives straight for her pussy, and my tongue comes out, and I lick her slit, the taste of her tingles on my tongue. "Fuck," she hisses out as my tongue slides between her lips and finds her clit. The minute my tongue touches it, her back arches. "Yes," she pants, and I use one of my hands to open her lips so I can see her. I suck her clit into my mouth, remembering how sensitive it was. Playing with her clit with my tongue going back and forth, I slip two fingers inside her. "Mmmm," she says, her hand going into my hair. Her nails dig into my head, pushing me into her pussy. My fingers fuck her at the same time as my tongue moves back and forth. I can feel her pussy getting tighter and her panting getting deeper. "Right there." She lifts her hips and moves with my fingers. "Faster." Her legs start to tighten around my head. "Travis." She moans my name and comes on my fingers, her juices running down my fingers. "Oh, God." She tries to close her legs even more, but I don't stop moving my fingers. "Sensitive," she says, and I look up at her.

"I know." I graze her clit with my teeth, and this time she comes again. The moan fills the night, and if anyone was around, they would know exactly what was going on. I slide my tongue into her at the same time as my fingers and then lick up to her clit as she rides the wave over and over again. Her hips buck each time, and when I move my fingers faster and faster until I can't move my fingers anymore, I know she's going to come again.

"One more time, Harlow," I say, and I look up at her as she stares at me eating her pussy. Her eyes roll to the back of her head, and she comes harder than she ever has. My fingers slow down as her hold on my head eases up. Her legs fall to the sides, and when I slide out of her, all I can do is watch her chest moving up and down.

"That was." She licks her lips and opens her eyes. "That was." I crawl up to her, and her nose rubs against my jaw. "That was fun." I can hear the smile in her voice. "I bet it'll be just as good when I take your cock down my throat."

Twenty-Five

Harlow

"That was." I lick my lips with my eyes still closed. I am afraid to open them and for it to be a dream. The cool air breezes through me, and when I open them, he is on his knees in the middle of my legs. "That was," I start to say, getting my breathing back to normal when he crawls up and over me, and I rub my nose under his jaw. "That was fun." I smile at how stupid it sounds. That was fun. That was way better than fun. That was the best I've ever had, and I've already had him. It was like the best on steroids. I kiss his neck, and he leans back so I can see his face. "I bet it'll be just as good when I take your cock down my throat."

He groans, and I slide out from his grasp, standing up with my dress bunched up around my waist. I slip it over my hips, taking my panties with it as I stand here in the middle of the balcony, naked as the day I was born. "Hmm." He pushes to his knees, and his face is the perfect height of my pussy. His hands go to my ass as he slides his tongue between my lips.

"No," I say begrudgingly. "It's my turn." I move out of his grasp.

"It's not my fault, if you put your pussy in my face." He smirks, getting up to his feet. "I'm going to eat it."

I throw my head back and laugh. "Good to know." I close the gap between us, and when he bends his head for a kiss, I fall to my knees in front of him. My hands go to his belt as I look up at him. His eyes watch my every single move. "I think the time has come." I pull out his belt and unbuckle it. "For me." I open the button. "To get this." I pull down the zipper and push his pants over his hips. "Baby down." I palm his cock over his white boxers, and it's just like I remembered it. Long and thick, and I swear my pussy convulses thinking about sitting on it again. My fingers slide into the elastic at the top, and I slowly uncover his cock. "Down my throat." I lean in, licking the tip of his cock just like a lollipop and tasting his salty precum. I push his boxers down with his pants over his ass. My hand grips the base of his cock, and he moans. "See how much fun this is." I suck the tip of his cock in my mouth and then let it go. "Your cock." I take him just a touch deeper before letting go again. "In my mouth." I take him even deeper. "Down my throat." I try to take him all in, but he's too long and thick. My hand moves with my mouth, and I look up at him as I try to take him all the way in. His hand goes into my hair as his hips move with my mouth as he fucks my face.

"Harlow." He hisses out my name when I graze the head of his cock with my teeth and lick down his shaft to his balls. I look up at him when I suck one into my mouth and then move over to the other one. "Fuck," he says. He closes his eyes and puts his head back when I take his cock in my mouth again. "I'm not going to last," he says between clenched teeth. "I'm going to come," he warns me.

"Come in my mouth," I urge, taking his cock back down my throat, and he does just that. I continue sucking him until the last drop, and only then do I let his cock leave my mouth.

"That was," he says, his chest rising and falling. He pulls me up to stand in front of him. "That was." He rubs his nose with mine, his lips kissing the corner of my mouth.

"Fun." I try not to laugh, but I fail miserably, and the both of us laugh. He pushes his pants down and steps out of them, leaving him naked in front of me. It's been four years since I've seen him naked, and the memories don't do him justice at all.

"I'm ready to have more fun." He wraps his arm around my stomach and picks me up. I wrap my legs around his waist.

"I'd love to have more fun," I say, expecting him to put me on the cover, but he starts walking inside.

"Are we not going to have fun on the balcony?" I ask him as he steps into the house.

"Fuck no." He shakes his head. "I'm not going to have fun with you on a wooden balcony."

I wrap my arms around his neck. "We had sex in the front seat of your car with the steering wheel pressed against my ass," I remind him. Sex with Travis was always, and I mean always, good. From the very first time until the last time. We would have sex often, sometimes three times a day.

"Well, I think I can do better than a steering wheel on your ass." He chuckles. "And that was your fault. You literally climbed over the console."

"You spent fifteen minutes telling me how you were going to eat my pussy," I huff out, and then he throws me on the bed. I laugh, and my legs fall open.

"I'm about to do that right now," he says, crawling on the bed and burying his head between my legs.

"That's good." My hips come up to ride his face. "But I think your cock in my pussy would be better."

He gets on his knees. "Is that so?"

I sit up and jerk his cock. "That is so," I confirm and turn my head to see the side table and a bowl full of condoms. "Whoever was responsible for this room needs a raise." I tear the corner of the condom open and crawl over to him, ready to put it on him.

"I'll do that." He holds out his hand. "You get on your back, spread your legs, and get yourself ready for me." I gladly hand him the condom and fall back and spread my legs for him. I move my hand down to play with my clit as I watch him sheathe himself.

"I want it hard." I slip two fingers in me. "And fast."

"You." He crawls over to me, his cock
"Will take my cock." He slaps my clit wi'
rubs it up and down my slit. He slips th.
give it to you," he says right before slamming in.

My eyes roll to the back of my head, and he pulls
out and slams back into me. I feel so full. "You can do
it harder," I egg him on, knowing that he always gave
it to me the way I wanted it. I tilt my hips back to get
him even deeper, and his balls slap against my ass over
and over again. He fucks me like he's never fucked me
before, every thrust is harder than the last one, and I love
every second of it. My fingers strum my clit, and when
I'm about to come, he can feel it because he pulls out of
me completely and buries his face in my pussy, sliding
his tongue in a couple of times before slamming his cock
back in. "I need," I say, and the only sound in the room
is the sound of our skin slapping together. His hips thrust
in and out, and he bends to bite my nipple, and it's the
push I needed to go over the edge. "I'm coming." I try
to close my legs to make him stay put, but he just keeps
slamming into me over and over again. I think I'm at
the end of it when he pulls out and turns me over to my
stomach. He grabs me by the hips and slams into me, and
I come again, and this time so does he. He roars out my
name as he comes into the condom. He collapses on top
of me, and my eyes close. "That," I say when I feel his
head touch the pillow next to me. I turn my head to see
him with his head turned and his eyes closed.

He opens them, and I have never seen his eyes so
clear before. "That was out of this fucking world," he

ys, slipping out of me and going to his back. He closes his eyes and puts one hand on his chest.

My pussy cries for him to come back. "I mean, it was good," I joke with him, and he opens one eye to look at me. "I think we can do better."

"Is that so?" He smirks at me, and I get on my knees.

"Only way to find out is to do it again," I say, and he pulls me to him.

"I see us doing that," he says, pushing the hair away from my face. "A lot more."

"Oh, really?" I say before his mouth is on mine.

"I'M GOING TO start upstairs," I hear a woman's voice say. "And then come and help you guys down here."

My eyes flutter open, thinking that I was just dreaming I heard voices. But when I hear someone gasp, I know it's not a dream. "Oh my fucking God." I don't move because I'm not sure if I'm covered or not. I don't even know how long I've been sleeping, every single time I closed my eyes, we would snuggle up, and his dick would end up inside me. The last time, I collapsed on my stomach and fell asleep when he was going to get rid of the condom. My mouth feels like I have swallowed sand on the beach.

I look over my shoulder, and my eyes meet Shelby, who just stares with her mouth open and her hand moving to cover said mouth. The sound of footsteps running up the stairs has Travis opening his eyes. I watch Clarabella and Presley come to the top of the stairs and halt in their steps behind Shelby. Both of them have the same expression on their faces that Shelby has. Just Clarabella smirks at me and rolls her lips to stop from laughing out.

"Jesus Christ, Shelby," Travis hisses out from beside me. "What are you doing here?" He sits up now, and the sheet that was on his chest falls to his lap.

"What am I doing here?" she asks, shocked.

"Can the floor swallow me?" I'm shocked when I hear the words out loud. I thought I was thinking it instead of saying it. I look around to see if they heard me say what I just did

"Someone swallowed someone last night," Presley says, folding her arms over her chest I groan out and grab the cover and try to bring it over my head.

"Okay, all of you need to go downstairs, and we'll meet you there."

"I'll make coffee," Clarabella says, turning and going down the stairs.

"I'm going to go help her and discuss what we just saw." Presley steps down one step. "Come on, Shelby." She pulls Shelby beside her.

"Oh my God," I grumble, and if I didn't want to die before, I definitely want to die now. "This is so embarrassing," I say, getting up and holding the sheet to my chest as I get out of the bed. Panic is running through me as I look back at Travis, who is now naked, and his cock is up.

I hold up my hand to stop my eyes from looking at it. "It's a little too late for modesty." Travis gets out of bed.

"You sat on my face less than two hours ago."

"That was different," I hiss whisper at him, but the openness of the room makes my voice carry.

"It was still you naked," he points out, walking to the door and then thinking about walking out onto the balcony, and I shout his name.

"Cover yourself. It's light out," I hiss at him, and he grabs a towel that we used when we got out of the tub sometime during the night. "And get my dress." I point at the door.

"Well, there goes morning sex," he says, wrapping the towel around his hips at the same time the phone in my purse starts to ring.

Twenty-Six

Travis

I put my hand on the doorknob to go outside when a phone starts ringing from downstairs. "That's my phone," she says, clinging to the sheet in front of her.

"Can someone bring up the phone?" I shout down the steps and then go to walk outside. The sun makes me squint as I grab our clothes and walk back inside.

"Here," Clarabella says, handing Harlow her purse.

"Thank you," she mumbles and doesn't even make eye contact with her. The phone stops ringing. I smile at Clarabella as she turns and walks back down the stairs. "Can this be any worse?"

I laugh. "It could have been my mother," I say, and she glares at me, and I laugh. "We are two consenting adults who can do what we want." I try to smooth it over with her. The last thing I wanted was to wake up with my sisters barging in. Not after the night I just had. The best night of my life, and of course, it would make sense that it was with Harlow.

The phone rings again from her purse, and she opens it and looks at me. "It's Rachel." She closes her eyes and puts her head back. "Hello." She puts the phone to her ear. "Yeah, yeah, I'm fine," she says, looking at me. "Brunch sounds like a plan. I'll be ready in about an hour." I don't know what Rachel says, but two minutes later, she hangs up. "I need to get back to the hotel." She grabs her dress from my hand. "Where are my panties?"

"Outside on the front porch." I hear Presley from downstairs. "We thought it was a joke."

"Well, the joke's on all of you," Harlow says and laughs as she stands up. "I'm guessing you aren't going to turn around."

"You would be right," I say, getting up, and I hate that she is shy in front of me this morning. "But I will," I say, turning and dropping the towel from my waist as I put on my boxers. I hear the zipper from her dress at the same time as I zip up my own pants.

"How do I look?" she asks, and I turn around, and I can't help but smile.

"Beautiful," I say softly, and then my eyes go to her neck, and I put my hand to my mouth. "Your neck," I say, and she walks over to the bathroom, and she looks in the mirror.

"Did you give me a hickey?" she shrieks out. "What is wrong with you?" Her head comes out from the bathroom.

"It's not my fault." I hold up my hands. "I think it's when you were sitting on." She walks out of the bathroom and holds up her hand.

"I don't need a replay. I was there," she retorts, and I walk over to her and take her in my arms. She comes reluctantly. "This is crazy."

"Is it?" I ask her softly, and she doesn't answer. All she does is look up at me, and I bend to kiss her lips.

"I have to go," she says. "Rachel is going to be waiting for me."

I nod my head at her and slip my fingers in hers as we walk down the stairs. My chest hurts, thinking she is going to leave any minute. "Well, well, well, if that isn't the walk of shame," Presley says from the stool in the kitchen. "I don't know what is."

"There is no shame," I say, and Harlow untangles her fingers from mine.

"Can one of you drive me to the hotel?" she asks them. "Or point me in the direction, and I can Uber there."

"I'll take you," Clarabella says, coming to her. "I'll be back for you guys after I drop her off."

"Thank you," Harlow says and then looks up at me, and I can see that she has so much she wants to say, but she just nods at me and walks out of the house. I want to reach out for her hand and kiss her one last time, but I know with an audience present and the embarrassment that she is feeling, she will not be happy with me.

I watch the door close behind her and then see Shelby walk past me and look outside. I hear the crunch of the tires as they drive away, and only then does Shelby turn around and look at me. "Have you lost your goddamn mind?" she shouts at me, putting her hands on her hips. Definitely not what I thought I was going to be doing this morning.

"Here," Presley says, walking to my side and handing me a cup of coffee. "Before you answer anything, drink."

"Why can't you be nicer, like her?" I point at Presley and take a sip of the hot coffee. "And why are you yelling?"

"Because you have lost your ever-loving fucking mind." She throws her hands up in the air, and I just smirk.

"There was also fucking last night." Presley tries to make a joke, and we both glare at her. "Tough crowd."

"One, what happened between Harlow and me." I say her name again, and it's like music to my ears. "Is between us."

"It took you two years to get over her," Shelby points out, and I roll my eyes.

"I was busy building my practice." I try to shy away from the truth.

"Lies," Presley says from beside me, and I look over at her. "He never got over Harlow."

"What?" I ask, shocked, and Presley just shrugs her shoulders.

"You can't stand there and tell me that you actually loved Jennifer," she says, and the coffee that I took a sip of is starting to come up. I'm about to say something when she puts up her hand. "I'm sure you liked her plenty, but love." She shakes her head, sitting back down on the stool. She picks up her cup of coffee and brings it to her lips. "You didn't love her."

"How can you say that?" Shelby says and then looks at me.

"You." Presley points at Shelby. "Are full of shit." Shelby gasps at her while I hear the sound of tires again. My heart speeds up in my chest, and I wonder if Harlow decided that she didn't want to be dropped off and instead wanted to come back. The front door opens, and Clarabella steps in and shuts the door behind her.

"Okay, I rushed as fast as I could." She looks at the three of us. "What did I miss?"

"Nothing," Shelby and I say at the same time.

"Liars liars, pants on fire," Presley says. "Shelby was asking if Travis lost his goddamn mind. Then I told him that he never loved Jennifer."

"True," Clarabella says, and my eyes widen, and she looks at me. She laughs. "You can't actually stand there and tell us that you loved Jennifer." She looks at me, and I want to say that I did, but I look down at my coffee. "Exactly, you were never you," she starts to say. "I mean, look at this place. You bought this house and never brought her here." I swallow down. "You never even told her."

"It never came up," I lie to her. I will not tell anyone why I bought this house four years ago. No one, except for the woman who just walked out.

"Wait a second," Shelby says, holding up a finger. "When I asked you about the wedding night, you said that you would rent a room at the hotel."

"I did rent a room," I tell them. "I told you guys not to decorate here. I specifically said I wasn't coming here on my wedding night."

"You said you didn't want to bring Jennifer here, yet you brought Harlow," Shelby continues as if she's fucking Sherlock Holmes.

"Because he doesn't love Jennifer," Clarabella says, and I look at her. "When you are with Harlow, it's like you are you."

"What the fuck does that even mean?" I say, frustrated that everyone is all in my business and that all of this is coming out.

"You never really laugh," Presley says. "It's just like…" She doesn't know what word to say, so Shelby comes up with one.

"Boring," Shelby says. "You are very boring." Her face grimaces.

"But then, with Harlow, you are joking and laughing. You held her hand coming down the stairs," Clarabella says. "I never saw you kiss Jennifer. Not once."

I tilt my head to the side. "So we weren't touchy-feely." I drink a cup of coffee, and it tastes sour in my mouth.

"Can I share my thoughts?" Clarabella says, holding up her hand.

"Why, you've been holding back?" I laugh.

She rolls her eyes. "When you broke up with Harlow," she starts. "We couldn't even say her name. Every single time we saw you, you looked worse and worse." She wipes a tear away from her eye.

"Yeah, you looked like shit," Presley cuts in. "Your eyes were all sunken in. It was bad."

"And forget about us even saying her name. I remember once Mom mentioned her name, and you got this look in your eyes, and you left the house." I look down, remembering how hard it was for me. "Now you broke up with Jennifer yesterday, and you didn't even bat an eye."

"Also, we've said Jennifer a million times, and you didn't cry." Clarabella points at me. "Harlow walked out the door, and you looked like someone stole your ice cream."

"What do you want from me?" I ask all three of them.

"We want you to be happy, jerkoff," Shelby says, folding her arms over her chest. "And if Harlow makes you happy, own up to it."

"You are so lucky," Presley says, shaking her head. "If you broke up with me four years ago, and then you invited me to your wedding, the last thing I would give you was a blow job."

"Same," Clarabella says. "I would definitely kick you in the balls."

"She obviously still has feelings for him," Shelby says, and my heart skips a beat hoping she is right.

"Anyway, I'd love to sit here and chat about Romeo's love life," Clarabella says. "But we have a brunch to get to."

"Also, please note," Shelby says. "I'm not cleaning anything in this house."

"You made this mess," I say, looking around at the house.

"You had sex in this house," she counters. "And the last thing I want to do is touch something that your ball sack touched."

"I would die," Presley says, stepping away from the counter. "Did you do it here?" She points at the counter. And I try to hide the smile. "Oh my God."

"I don't think we did it in that spot." I point, and truth be told, we never left upstairs. "But it might be around there."

"I need a shower and disinfecting," Presley says, walking out the door. "Brunch in thirty. Don't be late."

"Why are we having a brunch if there was no wedding?" I ask.

"Because the food was ordered, and we only invited your friends," Shelby states, walking out the door and slamming it shut.

"I guess I'll find my own ride there," I say, shaking my head and looking around. I walk back upstairs to the bathroom and take a shower, showing up at the brunch forty-five minutes later in jeans and a polo shirt.

"There he is," Frankie says when I walk into the same room we were in last night. Except all the tables are gone but one round one in the middle. "Fuck, how are you not hungover?" he says when I get close enough to him. I take a look around and see it's only the guys that are here so far.

"Slept it off," I lie to him, and the door opens, and I

look over, expecting to see her walking in. But the only ones who walk in are Rachel, Victoria, and Lydia. The three of them are all wearing sunglasses.

"Please tell me that someone has a Bloody Mary?" Lydia says, going straight to the bar.

"Hey," I say to Rachel when she comes to say hi. "Where is Harlow?"

"Oh, she left," she says, and everything inside me shuts down. "She had an emergency and had to head out."

"Thank you so much, Harlow," Mrs. Marcus says as she grabs her cat and places it in the carrier. The cat had gotten out of her house and had a one-on-one with a raccoon. He came in and looked like the racoon got the best of him. But in the end, after three hours of surgery and two days of recovering with us, he's finally going home. "I don't know what I would have done without him."

"It was my pleasure." I smile at her and look into the carrier. "If there are any questions you have, you have my cell phone." She nods at me, opens the door to the examining room, and heads out. I walk over to the silver examining table and spray it down before I disinfect it. Usually, Donna comes in after, but I know that she was the last appointment of the day, so I don't have to rush to the other room. Putting away the bottle under the sink in the corner, I open the water to wash my hands.

"Hey," Donna says from behind me, and I look over my shoulder as she comes into the room.

"If you tell me that someone else called." I glare at her and she just laughs.

"I was coming to say." She drags out what she is going to say, and I have this dread run through me thinking that it's going to be another long night. "That I'm leaving for the day and no one else has called." Donna smiles at me. "I've forwarded all the calls to Tyler for the weekend."

"Thank you." I turn the water off and grab a paper towel to dry my hands.

"I left the files on your desk." She mentions all the cases I did today. I always chart in writing, and she puts it in the computer. "You can take them home."

I shake my head. "I'm going to finish them here and sleep for the next two days."

"Well, I was going to say you look exhausted." She tilts her head to the side. "But you've been a cranky little bee this week, so I decided against it."

I chuckle. "And I'm not cranky."

"Oh, you're still cranky, but I don't have to see you for the next two days, so you'll forget all about it." She turns to walk out of the room. "See you Monday." She holds her hand up over her head.

Walking out of my examining room, I head straight to my office. The light for the two windows in the corner makes the room just a touch brighter. The big wooden desk sits in the middle with two chairs in front of it and a love seat in the corner. Which had to be comfortable since sometimes I would finish surgery and just crash on the couch for a couple of hours.

I walk around my desk and see the manila folders stacked in the middle as I sit in the big brown leather chair and lean back, my eyes closing for just a second.

This week has been brutal in so many ways. Work has been nonstop, and I've even been called in the middle of the night to help with a couple of horses birthing their foals. Then called back when the placenta didn't come out, my days were going on twenty hours a day for the last three days.

To top all of that off, I was barely sleeping because every single time I closed my eyes, all I saw was Travis. He was smiling at me, he was smirking at me, he was on top of me, thrusting into me. He would shout my name and my eyes would always flutter open when I would get close enough to him. It was pure fucking torture, and I was over it.

My goal is to literally sleep all weekend long, right after I get my work done. I open the first chart and read the little notes that I scribbled down between patients and eating. It takes me about an hour to get through all of it. My mind is on autopilot when I hear the bell ring over the door. I look up from my desk, hoping and freaking praying that it's one of my family members and not someone who needs me.

I have to laugh at myself as I sit at my desk, not moving, and after a couple of seconds, I get up. If it was any of my family members, they would have yelled my name by now. I walk out of the office and down the hallway toward the reception area, and I stop midstep. It can't be, is the only thing I can think of. As my heart pounds in my chest, I feel the nerves fill my body as the heat rises up my neck. My hands shake just a touch. "Travis." I say his name, and I have to wonder if I'm dreaming. Is this a dream?

He turns around to look at me and I take him in. He's wearing khaki pants and a button-down blue shirt tucked in with white sneakers. The sleeves of his shirt are rolled up to his elbows and the two top buttons are open around his neck, showing you the smooth skin under it. Skin that I spent a good part of last Saturday licking. His green eyes light up when he sees me, his five o'clock shadow thicker than I remember. "Hey," he says as if him being here is a normal occurrence

"What are you doing here?" is the only thing that comes to my mind.

"I was in the neighborhood." He smirks at me, and I can't help but laugh.

"You took a plane?" I ask him, my head spinning around and around while my head is reminding me of the way he kissed me.

"No, I drove." He stares at me, and my stomach fills with knots.

"You drove six hours to be in the neighborhood?" I fold my arms over my chest before I do something stupid like grab him by the shirt and pull his lips down to kiss me.

"Actually, it was eight hours with traffic." He chuckles, and my whole body feels like it's been zapped with an electric shock. "Besides, how else would I be able to ask you to dinner?"

My mouth opens. "You drove all this way to ask me to dinner?"

"Well, I tried calling but you must have changed your number," he says, looking around. "And calling your office"—he shrugs—"seemed so impersonal." His eyes stare right at me. "And let's be honest, you would just avoid me."

"Okay, once." I hold up my finger, angry that he knows me as well as he does. "I didn't change my number." I take the phone out of my pocket, showing him the phone.

"I called you," he starts to say, and I hold up my hand.

"No, you didn't." I shake my head, walking over to Donna's desk and picking up the phone to dial my number. The phone rings in my hand. "See, working phone."

He grabs his phone from his back pocket and looks down at it. Putting the phone on speaker, it doesn't even ring and goes straight to my voice mail. "That's all I got. I called over a hundred times on Sunday. I texted you also."

"Well, there you are, lying because I don't have anything." I look down at my phone.

"Let me try," he says, typing out something on his phone and pressing send. I look down at my phone waiting, and nothing comes through. "See," he says, turning his phone, and I see that all the messages on his screen are green.

I put my hand in front of my mouth. "I think I blocked you."

"You don't say," he says, not the least bit shocked. I look down at my phone and dial his number, and his phone rings in his hand. "Oh, look, it's Harlow calling," he jokes and puts the phone to his ear and I hear it echo. "Harlow," he says as if he isn't standing in front of me. "How nice of you to call."

"Very funny," I say, hanging up the phone. "Okay, so maybe you are blocked."

"Well, unblock me," he tells me.

"I don't know how since you aren't a contact in my phone," I say, looking down at my phone, and he gasps.

"You deleted me as a contact?" he asks, shocked.

"No." I shake my head. "It's just I lost my phone, and well, I didn't have it saved to the cloud, so I lost all my contacts."

"Oh, wow." He folds his arms over his chest. "Blaming it on the cloud."

"I'm not blaming it on the cloud," I defend.

"Good, because no one really knows what the cloud really is," he points out and he isn't wrong. When the guy at the store explained it to me, I thought he had two heads.

"Anyway, we are going off topic here," I say, getting flustered.

"Yes, we are." He nods.

"Also…" I point at him. "I would never avoid you," I lie through my teeth. Even he knows I'm lying.

"So, if I had left a message, you would have called me back?" He stares right into my eyes.

"Yes," I say, hoping he changes the subject.

"You would have called me back right away?" Fuck, is the only thing I can think of when he asks that question.

"I've been busy." I throw up my hands in my defense.

"Exactly," he says. "So you would have avoided me, and then what?"

"And then you would take the hint and not call me back," I say, and I can see the hurt flicker over his eyes, and then he quickly recovers.

"Well, then, I guess it's a good thing I was in the neighborhood." His voice is soft. "So what do you say, Harlow?"

"About what exactly?" I ask him, knowing that we definitely should talk about what we did last weekend. But then as soon as I think about last weekend, I hope that we don't talk about it. I want to sweep it under the rug where it belongs and hope to fuck I can get over it and stop thinking about it. Except one look at him and I'm already replaying all the times I reached for him in the night. Or the way he never ever let me go, he always had to be touching me.

"About having dinner with me?" He smirks, and fuck, I wish I could walk over to him and lean my head back while he kisses me.

I shake my head. "I can't believe you drove all this way just for this."

"Well." He smiles at me, and then my chest fills. "I really, really wanted to see you." I just look at him, not saying anything. "Does that silence mean a yes?"

Twenty-Eight

Travis

"I can't believe you drove all this way just for this." She shakes her head at me, and I can't help but smile at her. The minute I saw her, all I could do was smile.

"Well," I start to say. "I really, really wanted to see you." I give her a second to answer, suddenly nervous that she is actually going to say no. "Does that silence mean a yes?"

"I need to change." She points at the blue scrubs she's wearing.

"That's fine," I say. "I have to check into the hotel anyway."

"Hotel?" She tilts her head to the side. "You booked a room?" she asks, shocked.

"Well, yeah." I look around her waiting room and my

heart can't calm down. Did I want to rent a room? No. Did I want to stay with her and take her in my arms the minute I saw her? Yes. Was I going to let her push me away? No. Was she going to fight me the whole way? Probably. "I'm going to go check into my hotel and then I'll swing by your house in about an hour and pick you up, okay?" Every single second that I wait for her to answer feels like an eternity. My feet move to her, and my hands go out to grab her face. My thumbs rub her cheeks. "Do you think you can unblock me now and send me your home address?" I smirk at her as my heart echoes in my ears. "It would be hard to explain if I have to go door to door and knock, looking for you."

She chuckles and looks down. "Fine," she says, reluctantly. "I'll unblock you." I can't help but lean forward and kiss her lips softly. Definitely not the kiss I really want to give her but I know that it's baby steps. "But only because I'm afraid that you'll knock on my father's door or my brothers', and then they'll shoot you."

I can't help but put my head back and laugh. "Fair enough." The burning starts in my stomach. I don't know if I would blame them for shooting me. I hurt her, and it's unforgivable.

My hands drop from her face when she pulls up the phone in her hand and adds me back as a contact. She starts to type something, and then the phone pings, and I take it back out of my back pocket.

Harlow: 2145 Villas Street
I text her back.

Me: I'll be there in an hour.

I press send, waiting for it to beep in her hand, and when it does, I just smile. "And just like that, you're back." She makes me laugh.

I kiss her one last time before I turn and walk out, taking a step before turning back. The door opens, and she stands there. "This isn't your father's house address, is it? Or your brothers'?" I ask, and she rolls her lips. "Why would you lead me to the lion's den?"

"Come to think of it." She puts her hands on her hips, and her eyes light up so bright everything settles inside me. "I should have."

I shake my head. "See you in fifty-five minutes, Harlow." I turn, finally making my way into the car and only when I sit behind the wheel do I finally breathe a little sigh of relief. I take one look back at her practice and smile. She did everything she said she was going to do. I can't be sorry that I let her go because of that, but ever since I laid eyes on her last Saturday, the regret has hit me harder than a wrecking ball hitting a concrete wall.

Checking into the little hotel is a breeze, and when I dump my overnight duffel bag on the bed, I walk over to the window, looking out. From the minute I found out she left on an emergency, I knew that I was going to go after her. There wasn't even a question in my mind. I acted normal the whole time, I laughed when I needed to laugh and listened when I needed to listen, but the whole time, I was making my plan.

It took me a couple of days to make sure everything

was covered with my shifts, but as soon as it was, I packed a bag and headed out. Sitting in the car for eight hours gave me time to play everything over and over in my head. The reunion went a lot smoother than I thought it was going to go. I thought she would have said no, but I think I caught her off guard. Looking down at my watch, I see that just ten minutes have passed, and instead of just standing here waiting, I walk back out toward my car.

I make a pit stop at a flower shop before heading to her house. Stopping in front of her house when the GPS tells me that I've arrived, I take a second to take in her house. The white house looks modern, but the four windows have brown wooden shutters, and the awning in the front is held up with the same wood posts. Two chairs are off to the side of the house with a table between them, and I wonder if she spends time out there sitting. I pick up the flowers wrapped in white paper before getting out of the car. My palms are sweaty, my knees are weak, and the whole time I walk toward the front door, I feel like my heart is going to come out of my chest. I walk up the two steps facing the two big brown doors. My hand shakes while I ring the doorbell as I try to calm myself.

"Coming." I hear from the other side of the doors when I hear the sound of the locks open. A smile creeps onto my face, only becoming bigger when I see her. Her hair is piled on top of her head, and I can see that the bottom looks wet. She must have just gotten out of the shower and my cock suddenly wakes up. "It's been thirty-five minutes," she jokes with me, moving aside so

I can step in.

"I couldn't wait any longer," I admit to her and bend down to kiss the side of her mouth. "I got these for you."

"Aww." She reaches out to grab the bouquet from me, and our fingers graze each other. "These are beautiful," she says of the white and pink peonies and roses that I picked out. "Come on in." She motions with her head, and I watch her ass sway right to left in the light gray joggers that she has on. She leads us toward the big family room that is attached to the kitchen. "So I know that you want to take me out to dinner," she says as she grabs a white wooden stool to open the cabinet on top of the stainless-steel fridge. "But I thought it would be nice." She grabs a big square glass vase. "If we could stay in, and I'll cook something." I look at her, wondering if she is joking, and when she doesn't even crack a smile, I know she is serious.

"Harlow, I don't care what we do as long as we're together," I say, without adding in that we should just order something instead.

"Wow," she says, putting water in the vase and then placing the flowers in them. "You would sacrifice your life just to have dinner with me?"

I shake my head when she laughs and brings the flowers into the living room and places them in the middle of the wooden coffee table. I look over at the mantel on top of the fireplace and see that there are five picture frames. She bends over and my eyes go to her ass once more, and when she snaps back up and turns around, she catches me staring. "Okay." She claps her hands and walks to me. Her smell of honey fills me when she gets close enough, and my hand shoots out to bring her closer to me. The softness of her long-sleeved white cashmere sweater feels like silk. It hangs low in the front and falls off her shoulder a bit, and I bend to kiss it. "I put my grandmother's chicken potpie in the oven when I got home," she informs me and I still don't let her go. "We can have a glass of wine outside while we wait."

"That sounds like a plan," I say, kissing her lips softly as my arm lets go of her waist. She walks back into the kitchen and I'm suddenly fucking jealous and angry that she grew a life here and I wasn't here with her. I know it's stupid since I was building my own life, but seeing her in her environment just makes it so much more real. She grabs two wineglasses and then walks to the fridge, taking out a bottle of white wine. "Do you want red?"

"I'm good with whatever you are having," I say and she pours white wine into the two glasses.

She hands me a glass and takes hers in one hand and the bottle in the other.

"Let's sit outside. The potpie shouldn't be long, and I've been cooped up in the office all day."

"Lead the way," I say and she turns toward the side where the back door is. She looks over at me to open the door for her since her hands are full. I step forward and lick my lips, kissing her again before opening the door and holding it open for her.

"Thank you," she says, walking past me. "Welcome to my oasis," she says and I look around at the big wooden deck that is covered with a round table with six chairs.

"Let's sit over there." She points at another level of her deck where there is a couch area that is also covered. I walk down the step and look around at the trees that are surrounding her.

A hammock in the corner of the yard sways back and forth. "This is relaxing," I say, looking around, seeing her slip her legs under her on the couch as she sits.

I sit down on the couch facing her, even though I want to sit next to her and touch her. "This is paradise," I say, putting my ankle on top of my knee and leaning back in the couch. My arm opens to drape across the back of the chair. "Do you spend a lot of time out here?"

She shakes her head, taking a sip of her wine. "Sadly, not as much as I want to."

I sit back and watch her. Fuck, I could watch her for hours, days, weeks, months, years. Fuck, I want to watch her forever. "Why are you staring at me like that?"

I shrug and take a sip of my wine. "You're beautiful," I say as the sun slowly starts to set on one side. The sky is turning a soft pink. "It's going to be a nice day tomorrow?"

"It's supposed to be nice all weekend long." She stares back at me and I smile, bringing the glass to my lips. "I'm going to go and check on dinner." She gets up and finishes the rest of her wine. "I'll be right back."

"I'm not going anywhere," I say, and she looks down and walks back into her house. "Not anytime soon."

Twenty-Nine

Harlow

"It's supposed to be nice all weekend long." I stare at him wondering what the fuck he is thinking. "I'm going to go and check on dinner." The nerves are going to take over my whole body and I need to step away from him for a second. I grab my wineglass and finish the rest of it. "I'll be right back."

"I'm not going anywhere." His statement sends shivers down my spine and I avoid his eyes. Walking back into the house, the cold air hits me right away. I close the door behind me and I can't help when my body collapses with my back against it. Ever since he walked out of my office this afternoon, I've gone over everything in my head. Why the hell was he here? Why after all this time, was he here? One night with him has sent my life into an upheaval.

Pushing myself from the door, I walk over to the oven and open it to see the potpie a golden brown. "It's smells delish," I say, walking over to grab two plates. I grab a big tray and arrange everything on it. After I add the utensils, I walk over to the fridge and take out the premade salad that I bought myself at lunch thinking that I was going to have a nice relaxing evening at home, instead of this. "What the hell is going on?" I mumble when I look outside and see Travis standing up, looking around. "Why the fuck is he even here?" Putting on the oven mitts I take the potpie out of the oven and place it on the tray. Taking off the mitts, I place them on the counter and take another look outside, seeing the sun setting right behind him. My stomach flutters when I see his silhouette facing away from me. He stands there with his hands in his pockets just looking off into the distance, and again I wonder what the hell was he thinking. "Get through dinner and maybe he will go back from where he came," I say, walking over to the door and opening it before going back and grabbing the tray.

He must sense me coming because he turns around and rushes to my side to grab the tray from me. "Why didn't you call me?" he asks as he takes the tray from my hands.

"Well, because it's just a tray of food and I could carry it," I huff out, walking toward the couch area to grab the wine and the bottle. When I walk back to the table area, he has the tray in the middle of the table and he's setting the utensils on the place mats. The sun went down a lot faster than I thought it would and the little fairy lights that I have wrapping around the trees are starting to turn on. It gives it a whimsical glow. I'm not going to lie, but lying in the hammock with the lights on and listening to sounds of nature is relaxing.

"This smells amazing," he says, and I look over at him as I pour him another glass of wine and then fill my own glass a bit more than I should.

"You sound both shocked and amazed by this." I try not to laugh as I sit down in front of him.

"That's because I am." He doesn't lie to me, which I guess I should give him props for.

"Well, I can use an oven like no one else can," I joke with him and cut the pie in fourths. "It's hard to fuck up when all you have to do is set the temperature and put on a timer."

I hold out my hand for his plate and he hands it to me, our fingers graze. "Didn't you burn a pizza pocket?"

I glare at him as I put a big piece on his plate. "That was in the microwave and I pressed an extra zero by accident."

He laughs as I hand him his plate. "Didn't you have to buy a new one?"

"No," I say, putting my own piece on my plate and sitting down. "I just chose to because I couldn't scrape out the cheese and it smelled bad." I roll my eyes. "I can't believe it exploded," I say, laughing at myself. "Who would have thought."

"It was a massacre," he adds in and waits for me to pick up my fork before he picks up his own.

My stomach is so twisted in knots I barely eat anything, and when he grabs his glass of wine and leans back in his chair, I ask him what I've been dying to ask him ever since I saw him standing in my waiting room. "Travis." I say his name, grabbing my own wine and take a shot for liquid courage.

"Harlow." He says my name and I ignore the smirk on his face. If I wasn't so nervous, I would laugh at how crazy this whole thing is. If I wasn't so nervous, I would make a joke about it. If I wasn't so nervous about all of this, I wouldn't be able to ask him the loaded questions. But he is here and it's been four years; if I get anything out of this, it will be the questions answered I've asked him in my head the last four years.

"Why are you really here?" I ask him. My heart is starting to pick up its pace and the back of my neck suddenly feels like it's on fire.

My eyes never leave his as I wait for him to answer the loaded question I just asked him. "I missed you," he says, and I don't know if it's the nerves or the wine or a bit of both but I laugh.

"You were getting married last week," I say, the words tasting like bile in my mouth. "And you missed me?" I shake my head and laugh bitterly as I take another sip of wine. "You broke up with me." Fuck, I want to kick myself for making it sound like it still bothers me.

"I broke up with you," he says, putting his glass of wine back down on the table. Then leans back again in the chair, folding his hands in front of him, looking calm, cool, and collected. Irritating me even more, because he looks so fucking good doing it. "Because I was an idiot."

My mouth gets dry all of a sudden and all I can say is, "Keep going." Trying to get my heart to calm the fuck down.

"I broke up with you because I knew I couldn't do the long-distance relationship." His eyes never leave mine.

"Who said you had to do that?" I lean forward, putting my glass on the table. "Who told you that we had to be in a long-distance relationship?" I throw up my hands as he opens his mouth to say something, but I cut him off. "You didn't even ask me. You never had a conversation with me." The hurt from four years ago is now suddenly front and center.

"But your family is here," he says softly, and I have to wonder if he is feeling like he, too, is back to that moment four years ago. "And you had everything mapped out for you."

"Plans change," I finally say to him. "Things change. You didn't even sit down and talk to me about it." I try not to cry, I try to fight away the tears as hard as I can. I shake my head, angry that it's still getting to me and knowing that whatever happens from here, I have to know what the fuck he was thinking four years ago. "How could you just have made that big of a decision on your own without so much as talking to me about it?"

"I didn't want to make you choose," he says, looking down.

"Again"—my voice rises just a bit—"you never even fucking asked. Like, how could you just do that? I sat down that day trying to wrap my head around what the hell you did." I finally admit to him. "You tossed away our relationship like it was nothing."

"I never ever wanted to toss you away," he finally snaps. "You think it was easy for me to do what I did?" He points at my chest. "You think walking away from you was easy for me?" He isn't the one giving me a chance to speak. "Do you think any of that was easy for me? I walked around in a daze for years," he says. "Not singular either." And maybe it's just the pettiness in me or maybe it's the fact that I'm still bitter, but I roll my eyes. "You had a plan set in place." His voice finally goes down a touch. "You never ever wavered on that plan. What kind of an asshole was I going to be if I just erased all your dreams?"

"I really want to know who you had a conversation with regarding me and my dreams." I almost smack my hand on the table, the sadness definitely replaced by anger. "I would love to know where this conversation took place." It's his turn to roll his eyes. "I mean, at the very least, I should have been included in those discussions since it had to do with my future and my life. Don't you think?"

"I couldn't do that to you." His voice is almost in a whisper. "The thought of making you choose me or your family, I just couldn't put you in that position." He shakes his head. "Have you pick me or your family; how would you be able to do that?" I can see how torn up he is about it even after all these years. "What if you picked me and regretted it and then resented me?"

"I loved you with everything that I had." I put my

hand to the middle of my chest where the pain is starting to form. "And you just threw it away."

"I didn't throw it away." He shakes his head. "I let you go so you could do this." He raises his hands toward the backyard. "So you could build the practice that you always thought you would have. I sacrificed myself for you." I see him blinking away his own tears. "That was the single hardest thing I ever had to go through." I see his Adam's apple move up and down when he swallows. "Even harder than when my father died." His voice cracks and I gasp in shock. Never once did I think that he hurt as much as me, or maybe I just didn't want to think about it. Maybe I wanted him to hurt for hurting me, but I never ever thought it would be as bad for him as it was for me. Because he was the one who let me go. "What if I had asked you to come with me?" He looks at me and I see the pain in his eyes. "Would you have come with me?"

"It's too late for that," I answer honestly, not willing to go back to that time. Not wanting to go back to the same question I asked myself over and over again. "It's too late for that," I repeat again, shaking my head.

Thirty

Travis

"What if I had asked you to come with me?" I look at her and the pain from letting her walk away from me four years ago leaks out into my soul. The wound that I thought faded and left a scar is now bleeding out. "Would you have come with me?" I ask her the words that I should have asked her four years ago. The question that could have changed both of our lives.

"It's too late for that," she answers, shaking her head. "It's too late for that," she repeats the words again.

"It's never too late." I hate that I'm sitting in front of her and not next to her where I can touch her. I hate that we are having this conversation over a dinner table and not with her in my arms. "What if I told you that I never should have let you go?" I see her bottom lip tremble.

"Not this past Sunday and not four years ago."

"Travis." She says my name and I'm not sure if it's a plea or a question.

"Letting you walk out of my life is the biggest regret of my whole life." After four years, she deserves to have it all. We both do. "Hands down, the worst day of my life. Hands down, the worst decision I ever made. Hands down, the biggest regret I've had."

"You were going to get married," she says, her voice in almost a whisper. "You were literally at the altar getting ready to get married."

"Yet, here I am," I say. "Sitting at a table with you. Where I'm meant to be. Do you think I would be here if I wasn't meant to be here?"

"I have no idea." She shrugs.

"You walking into the church was a sign. I knew that I didn't love her. At least, not the way I should. Not the way someone should when they are going to be married. Do I love Jennifer? She's a great person." I swallow the lump in my throat. "But what I felt for you." I shake my head to correct myself. "What I feel for you, it's so much fucking more."

"How can you say that?" she asks and I can see the struggle she is going through and I hate that we are doing this.

"Because I can," I finally say. "Because it's the truth. Because after four fucking years, it's time to get it all out there." The nerves run through me. "Four years ago, I let you go without talking to you. I was wrong," I admit. "Four years ago, letting you go shattered me.

Literally." The lump in my throat forms into the size of a golf ball. "I don't even know how I made it through the exams, and to be honest, I don't really remember much of anything for a good year. It was like I was in a daze. I got up every day, did what I had to do, and then the next day started over again. Like *Groundhog Day,* except it was my life." If I give her anything, it will be the whole picture, the good, the bad, the ugly. "For two years, no one could say your name around me." I look down at my hands and they nervously tap the table as a tear slips out. "I couldn't even think of you without having this crushing pain in my chest. It was hard to breathe, and then I met Jennifer and she was nice. I knew that what I felt for her wasn't love because it was nothing, and I mean nothing, like what I felt for you. I figured that what you and I had was something that you will never get again." I smile sadly. "So I settled on just feeling content. I told myself it didn't matter that my heart didn't speed up when she called my name. I told myself that it didn't matter that we would go sometimes weeks without seeing each other. I told myself it was fine that I wasn't attached to her. I told myself all these things because I knew deep inside me, you were the only one I would ever feel that with and I had lost you." I wipe the tear that is coming, the pounding of my heart in my chest is echoing. "I remember my father once telling me a story about how he knew my mother was the one. How he would get antsy if my mother wasn't around. How just her being in the room would make him feel okay. How with just one little touch from her and he would settle. I knew that was what you should feel. I knew that because I felt it with you." I swallow the guilt. "But then I felt none of that and I thought it was because you only get one love your whole life, and I knew you were it." Now that I'm sitting here looking at her, talking to her, touching her, I know that there is going to be no one else for me. That she is it. She was always meant for me. We were always meant for each other.

"Travis." She says my name and I look at her, seeing tears running down her face. "This is." She shakes her head. "It's just too much."

I shake my head and push my chair away from the table, getting up and going to her. I turn her chair to face me with her still seated in it. She bends her head, not showing me the tears, and I squat down in front of her. "Harlow." I say her name as her hand comes out to wipe away the tear that is escaping out of the corner of her eye. I put my finger under her chin and raise her eyes to look at me. "This is everything." I rub my thumb over her cheek, wiping the tear that is rolling down her cheek. "Seeing you again, it just." I stop speaking because the lump is so big. "It made me see that there isn't anyone out there for me but you."

"Travis." Her lower lip trembles.

"I'm not letting you go this time." I pull her to me and kiss her lips. I taste her tears on her lips.

Her hand comes up to hold my face. "I don't know what the right thing to do is," she says, looking into my eyes while she rubs her thumb back and forth over my five o'clock shadow. "You hurt me like I've never thought

I could hurt," she tells me, and I know that hearing this is going to kill me, but to get to the future, we have to talk about the past. "You making that decision that changed both our lives without so much as talking to me. I just don't know."

"There are no words that I can say that will make what I did okay," I admit. "None. I would say I'm sorry but that isn't even close enough." I lean in and rub my nose against hers. "But I'm going to die trying," is the last thing I say before she leans in and kisses my lips. She slides her tongue into my mouth and I know without a shadow of a doubt that she was made for me. I tilt my head to the side and take the kiss deeper, her legs opening up so I can get in the middle of them. She scoots to the front of the chair, and when I wrap my arm around her waist and stand up, she wraps her legs around my waist.

I turn to walk into the house and she lets my lips go as she buries her face in my neck and lays her head on my shoulder. "I love you," I say when I step into the house and I look down at her.

"By there." She points at the hallway off the side of the kitchen, away from the living room, and I walk into her bedroom. Her bed is already undone when I walk into the room and sit on the bench that is right in front of her bed. She unburies her face from my neck. "Kiss me," she says and I groan out before my hands go to the back of her neck, roaming up and getting lost in her hair, pulling her head back, and leaning forward to kiss her neck. "No hickies," she says. "I had to wear a turtleneck for the last week."

"But your skin." I nip at it. "It's so clean."

"It's the month of May in the South." She pushes up her shoulder to stop me from marking her. "You can give them to me anywhere you want," she says. "Just not my neck."

"Anywhere?" I ask her, thinking of all the places that I'm going to mark her.

She pulls her tank top over her head and tosses it to the side. "Anywhere." She stands in front of me with her tits on display for me. I can't help but groan as my hands come out and take one in each hand.

"Define anywhere?" I ask, bending and taking a nipple in my mouth, biting, and then sucking right next to it. Her white skin is turning a touch red. "What about here?" I ask her, going to the other nipple and repeating the same thing.

"That's okay," she murmurs and her head falls back, giving me complete access.

"Yes," she pants as I make another mark on her and I get up, turning her and setting her down on the bench where I just stood from. I get on my knees in the middle of her legs. "Tell me." She puts her hands to the sides of her hips. My hand moves on top of hers, "Lift," I say. She lifts up and I slip her pants and panties off her and she sits in front of me naked while I toss her pants right on top of her shirt. She leans back on the bed and stretches her legs open for me. The little landing strip calling my name, I lean down to kiss her inner thigh. "What about here?" I bite and then suck in. "Is this okay?" All she does is watch as I move to her other thigh and leave another mark. "And what about here?" I lean in and lick her slit, my tongue slipping into her and then going to flick her clit. "Can I do it here?" I suck her clit into my mouth.

"Why is it like this?" she pants as I put each leg over my shoulder.

"What do you mean?" I ask her between licks, as she tilts her hips and leans back on her elbows on the bed.

"Why is being with you so good?" she says, looking down at me and I take one more lick before I answer her.

"Because you were made for me."

Thirty-One

Harlow

I smell the coffee right before my eyes flutter open and I see the sun coming into the room. I stretch my hands over my head and groan out, my muscles tight from all the exercise I did last night, and then again this morning. There is sex and then there is sex with Travis, and no matter how much I try to deny it, everything with him is better. And I mean everything. I look over toward the clock and see that it's just a little past ten. I turn to my side and reach out to find the spot next to me warm but empty. I get up on my elbow. "Travis?" I say his name and hear movement coming from the kitchen.

I lay my head back down on the pillow and cuddle into the bed, closing my eyes again. "Morning," I hear him say and open my eyes again, seeing him standing by my bed wearing his white boxers and holding two cups of coffee in his hands.

"Good morning." I smile and get up, holding the sheet to my naked chest. He hands me a cup of coffee and I grab it with my empty hand. He puts his knee onto the bed and then leans in to kiss my lips.

"Did I wake you?" he asks, getting into the bed beside me.

"The smell of coffee did," I say, taking a sip of the hot coffee. Sitting with my back to the headboard I look over at him. "How did you sleep?"

He sits with his back toward the headboard also and takes his own sip of his coffee. "Great." He smirks. "Especially when I fall asleep and then wake up with my dick in your mouth."

I chuckle and shrug. "You were poking me in the ass with it. What was I supposed to do?" I look over at him and lean over to kiss his shoulder. "Besides, I didn't hear you complain."

"If my cock is going to be in your mouth." He stares at me with a smirk. "You will never hear me complain." I laugh and try to push down the feeling that is creeping up in my chest. I know exactly what it is; it's fucking happiness. It's something I haven't felt fully for four years. It's something I never thought I would feel again. It's something that I'm almost afraid of feeling. "So what do you usually do on the weekend?" he asks me.

"Work." I put my hot cup of coffee down on the side table and get up.

"Where are you going?" he asks, sitting up.

"To the bathroom," I say, walking across the room and feeling his eyes on me. I don't bother closing the door behind me because he's seen everything already. "Holy shit," I say, walking over the wet towels on the floor and then seeing the bathtub still full. I lean over and drain the tub. "I didn't think it was this much water." I laugh when I remember riding him so hard that I heard the water splashing but didn't pay attention to it at the time. He was also the first one out of the tub, so he cleaned most of it up. "I'm going to make a note not to fill it up so much the next time."

"That would help," he says from the bedroom and then I hear the sheet rustle and his feet walking toward the bathroom. "Want me to put the towels in the wash?" he asks, leaning against the doorjamb. His boxers show the outline of his cock and my body tingles.

"Stop talking dirty to me." I wink at him, walking to the sink and looking into the full-length mirror. "What in the hell?" I say, walking even closer when I see the red spots all over me. It's a mixture of hickeys and also beard burn. "I look like I got attacked by a swarm of bees."

He just laughs. "You also have a couple on your ass." He points at me and I turn around to see that I have one on each ass cheek. I look over my shoulder on each side and then glare at him. "You said I could do it anywhere but your neck."

"You took that really literally." I laugh. Walking to him and standing in front of him, I get on my tippy-toes and kiss him under his chin. One of his hands goes to my hip as he pulls me to him. "We need to eat," I mumble, not moving out of his grasp as I rub my nose across his jawline. "Are you hungry?"

"I'm famished." He picks me up and before I know it his mouth is between my legs.

"Where are you going?" I lift my head after he gets out of bed an hour later.

"I'm going to cook us breakfast," he says, putting his boxers back on. "You get dressed." I smirk at him. "You being naked got us sidetracked again."

"Does my nakedness offend you?" I poke out my tits.

He groans and walks away and I can see him adjusting himself. "Just cover your lady parts," he says over his shoulder and I can't help but laugh. I get out of bed, putting on shorts and a tank top but no bra or panties. Fixing the bed, I walk into the kitchen and see that he's already got bacon in the pan and is scrambling eggs.

"It smells good in here," I say when I get beside him and I kiss his back. "Let me make you coffee." Side by side, we get ready to eat. He takes out two plates, filling them with eggs, bacon, and sliced toast.

"I could get used to this," I admit, sitting next to him at the small kitchen table I have. I smirk at him and eat my eggs. I sit and try not to think that he's going to leave eventually and then what? I look at my plate and try to avoid his eyes.

"What do you want to do tonight?" he asks and I shrug. My fingers start to tap the tabletop as I think about what I was supposed to do tonight.

"I'm supposed to meet up with my cousins at the bar tonight," I say, looking over at him. "But we don't have to."

"Might as well get it over with," he says, getting up with his empty plate. He puts his plate in the dishwasher. "I have to go and get my things at the hotel."

I shake my head. "You really rented a room?" I ask, semi-shocked. "I thought you were pretending."

"Yeah," he says, laughing. "I didn't know what your reaction would be when I got here and I didn't want to assume I would be spending the night so…"

I shake my head. "Why don't we get dressed and go pick up your things, have sex, and then come back here?" He looks at me. "It's a hotel room; it's like sacreligious that you don't have sex in the bed."

He just shakes his head. "Whatever you want," He kisses my shoulder and we get dressed. We go to his hotel room, where we do in fact have sex on the bed.

"ARE YOU NERVOUS?" I look over at him from my side of his car and he just shrugs. My stomach feels like I've been on a roller coaster going around and around.

"I mean, the good news is that if I get shot, you can help take the bullet out. The bad news is they might shoot me in the dick," he says, taking my hand in his and bringing it to his lips.

"Well, if it's any consolation." I turn in the seat when he puts the car in park. "They promised to be on their best behavior."

"Oh, goodie," he says sarcastically when he turns off

the car and gets out. He opens my door for me and holds out his hand for me to grab. "You look good." He smirks, pull ing me close to him. I spent way too long picking out this outfit of white jeans and a baby-blue silk tank top with spaghetti straps that criss-cross in the back. I even put on blue heels, which I never do because I always go for comfort, but something about going out with him tonight made me want to dress up. He slips his hand into mine as we make our way over to the bar. The sound of music fills the parking lot, and the closer we get, the more my stomach aches. "Here we go," he says when we get to the door and I pull him to me before he has a chance to grab the door handle.

"If you want to leave, all you have to do is say the word," I say so he knows that I'm on his side.

"If you could show up at my wedding." He smirks. "I'm pretty sure I'll be okay with your brothers and cousins." He kisses me and pulls open the door.

"Yeah, but I didn't dump you," I say right before he steps inside and stops.

"This is bigger," he says, looking around, and I nod my head at him. Ever since Amelia took this place over from my aunt Savannah, she's expanded it four times. It is the it place to be on a Saturday night.

I walk with Travis's hand in mine as we make our way over to the bar in the back. It's the bar my family sits at when we are here, and I know right away that they spotted us when I see my brothers, Reed and Quinn, share a look. "Hey," I say when I get close enough. My sister-in-law, Willow, turns her head first to say hi, and her eyes widen when she sees Travis behind me. She leans over to whisper something in Quinn's ear and if I know her right, she probably told him to calm down.

"Well, well," Hazel says when she sees me. "Look what the cat dragged in."

I throw my head back and laugh and I see Hazel's hand go to Reed's knee to keep him in his place. "Guys," I say, taking a deep breath. "You remember Travis," I introduce, as if they could fucking forget him.

He nods at them. "Nice to see you guys again," he says diplomatically.

"Where's your wife?" Reed asks, without skipping a beat, looking straight at Travis.

"Right next to me," Travis says, without thinking twice, making everyone stop talking. "I mean eventually, that is."

Willow laughs. "Shit, you should have seen the look on your face." She points at Quinn, who just glares at her.

"Listen," I say and they all look at me. "We might as well get this over with. I don't want to hear anyone's bullshit. It's two friends that have…" I think of the word.

"Rekindled," Hazel says for me.

"Yes." I point at her.

"Two friends that rekindled their friendship." I look up at Travis, who stares at me.

"So, friends that do benefits," Willow says. "I never had that." Quinn turns to look at her and shakes his head.

"Never going to have that either," he mumbles, and Amelia comes to me with a glass for me and beer for

Travis.

"Nice to see you," she says, handing him his beer as he nods at her. "If you fuck up, I'm going to let them shoot you."

"Good to know," he says, taking a pull of his beer, and I can't imagine what it must be like for him. I mean, I went to his wedding, but I wasn't the one who dumped him. I don't even think I would have had the balls to go if the roles were reversed.

"Okay, are we done?" I ask, taking a sip of spiked sweet tea, then looking up at Travis and smiling. He lets go of my hand and puts it around my shoulders, pulling me to him and kissing my head.

"All good, baby," he says softly, and I'm about to say something when I hear: "What the fuck is this?" my cousin, Chelsea, says from behind me, and I turn to see her standing there with her hand on her hip.

"Okay, maybe I should have warned them that you were here," I mumble, and he just shrugs, not caring.

"Didn't you go to his wedding last week?" she asks, shocked, as she looks from me to Travis.

"There was no wedding," Travis reports.

"Oh my God," Mayson, her husband, says from behind her. "I told you going to that wedding was bad luck."

I put up my hand. "Okay, one." Closing my hand and putting up a finger. "I didn't have anything to do with the wedding not taking place." I look at all of them. "And two, I'm not bad luck."

"You aren't bad luck." Travis bends to tell me in my

ear. "You are the best luck."

"I just threw up a little," Quinn says, putting a hand in front of my mouth. "Good to know you're still a lovesick puppy."

"Eww," Reed says. "Remember when he sent her flowers every single day of winter break with poems?"

"It wasn't poems," Travis says, defending himself. "It was lines from her favorite romance books."

"That makes it even worse," Quinn says, and Willow shakes her head.

"What? Like, you wouldn't send me flowers?" she asks Quinn, who side eyes her, bringing his beer to his mouth.

"He wouldn't bring you flowers," I say. "He would plant you a whole fucking field full of them."

"Gross," Reed says and that has all of us rolling our lips.

"Didn't you leave a rose in her car for two years when you got back together?" Quinn points at him. "And you kept doing those stupid Facebook posts about love and her. I'm surprised they didn't block you with all the times I had you reported." We all laugh and Travis walks over to sit on a stool and motions with his head to come to him.

I walk to him while Mayson sits next to him on the stool. "So, besides not getting married, what else have you been up to?" he says, and we all laugh as Travis opens his legs for me to step between. His hand goes to my hip and it feels like old times; the guys joking with each other while the girls just gab.

Travis bends and kisses my shoulder and I look at him from the side. "You okay?" I ask, putting my hand on his cheek.

"Never better," he says with a smile and I lean to him and kiss him. "Never better." I smile at him but the reality of it is that eventually he's going to leave and we are going to be back to square one. I take a sip of sweet tea while my head yells at me that it'll be fine, yet my heart stops feeling the fullness that it felt all day.

Thirty-Two

Travis

"I'll be back." I smile at her and can tell something is wrong. She tries to avoid looking at me and I want to drag her out of the bar and ask her. But instead, I sit down and try to get her family to like me again. I mean, I don't know if it's going to help. I also don't know if they will ever forgive me for what I did to her, but that they didn't take me out in the back and beat the shit out of me is a start.

I bring the beer to my lips as I look over and see her coming back from the bathroom. She smiles and laughs at something that Amelia just said when a guy steps in front of her. My insides burn the minute he leans down and kisses her on her cheek. She smiles at him as they joke, my hand squeezing the bottle in my hand harder and harder. She nods her head at him and steps away and I watch him watch her. The nerves fill my body, and when she gets back to me, she smiles. "Friend of yours?" I motion with my head toward the guy, knowing that it's fucking dumb.

"I don't think you can call it that," she says, grabbing her drink. "Acquaintances is a better word for it." She takes a sip. "Don't forget you were with someone."

"I didn't expect you to wait for me," I answer her honestly and it's the truth, but to see in front of me that she had a whole life, it's going to sting and I'm going to have to live with it. "Give me a kiss," I say and she laughs.

"So everyone can know I'm off-limits?" She shakes her head and leans in to kiss me. "Does that make you feel better?" she asks, and I look up at the guy to see that he was watching her.

"Little bit," I say, kissing her again. "Little bit."

She puts her drink down and steps between my legs. "If you want." She wraps her arms around my neck. My hand is gripping her hip and pulling her even closer to me. "We can leave here and I can show you all the ways that I've missed you."

"We are right here," Reed says next to me. "Like, we can hear you." His face grimaces.

I get up. "This has been fun but," I say, putting my hand around her shoulder. "She looks tired."

"I mean, if she is going to look as tired as she did last Monday, you have a lot of work you have to do," Hazel says, snickering. "She was exhausted."

Willow gasps. "Is that why you couldn't walk properly?"

"Good night, everyone." Harlow lifts her hand and slips it into mine. "It's been fun." She pulls me away from the group.

We step out into the darkness and I look up at the stars in the sky. "You know what we've never done?" She looks at me and I just watch her. "We've never had sex in a hammock."

"There is a reason for that," I say. "And it has to do with breaking my dick."

"Ugh, fine," she says. "Definitely don't want to break that." She smiles at me and I can't help but bend down and kiss her. My tongue slides into her mouth as I taste the sweetness from the tea. "You keep kissing me like this and we are having sex in the back seat."

"I'm going to have to take a rain check on that." I open the door for her. "Your brothers didn't shoot me, but chances are if they find you riding me in the back seat of my car in a parking lot." I look around. "Fuck, I'd shoot myself in the foot." My hand goes to her hip and then moves under her silky shirt, finding her lace bra. "Next time, wear a dress and I'll finger-fuck you all the way home."

I pinch her nipple and she groans and arches her back. "I can take off one leg."

I shake my head and the whole ride back to her house she's like an octopus, with her hands everywhere. She is leaning over kissing my neck, while her hand gropes my cock, and finally when I pull into the driveway, she unbuckles her seat belt and has my cock out and her mouth is swallowing me. I stop the car as she gets on her knees in the passenger seat. My hand reaches out to rub her pussy outside of her jeans. She moans with my dick in her mouth and then I slide my hand up and into her jeans. Her stomach is shivering when my hand gets between it and the lace thong she is wearing. My finger slides right into her and I slip another one in. My thumb squeezes her clit as I move my hand. With her jeans so tight I'm restricted, but it doesn't stop her from coming all over my fingers. She lets go of my cock, sitting back in the passenger seat, and in a blink of an eye she has one pant leg off and she moves over me and sinks down on my cock. "So much better," she says and my hands rip the silk cami over her head but I don't shatter the lace that is covering her tits. She rides my cock as I work her nipples, my mouth over one and my hand on the other. I pinch and pull one while biting the other. "I need you deeper," she pants, fucking me faster and faster, putting her hands on my shoulders as she tries to get deeper. "Travis." She cries my name and throws her head back and arches her back as she comes all over me. The sound of the horn blares from her back, and I don't even give a shit because my balls pull tight and I come inside her. She falls on my chest as my hips move up and down emptying into her. We've had sex everywhere and this time it was almost barbaric.

"That was," she says, trying to catch her breath. "So freaking good."

"I need a minute," I say, as her pussy squeezes my

cock again. "Just one minute and then I'll carry you inside."

"Do you think," she says, looking at me, rotating her hips, "you can carry me inside with your cock inside me?" She moves her hips up and down.

My hands go to her hips, making her stop moving. "You keep moving like that, I'm going to fuck you on the hood of the car," I threaten and she just smirks. "Fuck." I grab her around her waist and pull her down on me as I open the door, putting one foot out and then the other. She wraps her legs around my waist and I walk to the front door, her hips going around and around. I open the door and the minute I'm inside I place her ass on the table at the front door. "Hold on," I warn and her legs go to the sides as I fuck her hard.

"Yes," she cries out as I slam into her over and over. "Right there," she says.

I know she's close, so I pull all the way out and slam in once, then pull out again, and she moans this time. I pick her up and turn her around. "Bend over," I demand and not only does she bend over, she puts one knee on the table to give me even better access. I bend my knees and slam into her. My hands on her hips pick her up every time my cock slams into her. The sound of flesh slapping against each other, along with her moans every single time she comes on my cock, drives me crazy.

"I'm going to come," she says over her shoulder, and I feel her hands from between her legs playing with my balls. "Right there," she urges and her eyes start to close, her head falls forward, and she comes on my cock again but this time I come with her.

"That," she says, lying on the table in front of her. "Has to be the best sex we've ever had."

"Well, only one more thing to do," I say, slipping out of her, and she looks over at me as I slap her ass. "Try to up it."

"Got to catch me first." She winks at me and runs to her bedroom.

"Two DAYS IN a row," she tells me when she sits on the chair in front of me. "I don't know what I'm going to do tomorrow." She tries to make a joke of it, but I can see it bothers her and she's been quiet ever since this morning when I mentioned I would have to leave soon.

I take our plates filled with pancakes and sausage and sit down next to her. "So," she says when I sit down. "Are we going to talk about what happened last night?"

I look over at her, cutting a piece of pancake and eating it. "You have to be a bit more specific, there was lots that happened." I wink at her. "Some very good things happened."

She laughs. "Well, let's start with us not using condoms." She points at my dick and my eyes widen.

I swallow down my food hoping that I don't choke. "Are you not on?" I ask her, knowing she was always on the pill when we were together.

"It's not that I'm worried about," she says, looking up. "Are you…" She is thinking of the word and I finally get what she's trying to say.

I gasp, looking at her with big eyes. "I've never had sex without a condom, well, except with you." I shake my head and take another bite of the pancake.

"You were engaged!" she shrieks out at me and I look over at her.

"I'll repeat myself again," I say as I slowly nod. "You were the only one I've had unprotected sex with." I tilt my head to the side. "Are you?" I ask her, raising my eyebrows.

"Oh, don't you even dare," she says to me and I hold up my hand.

"Are we really going to do this right now?" I ask her, knowing that we have to talk about me leaving, but her trying to start a fight with me right when I'm leaving must be her trying to prove it doesn't bother her.

"We are having a conversation." She glares and I know for a fact that she is trying to fight with me; this is her being scared. "Are you going to ask me again if I had sex with people unprotected?" She folds her arms over her chest and I look at her.

"What's wrong?" I ask her and I can see her eyes shift.

"What do you mean?" she asks, trying to act stupid, but she must have forgotten how well I know her.

"I mean, yesterday at the bar you went off in your head and avoided my eyes," I remind her, and I can see in her eyes that she is surprised I caught it. I put my fork down and turn on the chair to face her. "What is going on?"

She shakes her head. "What is this?" she finally

says. "Like, what are we doing?" I put my head to the side. "I don't mean that; I mean, this you-and-me thing. Like, is it a fling? Is it friends with benefits? Are we acquaintances?"

I glare at her. "I know we are definitely not going to be acquaintances."

She huffs, throwing her hands in the air. "I'm being serious, Travis."

I reach out to touch her, pushing the hair away from her face and look into her beautiful eyes. "I don't have the answers," I answer her honestly.

"You don't do long-distance relationships," she reminds me, her voice going soft, and there is the fear written all over her face.

"I said a lot of things." I pull the chair closer to me.

"What does that even mean?" she asks.

"It means that we are going to do what we need to do." I smile shyly at her. "I will come here, you come there." I swallow down the lump in my throat. "I'm not losing you, Harlow," I confirm the only thing I'm sure of. "Whatever happens, I'm not fucking losing you again." She looks up at me and I can see the tears in her eyes. "Tell me you understand what I'm saying." I lean over and kiss her on the lips. "I'm here for the long haul." I cup her cheek with my hand. "Whatever it is, we will make it work."

She nods her head at me, and when I get up and get my bag from her room, everything inside me hurts. And I mean everything; there is a tightness in my chest. My stomach is in knots, the back of my neck feels like it's on fire. She walks out of the house with me and stands beside the car. I put my bag in the back seat and then turn to her, pulling her into my arms. Her arms go around my waist. "I'll call you when I get home." I bring her to me and she rests her head on my shoulder, my hand rubbing her back. "And we'll get our calendars out and start looking at dates." She nods her head and steps back and I can see her rolling her lips trying to keep strong. I lean down and kiss her one last time before getting into the car. She doesn't move from her spot by the car, and when I drive away, I watch the rearview mirror until I can't see her anymore and I finally let the pain in my chest out. "Fuck," I hiss out and I want to punch something.

My phone rings and I think it's Harlow and I want to turn the car around and go back to her. I look at the call display and see it's Bennett. "Hey," I greet, putting it on Bluetooth.

"Hey yourself." His voice fills the car. "I'm at your house and you aren't here."

"Yeah," I say, getting on the highway. "I went away this weekend."

"You went away?" he asks, shocked. "Like, on your honeymoon by yourself?"

I laugh, imagining his face. "No. I went to see Harlow."

He whistles out. "Oh, snap." I don't say anything. "Are you sure that was a good idea?"

"No, it fucking sucks," I admit. "But I can't stay away from her." My hands grip the steering wheel so hard my knuckles are white. "I just left her house and all I can say is it fucking sucks."

"But you broke up with her for this very reason. Plus, not to be a Debbie Downer and all that, but you were engaged less than a week ago."

I groan out, "I'm going to have to admit that marrying Jennifer would have been a colossal mistake." The bitterness starts to form in my mouth. "And it's safe to say we would have divorced in the end."

He lets out a huge breath. "You don't know that."

"Actually," I admit. "I know that for a fact. It wasn't love. Fuck, one look at Harlow on my wedding day and I knew that what I felt for Jennifer was nothing. I'm not proud of it and I'll never tell anyone but you that. But, man, with Harlow it's this overwhelming feeling that fills my whole body. Fuck, it fills my soul. I want to hold her, touch her, listen to her talk." The chest that had pressure on it just a couple of minutes ago now has even more pressure. "I just want her."

"Well, that is all good and everything, but it doesn't erase the fact that she lives in a different state. And I'm not talking a town over."

"Trust me, I know," I huff out. "It's a six hour road trip."

"You drove?" he gasps. "What is wrong with you?"

"I had time to spare," I lie to him and he laughs.

"No, you didn't. You took your car because if she told you to fuck off, you could lick your wounds all by yourself for six hours." He laughs and I hate that he knows me as well as he does.

"It was eight with traffic," I say, and he just laughs

louder. "I'm hanging up."

"I'll come and see you tomorrow," he says and I hang up the phone. I spend six hours driving back to my house, and when I get into the driveway, it's night out.

I grab my bag and walk up the steps, the whole time I miss Harlow like I've never missed her before. Every single step feels heavier than the last, and when I unlock my door and step inside, I stop in my tracks. The boxes are all gone. I put the bag down and walk into the kitchen and look around to see it empty. A white paper sits on the counter with my name on the top.

I sit on the stool and read it.

Travis,

Sorry we weren't the right person for each other.

All the best,

Jennifer

I shake my head and put the paper down and wait for it. I wait for some little twinge of regret. I wait for some little pain that she isn't in my life anymore. I wait for anything but instead I get nothing.

I take my phone out and call Harlow, a smile fills my face knowing I'm going to hear her voice, but instead of her saying hello, it goes straight to voice mail.

"You better not have blocked me," I say into the phone nervously, trying to calm myself down. "Call me back."

Thirty-Three

Harlow

listen to the voice mail and laugh when I hear his voice. "You better not have blocked me." He laughs nervously and I look over at the clock, seeing it's a little after 1:00 a.m. "Call me back."

Walking into the house, I head straight to the kitchen and wash my hands. Grabbing a bottle of water, I send him a text instead of calling him.

Me: Sorry, had an emergency. Just got home, call you in the morning.

I walk back to my room and strip off my clothes, turning on the water in the shower, I step in. I'm so freaking tired and my back hurts from bending over for the last four hours. Closing my eyes, I put my head forward for a couple of minutes. I'm grabbing a towel when my phone rings and I groan out loud thinking it's another emergency, but I smile when I see that it's Travis and he's FaceTiming me. I press the green button and walk to the bed, sliding in on his side. His scent fills me all around and the little pang in my chest is just enough for me to feel it.

His face comes onto the screen and I see that he's in bed and I miss him. "Did I wake you?" I ask, putting my head down on the pillow, wishing he was here with me.

"I thought you blocked me again," he mumbles and I can't help but laugh at him.

"You know where I live," I remind him. "So there really is no use in blocking you." I look at him. "How was the drive home?"

"Long," he says, and I see that he's not wearing a shirt. "Where were you all night?"

"A coyote got through the fence and a calf was stuck fighting him off," I say, closing my eyes.

"How is the calf?" he asks softly.

"Forty-seven stitches on one leg," I say. "And lost a chunk of his shoulder but I think he'll be fine."

"Ouch," he says, hissing out.

"I wish you were here," I admit to him, even though I said I wasn't going to. Watching him drive away from me was torture. I kept repeating to myself over and over again. *It's fine, I'll see him soon.* But it was as if my heart didn't believe what my head was telling it.

"I wish you were here," he says and his eyes close a bit. "When is your next day off?"

"I'm on call this weekend," I say. "I think I can

perhaps get off the week after next." He groans.

"What about you?" I ask and he gets on his stomach.

"I'm on call for the next two weekends," he huffs. "That's fourteen days."

"Is that what two weeks means in the city?" I joke with him and he just glares at me. "I'm going to go in tomorrow and check." My voice goes soft. "Does that make you feel better?"

"No," he pouts. "It would be better if you were here."

"Now let's say I was there," I start. "What would I be wearing?" I wiggle my eyebrows and for the rest of the call I show him my magic wand that I keep by the bed.

The alarm sounds six hours after I've fallen asleep, and I reach over to grab my phone right away. I slide the phone under the covers with me and slowly open my eyes when I see that I have a bunch of text messages waiting for me.

Travis: Good morning, beautiful. I tried to get coffee delivered to you but it's not available in your area.

I have to laugh loud at this one and shake my head. "Oh, my city boy," I say, turning on the other side and reading the other ones.

Travis: Waking up without you is not the same.

"Isn't that the truth," I mumble.

Travis: I miss you.

Travis: Have the best day and call or text me when you can.

Travis: P.S. You're beautiful.

I smile and start typing him a response

Me: What a way to wake up. I mean, it's almost my

third favorite way to wake up. I'll let you guess what my number one and number two are.

I miss you more. The bed isn't the same without you holding my boob, I think one might have run away.

Call me if you can.

P.S. Have I told you that I miss you?

I press send and get off the bed, going to start the coffee machine before I walk to the bathroom and brush my teeth. The phone rings and I smile seeing his name on top. "Good morning, sunshine," I say, putting him on speaker as I walk back to the kitchen

"Good morning, beautiful," he says and his voice sends shivers down my body. I could just picture him standing in front of me. "Did you just get up?"

"I did," I say. "Are you at work?"

"I am, got in here early. I'm between patients," he says, and I wonder if he wears scrubs or not.

"Whatcha wearing?" I ask and he laughs.

"Pants and a shirt," he says and his voice goes low and I hear someone call his name. "I'll take a picture and send it to you. I have to go, baby," he says softly. "I'll call you later."

"Okay," I say and hang up the phone, putting it on the counter. "It's going to be okay for seven days," I tell myself and I wish it was that simple. Truth be told, the next couple of days are a shitshow. I miss his calls most times, and when I call him, he always sounds like he's asleep. I refuse to admit that he was right four years ago and that long distance is fine.

I'm sitting at my desk four days later when I hear the

bell ring, and my stomach flutters when I think it could be him. I mean, I know the probability of it being him is slim, especially since I spoke with him this morning and he was going into surgery. I speed walk to the reception area and see my mom coming in. "Oh, it's you," I mumble, trying to hide the disappointment.

"Well, hello to you, too," she says, looking around. "Where is Donna?"

"She is sick today," I say, turning and walking back to my office, almost stomping back like a toddler being told I can't have a snack before dinner.

"Are you moping?" my mother says from behind me and I look over my shoulder at her.

"I'm not moping, I just thought that you were someone else and you are obviously not that person. So…" I walk over to the couch and sit down.

"And who did you think it was?" she asks, sitting next to me and I look over at her. I take a second to see if she knows anything.

"You never come visit me at work." I put my elbow on the side of the couch and rest my head on my fist. "So this is a surprise."

"I just wanted to see my daughter." She avoids looking at me, and I laugh, knowing for sure now that she has heard something through the grapevine, and chances are she got ten different variations, and I should have known this was coming. I was just freaking crazy trying to get this weekend off that I didn't even think.

"What are you fishing for, Mom?" I ask, and she gasps, shocked at my question.

"Can't a mother visit her daughter at work?" She pretends to brush lint from her pants, but I know that there would never be a piece of lint on anything she wears. My mother was a model since she was a little girl, and even though she's settled to life as a country girl, she still has all the city in her. "So what I heard was that a certain someone was in town." She shrugs her shoulders. "And no one said anything to me about it." She folds her arms over her chest.

"Aha." I laugh, pointing at her. "You came for information."

She puts her hand to her chest. "I did not." She glares at me. "Why didn't you tell me?" She points at me. "Why do I have to find out from a stranger that my daughter was out and about with a man?"

I throw my head back and laugh even louder. "Out and about my ass, we went to the bar on Saturday, so whoever you heard from saw us there."

"Maybe." She tilts her head. "That was where people saw you. The question is why didn't you tell us he was coming to town?"

"I didn't know," I answer her honestly. "He showed up here on Friday." Her mouth opens, and I know she has so many questions. "Ask the questions, Mom."

"I don't even know where to begin." She throws her hands up, and I wait for her to gather her thoughts. "You went to his wedding the other week."

"I did." I nod at her. "And he did not get married."

"Well, obviously, he didn't get married. He came to see you." She rolls her eyes, and she doesn't even ask me why they didn't get married. "I'm just shocked, is all."

"To be honest with you." I take a deep breath. "You aren't the only one who is shocked."

"It's been four years," she tells me, and the burning starts in my stomach when I think about it. "And it's been a hard freaking four years for you."

"It hasn't been that hard." I try to sugarcoat it.

"Hasn't been that hard. You're kidding, right?" She shakes her head. "You were miserable for what? The last four years to be exact."

"I was not miserable. I was just finding my ground." I hold up my hands because I know she is going to argue with me, and I also know she isn't wrong that I have been miserable for the last four years. Not always miserable but I always felt something missing in my life. "It doesn't matter right now."

"You're right, it doesn't," she agrees with me. "What matters now is that he's back in your life, I assume."

"That would be a good assumption." I nod at her.

"So now what?" I just look at her. "Now that he's come here and you've"—she beats around the bush—"you've spent time with each other." I can't help but roll my lips and try not to laugh at her.

"We spent lots of time together." I wink at her and she groans.

"Harlow," she hisses, "Can you be serious for one minute?"

"Okay, okay." I hold up my hands. "I just don't know the answers to everything," I admit. "And not having the answers makes me all nervous. Like, when is the next time I'm going to see him?" I shrug my shoulders. "I have no clue. How do long-distance relationships work? How long can one go with long distance before they give up?" I get up from the couch and start to pace in front of her and she knows this is me working it out in my head. "I was happy," I say and she tilts her head to the side. "Okay, fine. I wasn't happy. I was content. But now that I see him again." I stop and the tears come without me even realizing. "I see him again and it's like the four years never happened. I feel exactly how I did four years ago. He still makes my heart flutter. His kisses make me breathless. One touch from him and I crave more. It took me four years to try to get over him and one hour with him to fall back in love with him. I just." I look at her as she wipes her own tears off her cheeks. "I just hate this." I put my hands on my head. "He broke up with me because he couldn't do long distance and refused for me to give up my dreams for him. And now we are doing long distance and it fucking sucks monkey balls with blue cheese dressing on it. I hate it and it's been four days."

"Oh, Harlow," my mother says, getting up and coming over to me and she wraps her arms around me. "You have to follow your heart."

"What if my heart is afraid of getting hurt again?" I say, putting my head on her shoulder.

"What you feel for him," my mother says as she rubs my back, "you will never feel for anyone else, this I can guarantee you."

"But love is supposed to be easy." She just laughs.

"The last thing that love is, is easy." I can't help but laugh at the irony of it, and she lets me go and holds my face. "If it was easy, no one would want it."

"I love him," I share and she smiles at me. "Like not just, oh yeah, I love you. It's like the I love you so much it hurts when I can't kiss you."

"Why do you think I travel with your father when he leaves?" she asks me. "Why do you think that is? It's because I just can't live without him."

"Well, that doesn't help me at all," I reply, and she laughs. "Let's go and get you something to eat."

"I don't want to eat. I need to find someone to take my place this weekend so I can go and see my man."

"Well, then, let's get you to your man." She smiles at me and the little voice in my head is already making plans.

I park my car in the driveway and the phone rings right away. When I see it's her, I can't help the way my chest contracts when I see her face. "Hey," I answer after one ring. The smile fills my face as I get out of the car. Pushing my shoulder up to hold the phone, I take out the flowers that I stopped by to get for her.

"Hi," she says and she sounds exhausted. She's been on call for the last ten days; I look at my watch and see that it's past 7:00 p.m. "I just got out of surgery." I stop walking midstep when I hear those words.

"Weren't you supposed to be on your way here?" I ask her. The last text I got from her was, "leaving in an hour" and that was at three.

"I was and then I got an emergency call and I had no

time to text you." I close my eyes and then turn to sit on the front steps. "I'm so sorry."

"It's been over two weeks," I remind her and I'm pissed that our plans have changed yet again. Last week I tried to get out to see her, but then shit came up and I had back-to-back emergencies, so I just couldn't leave. We've been talking about this weekend for the past week. I didn't even make any plans except to get food in. I was going to lock the door and only open it when she had to leave. I missed her more than I could put into words, and every single day I was getting crabbier and crabbier, to the point where they were scared to talk to me.

"You don't have to remind me, Travis," she says, and I can hear that she is pissed also. "I know exactly how many days it's been," she huffs. "Even if I forgot, you would remind me." I drop the flowers on the steps beside me. "I have to go and take a shower. I'm covered in guts and shit."

"Fine," I snap out. "Call me after." I look down at the phone and see my screenshot, which is the picture that she sent me this week. She was sitting in the middle of the field with her hair piled on her head. With one eye closed, she looked more beautiful than she ever did before.

I grab the flowers and head inside, slamming the door behind me. I toss the flowers onto the counter next to my keys and my phone. Pulling open the fridge and grabbing a bottle of beer, I twist open the cap, throwing it into the sink, not even giving a shit. I walk over to the couch and sit down, kicking off my shoes. Grabbing the remote, I turn on the television and just flick the channels while I finish my bottle of beer.

So much is going through my head, it's like a spinning merry-go-round. I finish the beer in three gulps and get another one. "I really fucked things up," I say to the television, taking another pull of the beer. "Should I have just asked her to come with me?" I look at the bottle in my hand. "I fucking hate this shit." I look at the television, not even knowing what I'm watching.

Playing the scenario in my head over and over again. Asking her to come and then wondering if we would be married by now. For sure we would be, I would be begging her to marry me. Would we even be living in this house? Get up grabbing another beer and then checking to see if she called me, I think about calling her but I'm afraid that she might have fallen asleep and I'll wake her.

The whole night I drink beer after beer while I make myself almost crazy with questions about what would have been. I lie on the couch sometime after eleven and my eyes close for a second. I hear the soft knock and my eyes flutter open to see the television still on. My head feels all groggy when I pick up my phone to see that it's just after 2:00 a.m. I see that there isn't a text from her, nor have I missed a call. My stomach sinks knowing that she is probably mad at me for what happened before. I contemplate getting up and going to sleep in my bed when I hear the knock again. I sit up, looking back at the door and getting up. I take four steps to the door and then hear a soft knock yet again. "What the hell?" I say to myself as I grab the door handle and the phone rings in my hand. I look down seeing Harlow's name at the same time that my hand opens the door. My hand stops halfway to my ear when I see her standing there in the middle of the porch with the phone to her ear. "Harlow," I whisper, and I wonder if I'm dreaming about her again. I blink a couple of times to make sure that I'm really seeing her.

"Hi." She holds up her hand with the phone in it. "Surprise," she says, opening her arms and my phone falls to the floor and I rush out to her. My arms wrap around her waist as I pick her up. She wraps her legs around my waist at the same time she grabs my face with both hands and lowers her lips to mine. I slide my tongue into her mouth and the both of us moan out. I turn around, walking back into the house, closing the front door with my foot.

She moves her head to the side as the kiss deepens, my heart hammering in my chest. "I can't believe you are here," I say when I let go of her lips. "Are you really here?"

"I mean, you could be dreaming." She smiles and her index finger traces my lower lip. "I just hope you're real."

I lean forward and bite her neck and then suck in. "Yup, real," I confirm and I just stare at her. She's everything and more. "I missed you."

"Show me," she says in a whisper. "Show me all the ways you've missed me." She reaches for her shirt and pulls it over her head. "Fourteen days." She leans in, biting my lower lip. "Fourteen times," she says, and all

I can do is toss her on the bed. It takes a whole twenty seconds to get us both naked. Our hands are frantic to touch each other, our mouths attach and never let go. There is so much I want to do to her but her hand grips my cock and pulls it to her vagina. "I really want to swallow you to the back of my throat," she says, letting go of my lips for a bit. "But I need you inside me more."

She doesn't have to ask me twice, in one thrust I'm all the way buried in her. Both of us moan out. She arches her back and I fucking swear she was made for me. She wraps her legs around my waist and it doesn't take me long until I'm roaring out her name at the same time that we both jump over the cliff. I hunch over her, not moving from inside her. "Are you really here?" I bend and kiss her lips.

"I'm really here." She smiles at me. "I didn't think I would be able to swing it, but I just couldn't go another weekend." Her hand comes up and cups my face. "Even if it's for just a little while." She leans up and rubs her nose with mine and she rolls me over for round two.

"Where are you going?" I mumble with my eyes still closed when I feel her try to move away from me.

She chuckles as my hand doesn't let go of her one boob. "I have to pee." I open one eye when I let go of her and see her slip out of bed and walk to the bathroom. "What time is it?" I turn to look at the clock.

"It's eleven," I reply and wait for her to walk out of the bathroom. All night we went at it, neither of us wanted to sleep and lose the time we had with each other. We finally drifted off to sleep sometime after eight, after we made an early breakfast. I hear the toilet flush and then the water turn on. She walks out of the bathroom right after and my cock wakes up. "I have to leave by two."

The happiness that I felt not too long ago now turns into anger. "You just got here."

"And I had to beg someone to take my place, but they can't do it all weekend, so I took what I could." She puts a knee into the bed and then crawls to me. "Don't do that face."

"What face?" I try to change my face but she knows me.

"The face." She swings her leg over my hips straddling me and leans down. "When this part right here." She points between my eyes. "Gets all scrunched up." She kisses the spot. "And then this dimple right here." She points at the right side of my cheek. "It droops." She kisses my dimple and my hands go to her hips.

"I don't want you to leave me yet," I admit to her and flip her on her back. "What if I tied you up and never let you out?" I ask her and her green eyes just light up when she laughs.

"That, my friend, is called kidnapping." I smile at her. "And I think you get arrested and put into jail."

"Ugh, fine," I say, trying not to ruin the last couple of hours I have with her, but the minutes fly by and in the blink of an eye I'm kissing her beside her car. "Are you going to call me when you get home?"

"I sure will." She lays her head on my shoulder. "And then you are going to check and see when you can leave."

"I will," I agree and the wind blows her hair into her

face. My hand pushes it back and I kiss her lips one more time before she gets into the car. "Drive safe," I say, closing the car door behind her.

"Bye, Travis." She smiles and I can see that she is blinking away tears and I wish she could stay. She puts her hand to her lips and kisses her fingers and blows me a kiss before driving off. I stand here watching until I don't see her taillights anymore.

I walk up the steps and sit on the top step, the pain in my chest getting stronger and stronger. I sit out here looking at nothing really, and then my phone rings in my back pocket. "Hello," I answer, not even checking to see who it is.

"Hey," Shelby says. "Don't forget dinner at Mom's in ten minutes." I look at the phone seeing that it's almost five. I spent the last three hours staring at nothing.

"Yeah, I'll be there." I walk back in the house and slip on socks and shoes, grabbing my keys and wallet. I don't look at the bed, not willing to just yet.

When I pull up to the house, I see that all three of them are sitting outside on the front steps.

I get out of the car and close the door behind me, turning to walk up the walkway. "Jesus," Clarabella says. "You look like shit."

I shake my head, only my sister doesn't sugarcoat things. "Oh my God, did an animal die?" Shelby asks and I sit down on the step next to them.

"Nope," I respond and the front door opens and my mother comes out and she smiles until she sees my face.

"What happened?" Her smile fades. "Who died?" She

looks at the girls, who try not to laugh at her.

"No one died," I assure them and lean my elbows on my knees. "Why can't I just look like shit?"

"You don't just look like shit," Presley replies. "You look like someone kicked your dog and then kicked you in the balls."

"Do you need to be so graphic?" my mother huffs at her and she just smiles at her.

"Harlow was down," I share and everyone just stops even blinking their eyes. Even the animals in the trees sound like they stopped doing everything.

"Wait a second." Shelby holds up her hand and then looks at me. "She came down to see you?"

"I went to see her two weeks ago," I admit to them and my mother walks over to the rocking chair. She grabs the chair by the arm and pulls it closer to us and sits down.

"You went to see her the week after your wedding?" She looks at me. "You said you went to a conference."

"I lied," I confess. "I didn't want to say anything in case she told me to fuck off."

"You slept with her on your wedding night and she didn't tell you to fuck off then," Presley reminds me and Shelby puts her hand to her mouth when my mother gasps.

"What?" she shrieks out and I glare at Presley. "You slept with her on your wedding night?" She rolls her eyes and shakes her head. "Are you out of your mind?"

"Probably," I admit to her. "Probably. Because now I love her even more than I did before and it's so fucked up." My sisters look at me with their mouths hanging down. "I broke up with her four years ago for this exact reason."

"You broke up with her four years ago because you're an asshole," Clarabella tells me and it's my turn for my mouth to hang open. "Oh, come on, you don't think that what you did made any sense whatsoever."

"How could I have asked her to choose?" I ask, getting defensive.

"I know how." Shelby puts her hand up like she is in a classroom. "Harlow, I love you and I don't want you to move back home."

"It's not that easy," I declare, shaking my head, the pit of my stomach burning.

"But it is that easy. It's like *pick me, choose me, love me*," Clarabella says, and my sisters all nod and sigh.

"Four years ago, I let her go because I didn't want her to choose between going back home and being in this fucking spot."

"And what spot is that?" my mother asks.

"It's the spot where I miss her so freaking much I'm unbearable at work. It's the spot where I don't even sleep properly because all I want to do is dream of her, and when I don't, I wake up pissed. It's the spot where everything around me seems dull, almost like it's in black and white and she is the color in the world." The pain in my chest comes on full force now. "It's the spot that I didn't want to fucking be in and I'm here. I want out."

"One," Shelby states, putting up her finger. "If you weren't my annoying brother, I would barf at all the things you just said. And two, why don't you just ask her to move here?"

"She has a practice." I throw up my hands. "How much of a dick would I be if I said close down your practice and move here?"

"Well, if you are going to be as chipper and light-hearted as you are right here," Presley says. "Chances are that you are going to make everyone around you want to move away from you."

"You love her," my mother says.

"I do," I admit. "More than I did before, more than I will any other woman in this lifetime."

"I waited to see the light come back into your eyes," my mother says softly, and she uses her thumb to brush away the tear from the corner of her eye. "And when you brought Jennifer home, I was over the moon. I thought my boy is back." My sisters groan out at the same time. "Shut up, you three." She glares at them. "I kept looking at you, hoping to see the same light in your eye that you had with Harlow. I kept waiting for you to laugh like you did with her. I kept waiting for you to be like this." She points at me. "The whole time you were with her, you never had that light. You were dull."

"Jeez, thanks," I say, laughing at her. "Nothing like your mother telling you you're dull to brighten your day."

She gets up. "The answers are right in front of you." She puts her hands on her hips. "You know what the answer is." I just look at her, not sure when she says what my head has been screaming at me to do. "If you want her, go to her."

Thirty-Five

Harlow

"I'm so sorry, Harlow," Delores says from the phone and I close my eyes.

"It's not your fault you fell and broke your leg." I shake my head and look up at the ceiling of my office. "You just focus on getting yourself better," I say. "Don't worry about anything." I put the phone down.

"Why?" I want to bang my head on the desk. Donna comes into my office, and I look at her. "Is this a sign that we should just go our separate ways?" Delores was transferring over from the vet across town to join me and yesterday while on call she fell and broke her leg in three places.

"No." She shakes her head. "It's almost as if the universe wants to see how much you will fight for each other." She shrugs.

"Well, I'd like to sit down with the universe and tell it to fuck off." I put my head back and I can feel the headache coming on.

"In other news, I'm out," she says, turning around. "I will see you in the morning."

I nod at her, not saying anything, and when the phone rings and I see it's Travis, the burning in the pit of my stomach moves to my chest. I press the green connect button and see my face in the screen with the white circle going around and around. His face then fills the screen and the burning in my chest turns to a crushing pain. "Hi." I see his green eyes light up when he sees me and I miss him so much. I tried to put it into words the other day and I couldn't. It's this overwhelming need to be with him. The last two weeks have been hard, even though he flew down one day to surprise me, I then was called on an emergency and we spent a full three hours together. Then he had to leave and we haven't been able to make our schedules sync. "Oh, no," he says, smiling sideways. "That look is not a good look."

I try to blink away the stupid tears that come. I'm a grown-ass woman and I'm going to cry because I can't see my boyfriend. Who the fuck does that? Oh, I know, me. "I just got a call from Delores and she broke her leg." His eyes widen. "So she is out for a good month, if not six weeks."

"Great," he says, huffing out and putting his head back. "Not the news I was looking for today."

"I know," I say, frustrated with this whole fucking

situation. I just want to be able to spend the weekend with him. Friday to Monday without counting down the hours. I want to be able to go out to dinner with him and then go home and just chill on the couch. I want to wake up with him in the morning and have breakfast. I want to do what normal couples do instead of holding our breath for our next visit. Or trying to get someone to take my place for a day so I can rush to him. I'm just fed up with the long distance and I'm frustrated that he was right all along. Which makes me pissed off and irritable. I tilt my head to the side. "I was not expecting her to say that when she called."

He takes a big deep breath and looks at me. "It's fine," he tries to say, and I snap.

"It's not fucking fine." I slap my hand on my mouth, the calm, cool, collected Harlow is gone. The one who was always trying to sugarcoat shit is gone. The last phone call was the straw that broke the camel's back. I didn't even have time to process it before he called and I'm not sure it would make a difference. "It's not fucking fine!" I shout again. "Nothing about this is fine. Not one fucking thing." I throw up my hands. "I hate that I haven't seen you in over a week. I hate that the last time I saw you I spent three hours with you. I hate that I haven't been able to fall asleep beside you. I fucking hate it!" I shout and then finally take a breath.

"Are you done?" he asks calmly, making me glare at him.

"Does it look like I'm done, Travis?" I hiss at him.

"You're sexy when you are mad," he states with his

smile that makes me forget everything I was thinking about before.

"Stop trying to make me feel better," I snap at him, and if he was in front of me, he would probably pull me to him and just hold me, which makes me even madder. "You were right," I admit. "This long distance is." I stop talking before I say it's not working out. "It's a lot."

"It's a learning curve." He tries to be the voice of reason. "I wish I could swing coming to see you, but Micehlle just gave birth early and Roy just took off on vacation." He mentions his two partners.

"It's fine," I say, ignoring the panging in my chest. "Besides, knowing our luck, you get here and I'd be called away for ten hours and then what?"

There is a beep on his side and he looks down. "I have to go," he says and all I can do is look at him. "I'll call you in a bit." I don't answer him because there is a lump stuck in my throat. "Hey," he says when I look down. "Harlow." He says my name so I look up at him. When my eyes meet his, he just smiles sadly. "We'll work it out," he assures me softly and I want to argue with him but another beep goes out.

"Go," I say and I press disconnect before he does. "Fuck," is all I can say as I turn my chair and look outside at the sun that is slowly setting. When I stand from my chair, my body feels like it's been run over by a Mack truck. Every single step hurts, and when I get home, I barely make it up the steps before turning and just sitting in one of the chairs.

I feel the phone buzz in my pocket, and when my

hand reaches for it, I see it's him. I let it ring until it goes to voice mail and then hear the sound of rocks and I look up. The black truck stops right behind mine and I watch my father step out.

He takes two steps up and stops when he spots me sitting in the dark. "What in the Sam Hill are you doing sitting outside in the dark?" He walks over to me and then stops when he sees me. I probably look like a wreck; tears are smeared all down my cheeks for sure. "Who died?" I try to laugh but instead a sob just comes out of me and I put a hand to my mouth. He squats down in front of me, grabbing the other hand in his. "Harlow," he whispers in a plea. "I'm not going to lie, you are really freaking me out right now." He looks around and I can imagine he's wondering how he can call someone without leaving me.

"I'm fine," I say and then sniffle. "I mean, I'm not really fine."

"What is it?" he says, pushing away the hair from my face. "Whatever it is, we can get through it. Are you sick?" he asks and I shake my head.

He puts his head down on my legs. "Thank God," he utters. "I thought you were going to tell me that you're dying." He laughs uncomfortably. "Gotta say you took a million years off my life."

I laugh and wipe the tear off my cheek. "I'm not sick," I reassure him. "But I'm not happy, Dad." I say the words I've been scared to say out loud in the last four years. "I tried to be happy, I did." I smile at him but the tears come. "But it's just my heart is empty here."

"Harlow," he whispers and I can see his own tears in

his eyes. "Honey." He cups my cheek.

"When he broke up with me, I told myself that it was going to be fine." I look down at his hand on mine. "And then I decided that I was not only going to open my practice here, I was going to fucking kill it." I smile through the tears. "And I did and then."

"And then you realized that you were just going through the motions." He fills in for me.

"Maybe I didn't see it." I swallow down the lump in my throat. "How unhappy I was. Maybe seeing him again, it just clicked, and now I don't know."

"You love him?" he quizzes and I'm not sure if he's asking me or telling me. "Like, you aren't using him just to say to fuck off."

"Dad," I gasp. "Why would you even think that?"

"I don't know." He shrugs. "I was just hoping that you wouldn't get hurt again."

"But being without him hurts more," I say. "It's crazy that I lived four years without him and now that he's been back in my life, I just miss him all the time."

"It's not crazy," he says. "It's normal. Hell, I've been with your mom for a long, long time and every single day I love her even more." He smiles big and his eyes light up. "I can't imagine a day without her."

"Yeah, well, I can tell you right now, it sucks ass," I complain. "I got home tonight, and I swear I thought my body was shutting down." I look down. "Will you help me?"

"Whatever you need," he tells me. "It's going to be hard," he says, and it's my turn to wipe the tear from his face. "But if that's what you want, we will make it happen."

"Thank you, for always being on my side."

"There is no other side I will be on." He gets up and pulls me up with him. "If he hurts you again." He looks down at me. "I will get your brother to rough him up a little."

I throw my head back and let out a laugh. "Good to know." He puts his arm over my shoulder, walking to my front door. "You know he's afraid you are going to shoot him."

He chuckles. "I mean, you just never know." He winks at me as I open the door for him. "Tomorrow we sit down and start making a plan," he tells me. "Now go get your stuff." I just look at him. "Your mother isn't going to let you stay here all night with you crying and stuff."

"Who is going to tell her?" I fold my arms over my chest.

"I'm not lying to her," he tells me, mimicking my stance. "Do you know what she does when she finds out?" I roll my lips. "Last time she went seven days without saying a word to me. Do you know how many hours that is?" He shakes his head. "I slept with one eye open after the second day." I put my hand to my stomach and laugh. "Now go get your stuff."

I nod at him and turn around, walking toward my room. For the first time in the last month, my steps feel lighter. For the first time in the last four months, I can see the light at the end of the tunnel. For the first time in four years, I can feel my heart beating again.

Thirty-Six
Travis

I press the connect button on the middle screen. "Hello." Shelby's voice fills the car.

"Hey," I answer, looking around at the green trees as I drive down the road. "What's up?"

"Just checking in," she says, and I can imagine that she just spoke to my mother. Who is the only one who knows where I'm going right now. I can also hear that she's rushing somewhere, and knowing that she is probably at a wedding, this conversation is going to be quick.

"Checking in?" I chuckle. "Or calling to get the scoop?"

She gasps, "Can't a big sister call and check on her baby brother?" I can't help but laugh loud.

"Smooth. But I'm just getting to Harlow's house," I

say, turning onto the street and my heart starts to beat faster and faster as I get closer to her house. "And I haven't seen her in a while, so..."

"So, you are going to bang her on the porch." She roars out a laugh. "You'll last maybe five seconds."

"Goodbye," I say and then she cuts in right away.

"Good luck," she says, and I disconnect when I pull into the driveway and see that her car is there parked in the middle.

It's been a week since she's had a little breakdown, and I'm not going to lie, she's been more quiet than normal. It's almost as if she is pulling away from me, and every single day, I got itchier and itchier to say my plans.

Getting out of the car, I listen to the sound of calmness and smile when I look up at the house, knowing she's right in there. I jog up the steps to the front door and I have to laugh at myself when I see my hand shaking when I ring the doorbell. The last time I spoke to her she was just getting home and she was rushing to get off the phone.

I put my hands in my pockets as I wait for her to answer the door. I feel as nervous as I did on our first date. Even though we were talking way before we even went on that first date, I just knew what a big deal it was. I also didn't want to fuck anything up.

My heart speeds up even faster, my hands get really clammy, my knees are starting to shake, and now the nerves have moved from my stomach to the back of my neck. I reach out again to ring the bell and the sudden dread fills me. Maybe I should have told her I was coming. Maybe I should have told her my plans instead of just surprising her. All the maybes and the doubts run rampant through me. "Coming." I hear her voice and I don't have any time to prepare when the door swings open and she stands there. Everything that I was thinking before is suddenly gone with one look at her. She's wearing navy-blue loose shorts with a matching V-neck shirt. "Oh my gosh." Is the only thing she says before she jumps into my arms. "Oh my goodness." She wraps her arms and legs around me and buries her face in my neck. "Is this for real?"

I laugh as I step into her house and shut the door with my foot. "It's for real," I assure her, laughing, and she unburies her head from my neck. Her green eyes light up when she puts her hand on my cheek and leans in to kiss my lips softly.

I take a couple of steps into the house. "Why is it you're always carrying me?" She laughs and my heart skips a beat.

"I'll carry you every single day," I say and she tilts her head to the side. "I missed you." My arms squeeze around her waist even more, pulling her to me and it's my turn to bury my face in her neck.

"How long can you stay?" she asks softly as her hands go into the back of my hair.

"All weekend," I say, figuring I am going to start off slow.

She gasps, and I remove my face from her neck. "Like, all weekend. Like, sleeping and waking up?"

"Yup." I smile and look around, seeing the boxes

scattered all over the place. "What is all this?" I look at her and see that her eyes avoid me. "Are you moving?"

She slips her legs off my waist and slides down off me. "I think we should talk," she says and all the nerves I had before have come back. She slips her hand in mine as she pulls me to the couch with her. I'm trying not to panic at this moment, but everything is screaming at me that I should have spoken to her about my plans.

She slides onto the couch and tucks her legs under her and I sit next to her. "I think we definitely need to talk," my mouth says before my brain can catch up. I had this whole speech planned, the benefit from driving six hours is you have a lot of time to think. I look and see that there are more boxes. My heart feels like it's hammering in the middle of my chest. "Umm," is all I can say when I close my eyes and try to find the words that are clustered all around my head.

"Travis," she says and starts to say something else but I hold up my hand.

"I really need to get this out," I start, turning to look at her. I push the hair away from her face, needing to touch her. "The last week I've been going through all these things in my head." She smiles at me.

"I have also." She reaches out with her hand to hold mine. Her fingers link with mine and all I can think is that I want to hold her hand in mine forever.

"Actually, it's been longer than just last week." I swallow. "But when you called last week and another weekend of plans were shot, I knew that something had to give." I pick up her hand that is linked with mine and bring it to my lips, kissing her fingers. "So I made the decision that I'm moving here," I say, finally letting it out and she looks at me shocked. "I know that it may come as a shock to you, but after I looked at everything." A tear escapes her eye. "The bottom line is that I can't live without being near you so..." I smile as another tear spills out. "I spoke to my partners and they are going to buy me out."

"You can't do that," she says, getting up and my whole body goes solid like a rock. The happiness that I had two seconds ago turns to ice-cold feelings.

I turn to face her as she stands in front of me. "What do you mean I can't do that?" My stomach sinks thinking that maybe she doesn't want me to do this. Maybe she is over this and just thinking about that I'm going to be sick.

"I mean that you can't do that," she repeats and rubs the tear off her own cheek. "You can't do that because I'm moving."

"Well, I see that." I try to swallow but the lump in my throat grows bigger and bigger.

"No, you don't." She laughs and puts her hands to her mouth. "You can't move here because I'm moving to you."

"What?" I ask her and it's my turn to be shocked.

"That's what all the boxes are for." She holds her hands to the sides of her. "I'm selling my practice."

I shake my head, not sure I'm actually hearing the words that she is saying. "I'm sorry," I say, laughing at us and this whole situation.

"Well, let me see if I can explain it better." Her whole face lights up with a smile and if I didn't love her before with everything I had, this moment right here would be where it would happen. "Actually, this decision was made four years ago," she says and if I wasn't sitting down to begin with, this news would knock me on my ass. I hold up my hand and she holds up her own. "Let me talk, please." She waits and makes sure that I'm not going to say anything else. "Four years ago, I was going to tell you that I was going to take a job at the emergency clinic with you." My brain feels like it's going to explode in my head, and my mouth hangs open. "Yeah," she says. "I had decided that I was going to stay with you."

"But," I start to say as the pieces come together. The clinic telling me that they were short-staffed because someone who was going to take the job decided not to. I never even put two and two together.

"But you broke up with me," she says, shrugging. "And my plans changed, so I came home."

"Why didn't you say anything to me?" I get up. "You never even told me."

"I was waiting until you brought it up." She takes a deep breath. "I didn't want to just assume that you would want me with you, so I was waiting until you asked me." Her voice goes low. "And then you broke up with me, so there was no point in that."

The only thing I can say is. "But."

"So I called my father and told him I would take his offer."

"You had told your father already?" I hiss out. "Great." I put my hands on my hips. "If he didn't want to, he'll want to shoot me now."

She laughs and comes over to me, standing in front of me. She puts her hands on my hips. "I went four years without you." She looks up at me with all the love that she has always looked at me with. The look I thought I would never see again. "And it took one day for me to see that I really wasn't happy. I mean yes, I had my practice and it was thriving. Yes, I had my family all around me. I had everything that could make me happy, except I didn't have that missing piece."

"I can't let you give this up for me." I shake my head. "I wouldn't let you do it four years ago. I'm not going to let you do it now."

"Well, good news is you have no say in this," she sasses me. "The decision has already been made and I have three interviews on Monday."

"You did all of this without telling me."

"You did the same thing," she counters back at me and my hands come and hold her face. "I really think we should talk about how we communicate with each other." She laughs and I can't help but bend down and kiss her lips.

"I don't want you to sacrifice all of this."

"That's the thing, Travis," she explains. "I'm not sacrificing anything. I'm choosing me and my happiness." She gets on her tippy-toes and kisses under my neck. "Now that we have that settled, can we get naked?" Only she can shock me one minute and then make me laugh the next. Only she can argue that what she is doing for you is really for her. Only she can make everything better. Only she can make my heart beat without pain. Only her.

Thirty-Seven

Harlow

"That's the thing, Travis," I say, my chest feeling full for the first time in the last four years. "I'm not sacrificing anything. I'm choosing me and my happiness." I get on my tippy-toes and kiss under his neck, exactly where I can feel his heartbeat under my lips. His heart is beating as fast as mine and all I can do is smile. "Now that we have that settled, can we get naked?"

"Yes," he agrees and holds up a finger. "Just so I understand what is going on," he says and I rub my nose under his chin. "Four years ago, you were going to move with me."

"That is correct," I say as my hands go to the hem of his shirt, my hands sliding it up just a touch.

"So not only was I a total asshole," he continues

talking. "But I was stupid."

"That is correct." I give his neck soft kisses. "And dumb." My finger trails up his stomach.

"Really dumb," he confirms, and when I look up at him, I see that his eyes are closed as I move one hand down to cup his cock through his pants. "Harlow," he hisses out. "I really…" His voice comes out breathless as my hand rubs up and down twice. "We really need to talk." He stops talking when my hand goes to the top of his jeans and I slip in the tips of my fingers, touching the head of his cock. He groans when my nails graze the head of his cock. "We really need to talk," he repeats the words and my other hand leaves his chest and comes to unbutton his jeans.

"We should talk." My hand goes to the zipper as I pull it down. "But there is something else I could be doing with my mouth." I smirk at him as I sink down to my knees and pull his pants down, licking the tip. "I missed you."

Travis chuckles. "Are you talking to me or my dick?"

"A bit of both right now." I fist his cock in my hand. "A little bit of both," I say, swallowing down his cock as much as I can.

"Harlow." He hisses out my name, burying his hands in my hair. I work his cock with my hand and my mouth. I feel his cock getting bigger in my mouth when he steps out of reach and I moan at him.

He goes back to the couch and kicks off his pants and then rips his shirt over his head before lying down. "I think I want to use my mouth to do something else besides talking." He doesn't need to ask me twice and in three seconds I'm naked in front of him. I walk over to the side of the couch and stand at his side. His hand rubs the back of my calf going up, and then he slips two fingers into me. "Sit on my face." He pulls me to him and I throw a leg over his head, putting my knee beside his head. He doesn't wait for me to lower myself over his mouth; instead, he grabs my hips with his hands and lifts his head to lick my pussy. The second his tongue slips into me, all I can do is moan out before falling forward and swallowing his cock. I suck his cock with the same rhythm as he finger-fucks me. First, with one finger and then with another, my hips rotating every time he flicks my clit with his thumb. I let go of his cock when I'm on the edge of coming. "Right there." I don't even have the words to say what to do, the only thing I can do is ride the wave. His fingers and tongue seem to be everywhere and then I start riding his face. "Travis!" I shout out and I can feel my pussy starting to clench when he stops licking me. "Travis," I moan out as my fingers slip inside myself to push me over the edge.

He reaches out and rips my hand away. Sitting down on the couch, he holds out his hand for me and pulls me toward him. "Ride me," he says and I straddle his hips, holding his cock with one of my hands as I position myself over him, sliding down. My hands go to his hips as I raise myself up, and he tilts his head back. I lean forward and kiss him, my tongue sliding into his mouth. His tongue wrestles mine as I move up and down, his hands coming up to cup my tits. He rolls my nipples between his fingers and all I can do is let go of his lips to moan out. His hands go to my hips as our lips hover over each other. "Harlow." My eyes look into his as I rise and fall on his cock. "I love you," he says the words I've longed to hear for I don't know how long.

I put my hand on his face. "I love you, too." Leaning back down and kissing him, it doesn't take me long before I'm coming all over him. His hands hold my hips as I stop riding him and he thrusts his hips upward. He sits up straight, wrapping a hand around my waist as he lifts both of us and turns me, placing my back on the couch. He puts my legs over his shoulders, pushing himself deeper inside me. He fucks me harder and harder with each thrust, going deeper and deeper. "Travis," I moan out each time he hits my G-spot. "I'm going to."

"I know, baby," he says. "I can feel it." He licks his thumb and pushes down on my clit as he rubs it from side to side. "Fuck, you are so tight," is the last thing he says before I come all over his cock again. He thrusts back into me twice more before he comes right after me.

My legs fall from his shoulders and I close my eyes to get my breathing underway. He falls on top of me and kisses my shoulder before he buries his face in my neck. "I," he pants. "I," he says again and I can't help but laugh. "I have no words."

"One thing we do really well," I tease as I rub his back with one of my hands. "Is sex."

"Yes." He kisses my shoulder again before peeling himself off me. "Communication we can work on. Sex." He shakes his head and pulls himself out of me. "We got that down to perfection." He bends to kiss my stomach before getting up and walking to the bathroom. He comes out a second later. "Your bathroom is empty," he says, shocked. "There is like one roll of toilet paper."

"I don't use that bathroom," I say, standing up. "So I packed it first."

I turn to walk to my bedroom and I can feel him following me and he stops in his tracks. "Holy shit, it's empty."

I look around the room seeing ten boxes packed and labeled. The last week I've pretty much spent all my days in my house unless there was an emergency. "I've been trying to get it all done."

"You really were going to just up and leave and come to me," he says and I put my hands on my hips.

"Were you not doing the same?" I tilt my head to the side and he just puts his hands on his hips. "Exactly," I say. "Don't you get all shy on me."

He laughs and comes to me, pushing me into the bathroom. "Time to take a shower."

I don't even argue with him, and when I finally get out of the shower, the water is ice cold and my hands are pruned up. "I don't have anything for dinner," I inform him, wrapping a towel around myself. He steps out of the shower after me, grabbing his own towel. "I'm sure I can whip something up." I grab a shirt and ignore the way he tries not to laugh. "I cooked last time and it was fine."

"That was not you who cooked it, and you know it." He smirks at me and kisses my shoulder.

"You're lucky I like you." I glare at him, walking

out of the bathroom and going to the kitchen. I open the freezer and cheer when I see that I have a couple of frozen meals that my grandmother made for me. I slip them into the oven and hear him walking out of the room wearing his boxers.

"I found two meals. I don't know what they are but my grandmother made them, so they should be good," I explain, and he wraps his arms around my waist.

"Then I think we are safe." He laughs loud, letting me go and then going to sit down on the chair.

"There is the family barbecue." I look over at him. "Tomorrow for lunch."

I watch his face and see the nerves settle in. "Well, better now than on our wedding day." He laughs nervously and my heart speeds up. In this whole thing I never even thought about what happens next. "Hey," he says and I look up at him. "Later," he tells me. "Tell me who will be there?"

"Pretty much my whole family," I share and he groans and puts his head back.

"Good, so everyone who wants to shoot me in the ass," he says and I can't help but laugh.

"Not everyone." I look over at him. "My grandmother might still like you."

"Good to know." He shakes his head and we spend the night, just us, together.

When I pull up to the house the next day, the number of cars is staggering. "Jesus, it looks like it's doubled since I was here last."

"Lots of kids grew up," I reply, getting out and walking

in front of the car to meet him. He's wearing blue jeans and a white shirt and he looks just as handsome as he did when I first saw him. He slips his hand over mine as we walk toward the back of the house.

"Oh, look, it's the Bobbsey twins," Reed says when we see him. "Did you guys really have to dress the same to get that united-front look?"

Travis laughs and leans down to kiss my head. "I want to make sure everyone knows she's mine."

All Reed does is fake vomit and then yells across the lawn, "Harlow is here and she brought a boy!" All eyes turn to us and he squeezes my hand a little tighter than he should. He slaps Travis on the shoulder. "Welcome back." He snickers and then takes off to find Hazel.

"It's going to be fine," I mumble under my breath. "The first thing we have to do is say hello to my grandparents and then work our way down the family."

"That sounds like a plan," he mumbles back. "I mean, he's older now, so chances are if he shot me, he would miss."

I can't help but laugh as we walk toward my grandparents who are sitting together. "Well, well, well," my grandmother says with her head tilted to the side. "Look at what the cat dragged in."

"Oh, dear," I say, suddenly thinking that maybe this wasn't the brightest idea I've ever had. Perhaps I should have eased into it instead of just jumping into the deepest part of the river.

"Hello," Travis greets from beside me. "Mr. and Mrs. Barnes, good to see you again."

"Is it?" my grandfather inquires, leaning back in his chair. He wears his jeans and button-down checkered shirt with his white cowboy hat that he never goes without. He looks at me, and even though he's got the tough exterior, I can see the lightness in his eyes. There isn't anything he wouldn't do for his family, even accepting Travis after he hurt me. "Heard you got married." He glares at Travis.

Thirty-Eight

Travis

"Hello," I say nervously from beside Harlow. "Mr. and Mrs. Barnes, good to see you again." I nod politely and ignore the need to vomit. My eyes go from her grandmother to her grandfather.

"Is it?" her grandfather, Billy, says. He is the stamp of what a cowboy is. Every single time I've met him he's wore his white cowboy hat and jeans. He also has always scared the shit out of me. "Heard you got married." He glares at me.

"You must have heard wrong," I say, the pit of my stomach sinking.

"I'm a lot of things," he replies, sitting up in his chair. "But hard of hearing isn't one of them." His eyes go even smaller, and the glare would have anyone quaking in their boots.

"Oh, please." I hear laughter from beside him and turn to see Charlotte just shaking her head. "It took me six times to call you for breakfast this morning."

"Dammit, woman," he says, chuckling. "I'm trying to be serious." He leans and kisses her lips. "He was scared." He points at me, and I can't disagree with him.

"Oh, please," Charlotte says, then turns to me. "Welcome back." She smiles big. "I saved you this time. I won't the next."

I nod at them both and pick up my hand that is in Harlow's and kiss her fingers. "There won't be a next time."

"Well, I think there are other people here that are waiting to say hello to us," Harlow reminds me. "Or at least ask him if he's married." She hits me with her hip and tries to hide the smile while I groan.

"We'll see you later," Charlotte says, leaning back in her chair and looking out.

When we get far enough away, I look over my shoulder to see Billy still staring at me. "See, that wasn't so bad," Harlow says as we walk deeper into the yard.

"Easy for you to say, he didn't glare at you," I mumble and then bump into a girl who is running. Her pigtails are lopsided, and she smiles when she sees Harlow.

"Auntie Harlow." She jumps into her arms. "Gabriel is chasing me and telling me that he's going to take my nose." She covers her nose right away, believing he can take her nose.

"Elodie." She says her name, and my eyes widen;

when I saw her last she was just a little thing just learning to walk. "I'll protect you." She looks just like Willow.

She looks at me. "Who are you?"

"This is Travis," Harlow says. As soon as Gabriel comes behind her, he looks over at me and stands there with his chest puffing out. He's a teenager now, and he's definitely gotten bigger.

"My dad called you a ding dong," Elodie says, and Harlow tries not to laugh.

"That's not true," Gabriel says from behind her. "He called him a dipshit."

"Gabriel McIntyre," Harlow says his full name. "Watch that mouth of yours."

"Sorry, Aunt Harlow." He shrugs. "Just passing along the message."

"Well, do it kindly." Harlow kisses Elodie on the cheek and puts her down.

"How kindly do you call someone a dipshit?" Gabriel folds his arms over his chest, and if he was tatted, he would look exactly like his father, Ethan.

"I think it's ding dong," I joke with him, or at least I try to, and he laughs even though I know he really doesn't want to laugh.

"There you are," Quinn says when he gets close to us. "Mom has been looking for you," he says to Elodie, who leans toward him and he takes her in his arms.

"Dad," she says, and he looks down at her. "Is ding dong nicer than dipshit?" His eyes go right away to Gabriel.

"Oh, my," Gabriel says, trying not to laugh while he grabs his neck. "In my defense, I was just repeating what you said about Travis."

"Okay," Harlow interjects. "This is enough." She points at Gabriel. "You need to make sure everyone knows that he's not a dipshit and that he was never married."

She then turns to Quinn. "You need to watch your mouth in front of people before I tell Mom that you are swearing in front of the kids." Quinn just glares at her. "And you." She turns to me. "I'm sorry that this isn't as easy as I thought it would be, but I'm sure the next time will be better."

"One can hope," Quinn says and then Harlow glares at him. "Fine, I'll be nice." She folds her hands over her chest. "Nicer than I am."

"Now"—she looks at me, and all I can do is smile—"time to go see my parents."

"And to think I almost didn't come today," Quinn says. "Let me go first and hand Dad Elodie. He can't shoot him if he has a child in his arms."

I laugh and look around to see none of them laughing with me. "He's joking, right?" I say as Harlow slips her hand in mine and turns to walk away from them.

We stop and talk to a couple more of her cousins, and I do get the glare more often than not, but I know in the end they are being somewhat friendly because of Harlow. Instead of calling me a dick to my face, they are waiting for me to walk away before doing it. "Auntie Harlow." Sofia runs to her, and I stop in my tracks at her beauty.

Harlow's face goes into a huge smile when she sees her, and her arms automatically open for her.

"There is my girl," she says, hugging her, and my heart slowly starts to speed up when I see them together. She is giving all of this up for me. I swallow the lump in my throat. We walk side by side as she talks to Sofia about everything going on in her life in the past two days. We walk through the grass, and I smell the food and look over to see her father, Casey, by the grill with her two uncles, Beau and Jacob.

"Here we go," I mumble to myself and see the three men, all with a beer in one hand and spatulas in the other hand, look up and glare at me.

"Smells good," Harlow says, letting my hand go while she walks over to her father and kisses his cheek. She mumbles something in his ear while she walks over to Beau and Jacob.

I take a deep breath, seeing her smile with them, and then they all look over at me and nod hello. All but Casey; he just brings his bottle to his mouth and takes another pull of his beer. I put my hands in my pockets, knowing that I'm going to have to sit down with him eventually and get it all out. I'm more nervous about that than anything else. Not having his approval will hurt Harlow, and I can't do that to her. No one says anything to me, which is even worse than asking me if I'm married.

"Okay, we are going to go and see Mom," Harlow says, and I nod at the guys and turn around to walk with her.

"I can't eat any of the food," I say, and she laughs.

"I'll take the first bite." She stops walking and stands in front of me, wrapping her arms around my neck. "I'll take one for the team."

"Never." I shake my head and lean down and kiss her lips. The minute I kiss her, everything inside me settles.

"It's going to get better," she assures me, and all I can do is lean down and kiss her neck. I let her go and look over to see her father watching us. I stare at him, nodding, and then looking around to see Olivia with a little baby in her arms. Hazel sits next to her as I look back at Casey to see him still staring at me. I motion with my head to the side, and he just nods at me. "What the hell was that?" Harlow asks.

"That's me facing the music." I take a deep breath. "Go sit with your mom, and if I'm not back in twenty minutes, come find me." I bend to kiss her lips and see that Casey is walking toward the barn.

"Twenty minutes, he can have you dismembered and skinned," she deadpans, and my eyes widen. "I'm kidding." She puts her hand on my chest, and I look down to see that her hand is very bare without a certain ring.

"I love you." I pick up her hand and kiss the finger where a ring should be. A finger that if I wasn't such an idiot would probably have two rings instead of just one.

"I love you more," she says and turns to walk away from me. "Don't let him scare you."

I put my hands on my hips, shaking my head and turning to walk toward the barn. I take a look around to see that most of her cousins are here with their own kids. I step inside the barn and see Casey standing in the middle of the barn. His legs are spread shoulder width apart, and his arms are folded over his chest. I heard a rumor that he trained with the Navy SEALs for fun. "I have to give it to you." He starts talking first. "You got some big-ass balls showing up here." He laughs. "Even more balls by asking to talk to me."

I'm about to say something when I hear someone walking toward us and turn to see that Olivia is coming. "Harlow sent me in to be the peacekeeper," she says, smiling sideways at me. "I came to make sure that you," she tells Casey, "keep your head cool." She wraps her arms around Casey's waist, and I wonder if she is doing that so he doesn't charge at me. "Now, what did I miss?"

"He was telling me that I have big, um." I try to think of the word that is better than balls. "That I have some nerve showing up here, and I was about to say that I had to do it," I share. "Might as well get it all out now." He just glares at me, while Olivia just looks at me. "Before I start or say anything, I just want to say I'm sorry for how I acted."

"You mean when you were a dipshit," he says, and I have no choice but to laugh loud now.

"Casey Barnes," she says between clenched teeth.

"Yeah, when I was a dipshit ding dong," I add in the words Elodie said. "I never, ever wanted to hurt her. I couldn't let her give up her family for me." I take a deep breath in and slowly exhale it. "I know how much she loves her family and that she had a plan and I couldn't be the one who made her change it. Breaking up with her was the single hardest decision I've ever made."

"What about when you asked someone else to marry you?" he says, and I know he's going straight for the jugular with this question, and he is going to get all of the answers.

"When I broke up with Harlow, it took me two years not to have this pain in my chest." I shake my head. "When I met Jennifer, I liked her enough, but it was never like Harlow, and I thought to myself that what I felt for Harlow wasn't as big as I remembered. I kept telling myself that it was all in my head. But one look at her again, and it's like everything I was lying to myself about was right in front of my face." I run my hand through my hair. "I don't even think I would have been able to marry her that day. I knew from the moment I saw Harlow that I was making a mistake." I swallow. "I want to marry her." Olivia gasps, but I don't stop. "I know in my heart that she is the only one for me. I let her go four years ago, and now that I have her back, I'm not letting her go. You can hate me." I shrug. "For the rest of my life. I won't give her up for it. I'll take whatever it is you have for me. I was leaving my practice," I tell them both and they both look at me shocked. "I couldn't do the long-distance thing and I've already lost so much time I just couldn't do it. So I was going to move here and be with her. I can't live without her. I can't breathe without her."

"Oh, Travis," Olivia whispers, wiping the tear from the corner of her eye.

"You don't get it," Casey says, his voice softer. "You

won't get it until you have a child of your own. But we watched her for the last four years skid through life. She was here with us, but the light in her eyes was gone. She would laugh and smile, but you could see that it was just a front. It's the single hardest thing watching your kid not living life. She had everything she ever dreamed of, yet she was missing something." He shakes his head. "Then a month ago, she goes to your wedding, and the minute she came back, and I mean the second I saw her, that light was back. Her shoulders didn't fall forward anymore. Her eyes would light up when she smiled. She was back, at least a little bit of her was, and then her plans would change, and you could see the dim come back." My chest literally feels like an elephant has just decided to sit on it. "She came to me and asked me to help her, and as her father, I would help her do whatever the hell she wanted, even if it was to go back to you. Even though I don't think you deserve her."

"Let's be honest for one more second," Olivia sniffles. "He would think no one was good enough for her."

I can't help but laugh at her. "He isn't wrong," I say. "I don't know how I got as lucky as I did to get her not to only fall in love with me once but twice. I'm the luckiest man in the world and I'm going to spend the rest of my life making sure that she knows how lucky I am." I look down at my feet. "I know that you don't believe me and I've broken your trust. I know that I won't have your blessing right now, but I hope in time I will get it."

"Does that mean that if we don't give you our blessing, you won't ask her to marry you?" Casey says.

"As much as it hurts me to say this." I swallow, knowing that if he didn't want to shoot me before, he might want to now. "I'm going to ask her to marry me regardless of your blessing."

"Well, then," he says, looking at his wife, then looking at me. "Since you put it like that. I'll put it like this. If you hurt her again." He's about to say something when Olivia puts her hand in front of his mouth.

"I'll hand you the gun myself," I declare, and he throws his head back and laughs loud.

Thirty-Nine

Harlow

"Travis!" Shelby yells his name. "She's here," I hear when I get out of the car and look over at my parents parking behind me.

"Hey," I greet, putting my hand over my eyes to see her and smiling when Travis comes out of the house. He walks down the steps at the same time that my parents get out of the truck, and my brothers pull up behind them in another truck.

"You're here," he says. When he gets close enough, he puts his hands on my face and bends to kiss me. "Hi," he adds between kisses.

"Romeo," Clarabella says from behind us. "You want to get out of the way so we can get the things unpacked."

"Yeah, that sounds good," Reed says, getting out of

the truck. "You go and direct us and we will bring out the boxes."

"Um, Harlow," Presley says. "Besides two hot married brothers, do you perhaps have any available cousins?"

I shake my head and laugh as I walk up the steps to what my new home will be. This past week has been bittersweet. I've said goodbye to my family, and even though I said I wasn't saying goodbye, I got sad thinking that I wouldn't see them every day. We walk into the house, and I look around, seeing it almost empty.

"Oh my God," my mother says from behind me. "Um, honey." She looks over at Travis, then around the bare room. "Did you live here?" she asks, stepping in just as shocked as I am.

"He did," Clarabella shares. "Trust me, it's better now than before." My mother looks at him and then at me with tears in her eyes.

"What the hell?" Quinn says, carrying in two boxes. "Were you robbed?"

"As if anyone wanted his stuff," Shelby says, laughing.

"I didn't know how you felt about my stuff," Travis says. "So I got rid of it, and tomorrow we can go and pick out all new stuff."

"Oh my God," my father says when he hears my mother squeal.

"Great, now you've done it," I mumble to Travis when my mother rushes over to us.

"I'll do it," she says, looking around, taking out her phone. "Leave it to us. It'll be our present to you."

"You did it now," Reed says from behind Quinn.

"You've woken the beast."

"You." My mother points at Reed. "Who did your house?"

"Mom, we had to baby-proof glass tables," he says, dropping the box. "And everything was white."

"It was neutral, and it's fine," she hisses out and then looks at my father. "You see what you did. You did this." She puts her hands on her hips. "You turned them like this."

"Me?" My father points at himself. "How did this become about me? All I'm doing is moving my only daughter six hours away from me."

Now Quinn and Reed both groan out. "Here we go," Reed grumbles. "Can we unload the truck before it gets dark out, because I have to get back to the kids."

It takes them two hours to unload all the boxes, and when I turn around, there are boxes everywhere that furniture should be. I hug my parents and brothers and fight back the tears, telling them I'm going to go and see them next week. When they finally drive away from me, I turn and bury my face in Travis's chest. "Don't cry." He rubs my back, and I hear a car pull up in the driveway. I turn and see his mother getting out of the car. "I brought food," she says, walking to the trunk and taking out two takeout bags. "I figured you guys would be hungry."

"Great," Shelby says. "Shall I grab pillows and we can sit on the floor and have a picnic?"

"We can sit in the kitchen. There are stools there," Travis says and glares at Shelby.

"We'll make do," I say, wrapping my arms around his

waist. "Also, I wouldn't be surprised if we come home tomorrow and the house is fully furnished." I walk into the house and wonder if I should tackle the boxes today or start fresh tomorrow.

"Tomorrow," Travis says, bending to kiss my neck, and I shake my head and laugh that he knew what I was thinking.

"I'm starving, and there are only two stools," Clarabella says, grabbing a bag from her mother. "What do we have here?" She starts taking out the containers. "Pasta." She puts it on the counter. "Chicken." She takes another one out. "Rice, veggies, garlic mashed potatoes, grilled chicken, and sliders."

"I'll go get some chairs in the garage," Travis says, kissing my neck and walking to get the chairs.

"There are paper plates in this one," Shelby says, grabbing them and putting them on the counter.

"Does this count toward our weekly family dinner?" Presley asks, opening the containers for us to help ourselves. "I vote yes."

"This is a celebratory dinner," his mom says, smiling at me. She comes over and gives me a hug. "We are so happy you are here."

"I'm happy to be here." I smile at her, grabbing a plate and filling it.

"I don't think we've ever had a meal here," Clarabella says, getting on a stool.

"We had breakfast here the day of his wedding," Presley reminds her, and then her eyes widen as she turns to me. "I'm sorry."

I chuckle. "I'm fine with it." I shrug. "He's the one who gets reminded of it." I grab a piece of carrot. "Weekly."

"We had dinner here on his birthday," his mom says. "Last year."

I look down at my food, and I have this sudden feeling of sorrow that washes over me. "Yes, and he had the lemon cake," Clarabella says, moaning. "That was the best cake I've had in my life."

"I don't know about you guys," Presley states, and I look up at her. "But I'm happy that you are here."

"Thank you," I say.

"It's not just because you are nicer," Clarabella says. "And easier to talk to." I look at them, and then his mother clears her throat. "What? You can't tell me you don't see a difference in him."

"There is a huge difference," his mother shares. "It's night and day. Every time I would invite him for dinner, he would just say yeah and come alone. Now I ask him about dinner, and he has to check with you."

The talking stops when he comes into the room with two chairs. "That's all I found."

"That's okay. I can stand," I say and he comes over and grabs a plate, coming to stand next to me when we eat. The talking is free around the table, and when he helps clean up, his mother sends him to the store to get milk for our coffee tomorrow. Clarabella and Shelby also take off with Presley following them.

"Are you okay?" His mother looks at me, and I smile. "It's okay to miss home."

"I miss home," I admit. "But I'm happier that I'm

here." I look around the empty house, and I can see myself having coffee every single morning. But more importantly, I can see us building our lives here.

"Are you going to be okay living here in this house?" she asks, and I see her nervously wringing her hands. "He was engaged."

"Yes," I confirm. "But she didn't live here."

"That she didn't," she says. "She barely came here. I think she did once, and then she was going to move in when they got married." She looks down at her hands and then up again. "I didn't think I'd ever see him happy again." She blinks away the tears that are welling up in her eyes. "Every time I would ask him if he was okay, he would bark at me that he was fine, but I knew he wasn't."

"I know how that feels. He wasn't the only one not happy."

"When he told me he was getting married, I knew it was a mistake. God, I felt it in my bones. I tried so hard to be supportive, but then every time the wedding discussion came up, he just said I don't care, just do whatever. Who does that?" She shakes her head. "I bet you everything that I have if I ask him about your wedding, he's going to have a list of things that he wants done for you."

I can't help but smile. "I don't know Jennifer," I say. "And I don't ask him any questions about it because well, it's in the past, but I'm really, really happy that I got that invitation in the mail."

She looks at me, and I see her eyes twinkle. "I'm really, really glad I mailed it to you." She winks at me, and I gasp. "I knew that if he saw you, it would change his mind."

"What if I didn't come?" I ask her.

"I would have had to fake a heart attack," she says, getting up. "Now I'm going to go home and celebrate having my son back." She stops next to me. "And getting a new daughter."

I hug her, and then she walks out of the house, leaving me all alone. Walking over to the fridge, I open it to put the leftovers in it and spot a new jug of milk. "Oh, well played," I say to the empty room. "Well freaking played."

I finish cleaning the kitchen when I hear his car come back. He walks in with two jugs of milk. "Did everyone leave?" he asks, and I nod my head at him. He pulls open the fridge and then spots the milk. "She played me."

"That she did." I laugh and lean against the counter. "That she did."

"What did she tell you?" he asks when he leans against his side of the counter.

"None of your business," I scoff at him. "I didn't ask you what happened with my parents."

"I was too busy celebrating the fact I didn't get shot," he jokes, then looks at me. "I have to talk to you about something."

"What?" I ask nervously, standing straight up.

"Well, I was talking to my partners today," he starts saying. "And we were discussing bringing another vet in." My eyebrows shoot up.

"Just like that, out of the blue." I fold my arms over my chest, looking at him and seeing that he's lying.

"I mean, I did mention to them that you were moving in with me after I took back the offer for them to buy me out," he confesses, and I shake my head. "And I did mention that you were way better than me." He comes to me and pulls me to him. "And I also said you would only do it if we would be able to have the same shifts."

"I have no words," I say.

"Good, you start in two weeks." He kisses my lips. "Now, can we go and celebrate you moving in with me?" He picks me up and then stops when he gets to the stairs. "Shit," he says. "We don't have a bed."

"What do you mean you don't have a bed?" I ask, shocked.

"I assumed that you were bringing yours," he says, and I wiggle down.

"Why the hell did you assume that?" I shriek at him.

"You." He points at me. "You always said how much you love your bed, so I assumed you would bring it with you."

"Did I once say, hey, I'm bringing my bed?" I yell at him. "Not once."

"Let's go," he says, grabbing my hand and pulling me out of the house. He locks the door, and I don't even ask him questions. Assuming that we'll be going to a hotel and I'm suddenly so pissed at him. I sit in the car stewing mad at his idiotness when I see us pull up to the place where we spent his wedding night.

"What the hell are we doing here?" I ask, looking over at him. "Did you even get a reservation?"

"Don't need one." He opens the door and steps out,

and before I have a chance to open my own door, he's there, pulling it open for me to step out.

"I don't think you can just show up when you want to," I grumble when I get out of the car, and he fishes keys out of his glove box. I look around, seeing that it's as dark as it was that night, if not darker, since there are no lights on in the house. "I think we are trespassing."

He closes the box and then the car door. "No trespassing," he says before walking up the steps. "This is my house." I look at him with my mouth hanging open. "Bought it four years ago when I moved back." He unlocks the door. "It reminded me of you."

"You bought this house?" I point at the house. "Because it reminded you of me, and you were going to spend your wedding night in it?" I glare at him.

"That was never going to happen," he tells me. "She didn't even know about this house. The only ones who knew about it were my sisters and my mother." He pushes open the door.

"I have no words for you, Travis," I say, both shocked and lovestruck.

"I have three words for you," he says. "Welcome home, Harlow."

Fourty

Travis

"Would you stop calling me?" I hiss into the phone when I pick it up. Looking over my shoulder, I see if Harlow is there. It's a bit past noon, and I know she'll be up any minute now.

"I'm only calling you because we want to let you know that it's done and to know what time you'll be coming," Shelby hisses back at me, and I look over my shoulder to see Harlow coming down the stairs dressed in one of my shirts.

"Later," I whisper into the phone. "Just be ready." I hang up, putting the phone facedown on the counter. "Morning," I greet, and she walks to me with one eye still closed.

"I called you," she says with a groggy voice. "Like

three times." She wraps her arms around my waist. "Who were you on the phone with?"

"My mom," I lie to her and avoid looking at her. "Do you want coffee?"

"Does a bear shit in the woods?" She puts her head back, and I look down at her face and she gives me a shy smile. "I can't believe it's already noon."

"Go sit on the couch. I'll bring you coffee," I say and she walks into the adjoining living room. She was not kidding when she said that her mother would have things delivered the next day. By the time we got back from the cabin the next morning and started unpacking, the truck showed up. Not only that, Olivia had hired people to come and stage the house along with unpack the boxes. I didn't even know what to think but in a matter of four hours the house looked like it was out of a magazine, and for the first time it felt like a home.

I make the coffee while she gets on the couch and reaches for one of the throw cushions. It's been a month that we've been living with each other, and it's better than even I could imagine. She started at the clinic two weeks ago, and I was not wrong. She is way better than I will probably ever be. She goes through two patients while I'm still with one. "How did you sleep?" I grab the cups of coffee and walk toward her.

"Better if I woke up with you beside me and not a cold spot." She extends her hand to grab one of the coffee cups from me. She puts both hands on it, and just like every other time, she smells it before she takes a sip. "So good." She puts her legs on mine when I sit next to her.

"It's our first day off." She puts her elbow on the back of the couch, leaning her head on it. "What do you have planned?"

I swallow down and try to be cool, but the whole time, my mouth is suddenly dry, and I feel that I'm going to have word vomit. "I have to go and see something at the cabin. Then we can do whatever you like."

"I'd love to go to the farmers market," she says. "Someone said that the flowers are amazing."

"We can get dressed and go," I say, taking a sip of my coffee. My whole body is one big nerve. When she gets up and walks up the steps, I try to calm myself down.

"I have to shower," she says over her shoulder. "Care to join me?" She wiggles her ass just a touch as she walks up the steps, and she does not have to ask me twice. I leave my hot coffee on the table and run up the stairs two at a time, grabbing her from around her waist and carrying her to the shower.

"Is it hot out?" She sticks her head out of the walk-in closet naked. Her hair is in a white towel on the top of her head. "Is it a shorts or pants kind of day?"

"I think it's a shorts kind of day," I say, and she nods and goes back into the closet. It takes her thirty minutes to finish getting ready.

I'm texting Shelby when I hear her coming down the stairs and look over at her. She is wearing a pair of green linen shorts tied at the waist with the same-colored belt. Her white spaghetti strap shirt hangs perfectly and is tucked in with three brown buttons. She has never looked more beautiful; it's crazy, but it's true. Her hair hangs low over her shoulder, and I push it aside to bend and kiss her shoulder. "Are you ready?" I ask her, and she grabs her phone, and we walk out. I send Shelby a quick text that I'm leaving the house.

The sun is shining high in the sky without a cloud in sight. I open the car door for her, and she's busy on her phone. "Who are you texting?"

"Everyone," she says, putting on her sunglasses. "And no one is answering me."

"Maybe they are busy." I put the car in drive and make the thirty-minute ride to the cabin. My heart hammers so hard in my chest, I swear she is going to hear it any minute. My hands grip the wheel so tight my knuckles are white.

When we pull up to the cabin, I'm happy she doesn't see the surprise I had made for her. Her face is buried in her phone as she gets frustrated that no one is answering her. "How is everyone off their phones?" she huffs, walking up the steps, and I open the door.

She stops when she sees the rose petals at her feet. "What the hell is this?" she asks, looking around seeing balloons everywhere. She has a shocked expression on her face. "This looks like." She takes two more steps in. "The night of your wedding."

"Almost." Smiling, I grab her hand and pull her up the stairs toward the bed.

"Well, this is where we ended up." She laughs and gasps when she sees the MR. & MRS. that were not here the last time we came here. She looks at me. "What is going on?"

"Come this way." I pull her and walk to the door that leads to the balcony. Stepping out, I see the setup exactly how it was the first time I brought her here. The picnic basket sits on the cover and a bottle of white wine sits beside it.

"What is going on?" She looks around and puts her hands to her mouth.

"This is me doing what I should have done a long time ago," I say, as I pull her to stand in the middle of the blanket. She looks at me with tears in her eyes as she laughs and a sob comes out of her. She places her hand in front of her mouth to stop it but it comes out anyway. "Harlow," I say, my voice trembling as much as her hand in mine. "The first day I met you, something happened," I start to say and sniff my own tears back. "You literally knocked me off my feet." I smile at her as she wipes the tears away from the corner of her eyes. "And then by some fucking miracle we started hanging out. That night when I walked you home from the bar, the only thing running through my head was just kiss her." She puts her hand on my cheek now, her thumb rubbing back and forth. "We have so many memories together. But the one that holds a special place in my heart is right here. Right in this spot." I swallow down the lump in my throat. "You might not recognize this place. But it's the place I first told you I loved you," I say and she gasps and looks around. "The time when you promised me to be here on the best day of my life. The whole time I pictured this very minute." I smile at her and get down on one knee in front of her and her hands go to her mouth as she cries and flips her head down. "When I came back home, I bought this land and built this cabin, knowing that it was the only thing I had of you left. Harlow, four years ago I let you go and it was the single worst mistake of my life. But fate had other plans and the universe brought you back to me. I don't know what I did to deserve you, and I promise you that I will spend the rest of my life showing you how much I love you." I grab the red square box that has been weighing in my pocket for the last month. I open it and turn to show her. "Harlow Barnes, will you marry me and make me the happiest man in the world?"

"Oh my God," she gasps. "Is that my mother's ring?"

"It is," I confirm. "I asked them for your hand in marriage at the barbecue the first time," I say, and her shoulders shake. "It was a lot more intense than that, but your mother called me the day after and asked to see me. She told me it would be her honor to have you wear her ring." I look down at the ring. "If you don't like it, we can get you another one."

"I love it."

"So is that a yes?" I smile up at her, my whole body crawling out of my skin.

"There isn't any other answer," she tells me as she comes to me and grabs my face in her hands. "By the way, this is the last time you propose to anyone." She laughs with her lips on mine.

"Well, considering I never proposed the first time, it seems fitting." I take the ring out of the box. She holds her hand out for me, and I slide the ring on her finger. "I love you." I grab her around her waist and turn her in a circle, and here, right where she promised to be the best day of my life, she fulfills her promise to me.

Forty-One

Harlow

He wraps his arms around my waist and spins me in a circle as his lips fall to mine. "I love you," I vow between laughter and tears, my hand on his face. "I can't even," I say when he puts me down. I look down at the ring that used to sit on my mother's hand. I shake my head, not sure I'm actually awake, or maybe this is a dream. "I'm," I start to say and just come up speechless, my eyes never leaving the ring. "I can't." I look up at Travis. "My mother gave you this ring?" I ask, not even able to comprehend, and he nods his head. "For as long as I can remember, my father would buy her jewelry, and the one thing she never ever took off was this ring."

"Well, she wanted you to have it, and I didn't really want to take it, but then she said when she dies." And as soon as he says that, I groan out because of course my mother would threaten with death. "Yeah, well, it's good to know that my mother isn't the only one who uses that excuse."

"There is just." I shake my head. "There are so many questions I have."

"Of course, you do," he says, leaning down and kissing my neck. The phone buzzes in his pocket. "Ask away but know that my sisters found out I was doing this today, and well, if I don't answer them or go see them, they will come here."

I laugh, and I have to say I don't think I've ever been this happy in my whole life. Not when we were together, not when we got back together, not any other time. "Well, one, is this really the place where." I look around trying to find a spot that reminds me of that time.

"It is," he says, looking around also. "My parents own the land, and well, when we broke up."

"When you dumped me," I correct him, and he just glares at me. "Go on."

"I used to come and sit here by myself and then I just asked my mother if I could build a house here, so I did," he explains, looking around. "It was my escape from the world and the only place that was mine."

"But you were going to bring Jennifer here." I know I shouldn't care. I know that it's in the past, but well, I'm a girl and that's the shit we do.

"I was never going to bring her here," he assures me, shaking his head, and I don't know why but I feel suddenly happier knowing that this is just ours, which is stupid. "My sisters did all that. I booked us a room at the hotel."

"But," I start to say and his phone buzzes again. He takes out his phone, turning it and making me see it's his mom. "Let's go."

"Are you sure?" he says to me. "We didn't." He motions with his head toward the bed and I gasp.

"You think I'm going to have sex with you knowing your sisters and mother are waiting for us?" I shake my head. "And then show up all rosy cheeks and then she knows for sure we had sex."

I walk into the house. "She knows we have sex," he tells me from behind me. "But we can come back here after, then."

"Deal," I agree, looking around at all the decorations. "It's so pretty, much prettier than it was the last time." I laugh.

"We were also drunk," he fills in and I slip my hand in his as we walk out of the house. "I can't tell you how free I feel," he says to me. "That box was pretty fucking heavy in my pocket for the last month." I stop midstep

"You had this for the last month?" I gasp, shocked. "But," I start to say and he comes back over to me and grabs my face in his hands.

His eyes are so crystal green and light, his thumbs rub my cheeks. "It was the hardest secret I had to keep. Every single night I was like, just do it, ask her. But then I wanted to do it right. It had to be right."

I put my hands on his hips. "It was perfect," I whisper right before his lips fall on mine. I hear his phone beep again and I can't help but laugh loud when he groans.

"I'm going to block them all," he promises, walking to the car and opening the door for me. "As soon as we get there. Block all of them." He looks at me when I sit in the car. "You can help me since I've never blocked anyone in my life."

"Don't ruin this day for me." I glare at him. "You broke up with me and was engaged to another woman."

"Touché." He laughs, closing the door and walking around the car. I grab my phone and call my mother, wanting to share the news with her.

She answers after three rings and I can hear commotion in the background. "Hello!" she shouts out.

"Mom," I say, looking down at the ring on my finger. "I have some news."

"Oh, Harlow," she pants. "You caught me at a bad time. I'm setting up something with your father. Can I call you back?"

I look down at the phone when she disconnects without telling me she loves me. "What in the hell is going on down there?" I shake my head and look around to see that we are at the reception area.

"My sisters are setting up for a wedding tomorrow," he says and I open the door, getting out.

"I have to say." I wait for him to come over to my side and slide my hand into his. "I expected your mother to rush the car." He laughs and shakes his head while we walk up the steps.

"She must be busy," he says, opening the door for me and I step in. The sound of people shouting scares me and it takes me a couple of seconds to wonder what is going on.

My parents are there in the front with his family and behind them is everyone from my family, and I mean everyone. I put my hand in front of my mouth and sob out when I see them. "What is this?" I ask, but I don't have a chance to answer him because my mother comes to me.

"You didn't think that you would get engaged and we not be here," she accuses with tears rolling down her cheeks. "Congratulations, sweetheart," she says between tears, taking me in her arms. I feel my father put his arms around us and I look up at him, and all he can do is smile at me.

My head spins around and around as everyone comes to me and congratulates me. My grandfather kisses the top of my head, just like he always does, while my grandmother dabs her eyes. "I can't believe everyone is here," I say, looking over at Travis who is watching with a huge smile on his face. "I can't believe you did all this."

He holds up his hand. "Are you kidding me?" Shelby says, coming to give me a hug. "He was like groomzilla."

"I was not," he hisses and Clarabella looks at him and folds her arms.

"I refuse to even help you get married," she tells him. "Sorry, I just can't. He called us fifteen times a day." She shakes her head. "A day," she repeats.

"I wanted it to be perfect," he says.

"Well, it wouldn't be perfect without us," I hear someone say and turn to see all our of college friends. I bend, laughing and clapping my hands, and I can't help the laughter that comes out of me.

"Oh my God," I say when Rachel comes over to me and hugs me. "I can't believe you guys are here."

"He didn't really give us a choice," Lydia replies and I just look at Travis.

"It wouldn't be the same without these assholes," he states and Bennett comes over and hugs him.

"Congrats, buddy," he says and then comes over to me. "If you want, we can go behind the bar after and have another race." The laughter comes out of me right away when everyone moves away from us, going to their places and I finally see all the decorations that they put up. There are round tables everywhere with white linen tablecloths and small light pink rose bouquets are in the middle of the tables. White sheer sheets are hanging from the ceilings, going from beam to beam with little tea lights, making it magical.

"This is so perfect," I say, looking around.

"We have a dress for you to change into," Presley says. "Courtesy of your mother."

"I would expect nothing less." I chuckle and see my mother coming toward us.

"Are you ready to change?" she asks and I nod my head, walking to the back of the room where the changing rooms are.

I step in and I try to quiet my brain that is yelling at me. I sit down in the chair and look around at the beautiful blush pink dress that my mother picked out for me. "What's wrong?" Travis notices my change of mood right away.

"Um." I look around the room at my mother, who stands there with Shelby, Clarabella, and Presley. "Everyone is here, right?" I ask her and she looks at me strangely. "I think I said hello to everyone but it was a bit of a shock, so I'm not sure anymore."

"Everyone is here," my mother says and then I turn to Travis.

"If this is too much, we can stay in our clothes and just pretend it's a barbecue," he says and his eyes are clouded over a touch as worry covers his face.

"I was thinking," I say and put my hand on my stomach. "What if we got married?"

"Well, that's the plan," he announces to me with a smile.

"No, I mean now," I say, looking at everyone in the room. "Everyone we love is in that room, so why not just get married now?" I look at Travis, who doesn't say anything. "I mean, unless this is too much for you?" My stomach sinks when he doesn't say anything and then a smile just breaks out on his face.

"I bet your father that this would happen. I owe him a hundred dollars."

"What?" I ask, shocked.

"Your father called this," my mother says, grabbing me by the hand and pulling me out of the room and down toward another room. Bride is written in the middle of the door. "You." She points at Travis. "You can't come in here."

"I have already seen everything," Travis admits and

my mother glares at him.

"We told him not to," Clarabella says from behind me and now I turn. "He's the worst. Like, the absolute worst." She looks at Travis. "The worst."

My mother opens the door and there in the middle of the room is a mannequin with my wedding dress on it. "We have five other dresses," my mother says. "But this one."

I walk over to it and pick up the sheer sleeves, seeing that there are embroidered flowers all the way up to the shoulders. The embroidered flowers are all over the dress as it hugs the mannequin, and then kicks off at the knee with tulle and then the edge of the bottom has big embroidered flowers. My hand touches the fabric and the tears come to my eyes. "This is," I start to say. "It's beautiful." My mother doesn't say anything; instead, all she does is wipe away the tear that is coming out of the corner of her eye.

"We took a little piece of my dress," she tells me. "And then there is a little bit of Grandma's." She picks up the sleeves and I see that some of the flowers are beige but you can't even tell.

"But how did you?" I ask her and she tilts her head to the side like, are you even going to ask me that. "You probably had this done the day he asked you if he can marry me."

She laughs. "Just about."

"Okay," I declare, looking around the room at everyone. "Let's get married."

"She's serious," Shelby says, her eyes going big.

"You're serious."

"As serious as flies on shit," I confirm, and my mother groans as everyone laughs.

"Seriously, that's the best you can do?"

"What do you say?" I look over at Travis. "Want to be my husband?" He walks to me, standing in front and looking down into my eyes.

This man who I fell in love with, who then broke my heart and then just like that, mended it back together again. The man who every fairy tale is made of. The man who makes my stomach flutter. The man who makes me smile and frown. The man who I know I will love for the rest of my life. The man who I want to have babies with and I want to sit on the front porch with, holding his hand forever. The man who is my everything. "There is nothing else I'd rather do than make you my wife." He kisses me softly.

"Then it's settled," I say, looking at his sisters. "We're getting married."

Epilogue One

Travis

Ten months later

"So, when the doctor said to slow down." I look over at Harlow, who has her back to me as she writes down something in the chart. "You thought that would mean spending twelve hours on your feet?"

I put my hands on my hips as she turns around, and I see the roundness of her stomach. "Well, one." She holds up her finger. "I was sitting most of the day." She rubs her stomach, and I can't put into words what it feels like to be married to her. Every fucking day, I thank the universe for giving her back to me. And now that she's carrying our baby, I couldn't love her more. I mean, every day, I love her more and more. "And two." She glares, and all

I want to do is sit on the couch with her and rub her feet. "I'm fine. Besides, I have two weeks left, and I'll be on maternity leave for at least three months," she says, and I know that she'll get itchy about coming back after two months.

"Okay, but I think that you are pushing it just a touch." I try to reason with her, but I know, in the end, she's going to do what she wants to do. Just like the so-called engagement party that turned into a wedding. It was the best night of my life, watching her walk down the aisle with her parents beside her. I have never felt calmer and surer about anything in my life.

"Did you come in here to argue with me, or did you bring me a snack?" She cocks her hip and then stands straight again, and I see her face trying to hide something.

"What just happened?" I ask her as she rubs her belly.

"What's wrong is the whole day if I moved too much, I would get this pain in my lower back. Your child"—she points at her belly—"is being difficult."

I walk to her and put my hands on her stomach and squat down, kissing her stomach. "Hey, love bug," I say to her stomach. "Can you go easy on Mom?"

"I'm telling you it's a boy." She looks down at me. "It has to be."

"Or it could be a stubborn girl, just like her momma," I tease, getting up and kissing her lips.

When we found out we were pregnant, the doctor asked us if we wanted to know the sex, and Harlow was adamant about not knowing.

"Are there two arms and two legs? Does the baby

look healthy? That's all that matters."

"Ouch," she says and winces and then holds her stomach. "That was a sharp one. Kid must be on my nerve or something."

I put my hand on her stomach, and it's rock hard. "How long have you been having these pains, Harlow?"

She avoids my eyes. "I don't know. It's not like I was timing them," she huffs and then finally looks at me. "I might have maybe," she starts to say. "Perhaps." She rolls her eyes. "Probably did too much today." I'm about to say something when her eyes widen, and then I look down to see her scrubs wet. "Oh my God," she says and looks down also. "Oh my God."

"Is that pee?" I ask her, my whole body going on alert. "It's okay if it's pee."

"It's not pee," she states, her face going white. "At least I don't think it's pee," she says, and then I hear the water splash onto the floor. "Not pee."

"Are you sure?" I ask her, my heart starting to beat even faster while I try to keep calm.

"Are you freaking kidding me right now?" she hisses at me and then winces as she holds her stomach. "You think I pee rivers," she says the rest through clenched teeth.

"Okay, one." I hold up my hand as she hisses and pants. "That's, I'm pretty sure, a contraction."

She waits until the pain passes. "You really are like Einstein." She takes one step and then almost falls and I swear to God my life flashes before my eyes. "I'm fine."

"Don't freaking move." I point at her and then get my

phone out.

"Who the hell are you calling right now, Travis?" She tries to talk normally, but I can tell she's having another contraction.

"I'm starting the phone chain," I declare. "Your father just started to like me."

"He liked you a bit after we got married." She smiles through the pain, trying to be strong. "Then you knocked me up."

"Hey, it's me," I say when Casey answers the phone. "It's happening."

"What do you mean it's happening?" he asks, and I can hear him running. "It's happening!" he screams, and I hear what I think is Olivia. "Where are you, at the hospital?"

"No, her water just broke," I say, and he hisses out.

"And the first thing you did was call me?" he shrieks. "Get my daughter to the hospital. We are going to be there within twenty minutes." He hangs up, and I look at the phone.

"How are they going to be here in twenty minutes?" I ask, and she has another contraction.

"You think they wouldn't rent a house here?" she replies, shaking her head. "And I'm not going to pressure you or anything, but I think we need to get to the hospital."

I spring into action and go to her, picking her up. "Call my mother," I say as I carry her out.

Her hand is on her stomach, and I panic when she looks at me and says, "I don't feel well."

"Should we call an ambulance?" I ask her, even though I'm still putting her in the car.

"It will be about ten minutes, and I can have you there," I say, and she nods.

"Travis," she says. "You have to hurry."

I rush to my side, and I make it to the hospital in under six minutes, the drive a blur. I know that I honked so many times at one point I just kept my hand on it. I double-park, running in to get a wheelchair when I hear her yelling. "Travis!" She calls my name and I rush back to her. "I feel so much pressure."

"Jesus Christ," I say as the security guard helps me get her in the chair, the whole time she's yelling about it burning.

He radios someone inside and then looks at me. "Someone will be waiting for you at the sixth floor."

I rush inside as she puts her head back and places her hands on her stomach, crying out in pain. "It hurts." I feel like I'm in a daze as I speed down the white hallway and find the elevator waiting for us with another security guard. I press six, and it takes us what feels like an eternity to get to the sixth floor, and two nurses are there waiting for us.

They wheel her into the room, asking her questions. "How far apart are the contractions? When did your water break? Did you lose a mucus plug?" And all I can do is stand here in shock as my fierce wife breaks down and cries in pain.

They get her on the bed, and when they cut the scrubs off her, all I see is blood, and I'm about to lose my shit when the doctor waltzes in like nothing. "She's crowning," one of the nurses tells me and then smiles at me. "Come and help her." I walk to the side of the bed, afraid to touch anything or hurt her.

"Harlow," I say to her as another contraction rips through her.

"Breathe," I coach just like they taught me in the Lamaze class. "Look at me," I urge softly. "Breathe." She nods at me, and I can see her holding her breath and in fact not breathing.

"Okay, we need to get her an IV," the nurse says when the contraction finishes, and she looks at Harlow. "Let's get you ready to meet your baby." She nods her head and has enough time to take off her top and bra before another contraction comes.

"Okay," the doctor says. "Next one, why don't you try to push?"

"But I need drugs," Harlow announces, and the doctor laughs and then one look at Harlow, and he stops.

"It's way too late for that," he explains, and she puts her head back and sobs.

I hold her hand and push her hair from her face, my stomach in my throat as I worry for both of them. "You can do this," I reassure her, and she just shakes her head.

"My mom," she cries. "I want my mom."

"What's her name and number?" the nurse asks, walking around and grabbing the phone. We give her Olivia's number, and then we hear her talking. "Hi, this is Lara. I'm a nurse for labor and delivery. We have Harlow, and she was wondering if you were close." She listens to Olivia. "We'll send someone to get you." She puts the phone down and pages someone else, and I feel so helpless and out of sorts.

Two minutes later, Olivia comes into the room. "Mom," Harlow cries, and Olivia rushes to her bedside. "It's going to be okay," she comforts, and then she looks at me. "Travis is here. You're going to be fine."

"I want drugs," she says, moaning as a contraction is coming.

"Okay, I want you to push," the doctor says and starts to count. I hold her hand in mine as I count with her. She is a warrior, and four pushes later, the sound of crying fills the room. The doctor places the baby on Harlow's chest, and all she can do is sob out. The tears run down my face and Olivia's. "We have a boy," the doctor says, and all I can do is lean down to kiss Harlow's head and look at our baby boy.

"It's a boy," she says, kissing him. "He's so beautiful."

"You're beautiful," I say as this overwhelming feeling comes through me. It's a feeling that fills every vein in your body. It's a feeling that you will never forget. It's a feeling of a love so pure that nothing could ever be compared to it. "Thank you," I say to her, kissing her lips. "For being mine."

Epilogue Two
Harlow

Six months later

"What is all this fussing about?" I walk into the room and see Leo's feet and hands moving up and down as he cries. He stops crying for a second, and then when he sees me, he starts again. His eyes close as two big tears come out, and I have to laugh while I scoop him in my arms and kiss his chubby cheeks. "Now now," I soothe, rubbing his back as he sighs out in contentment, the tears now a thing of the past. "Did Daddy just put you down in the crib and expect for you to fall asleep on your own?" I ask while I walk over to the rocking chair. "The nerve of him," I say as I pull down my top and offer him my breast. He moves his mouth back and forth before finding my nipple and doing a huge deep sigh. "There you go."

"In my defense," Travis says, and I look up to see him leaning against the doorframe, his legs crossed at his ankles. His gray shorts hang low on his hips, and he's even hotter now that he's my husband. "He took a bottle not even thirty minutes ago and was sleeping when I left him." Everything about him turns me on, and I mean everything. I thought having a baby would slow down our sex drive, but it just made us crave each other more. That and the fact we have to make every second count. I can't tell you all the times that we had to put it on pause because Leo decided that he was done napping or just being quiet.

I smile at him and look down to see that Leo's eyes are getting heavier and heavier as he falls asleep. "Well, he needed a snack, then."

"Or you just can't hear him cry?" He chuckles and stands as he drags his hand through his hair that is still wet from the shower I left him in not too long ago.

My nipple slips out of Leo's mouth, and I pull my shirt back up, getting up and placing him back down in the middle of the crib. "Sleep tight, my prince." I bend and kiss him lightly on the cheek.

Turning to walk by my husband, my stomach still flutters when I'm close enough to him to smell him. I lean up and kiss his neck right where his heartbeat is. "Do you want to pick up where we left off?" I ask, wrapping my arms around his neck.

"I think I remember where we were." His hands go to

my hips as he picks me up, and my legs go around his waist. "I think." He starts kissing my neck. "That you had a lot fewer clothes on."

"Yes," I agree, my whole body ready for him to touch me anywhere he wants to. "I also think that your face was a little bit more south."

"You mean down under?" he jokes with me as he throws me on the bed, and he's about to get exactly where he was before when his phone rings from the bedside table, making us both moan.

"Next weekend," he says, rolling over and grabbing the phone. "I'm going to ask your father to babysit, and we are going to go away for twenty-four hours and have all the sex."

I get up on my elbows and laugh. "Just what my father will love to hear. Didn't he just start liking you again?" I roll my lips when Travis glares at me, grabbing his phone that rings again.

"I'm going to say you need a break." He shakes his head. "Oh, great, a group FaceTime." He presses the green button and sits down on the bed next to me as the circle goes around and around. We join the chat at the same time as Clarabella. "What is it?" Travis grumbles out while we see two more icons starting to join.

"I'm waiting until we are all on," Shelby says, and I can see that her eyes look like she's been crying, but her eyes sparkle. "Gosh, what has you in such a great mood?" she asks Travis, who just grumbles.

"Someone sounds like they have blue balls," Clarabella teases and laughs at her own joke when her mother joins.

"Mom, Travis is mean to me because we interrupted him and Harlow when they were making sexy time."

"We were not," I quickly cut in.

"How can they make sexy time?" his mother says. "It's six thirty."

"Can we focus on why I'm FaceTiming everyone?" Shelby asks as soon as Presley joins, and it looks like her hair is all over the place.

"Someone else was having sexy time," Clarabella says when she points.

"I'm hanging up," Travis says.

Shelby yells, "No!"

"Guys," she says and holds up her hand, shocking us all, "I'm getting married."

Dearest Love,

Another wedding season is upon us, and it looks like our very own Shelby will be walking down the aisle. Or will she?

It seems that a very suspicious e-mail is coming in right before she walks down the aisle that can change everything, especially since it's not meant for her.

XOXO

Made in the USA
Monee, IL
30 August 2022